mirror, mirror . . .

by the same author in English translation

Karin, a novel (1985, London; 1888, New York)

by the same author in the original Swedish

Puckelyggen
Flickan i Obaldine
Den Sommaren
Karin vid Havet
Ångestens Barn

To All My Family

Contents Page

Life is a pure flame, and we live by an invisible sun within us.
— Sir Thomas Browne

OVERTURE

A Stone Rose

She drifts about her big house. Alone.

It is rather old. English. Yet to be English not all that old. Dates only from the 1840s and has many grander and more antique sisters in this Sussex village not far from Brighton, the sea, the chalk cliffs; or from London – chaotic, noisy, Beatle-mad, wealthy, slummy, frivolous drugged up to the gills on tradition London. The advertisers' El Dorado, where money, its getting and spending, alike by those who have it and those who haven't, is the one and only motive.

Each morning before the mists have had time to lift, myriads of upper-class and upper-middle-class women drive their drowsy husbands, still warm from their beds, to Haywards Heath Station. Hair often shameless in curlers and faces smeared with Pond's Cold Cream, they fling a raincoat over their nighties and bare shoulders and drive off bravely, ejecting their husbands with a 'Bye, darling, see you this evening!' into the station where the men, jerked out of their slumbers by the raw morning air, join the jostling queue, stumble with their umbrellas through the dank ticket hall and rush upstairs to the platform, to be whisked away on another long day's journey into night in the charming, monstrous city of ads and posters where, patient to breaking point on their way to business meetings, they sit through endless minutes in despondent traffic jams as the pennies tick themselves away in the taximeter, or else with anxious eyes follow the ups and downs of sterling against foreign currencies, on the stroke of five to rush off homewards, sink down into a smoky, jolting, over-full compartment and drop off to sleep with open mouths and lolling heads over the evening paper. For forty-five minutes, almost an hour, they plunge again deep into the dream the bedside clock had disrupted; wake up; tumble out. Pass through the dreary station building and find themselves outside again, bedazzled by some astounding sunset, face to face with car and wife and a smiling or sullen 'Hi, had a good day at the office?'

I drift about in my big English house. Let my fingers trail over its wallpaper, probe to the ageless Sussex stone beneath. To its wisdom. Strength. Soul. Does stone have a soul? Up at the quarry the other day you showed me a solemn stone flower, hacked out in a single block; a dream carved in ochre, a sandstone risen star-like from death's grey quarry. A Tudor rose from some demolished Victorian church. All agog, you wanted to build it into the neo-Gothic façade of our already overburdened dwelling. But the more excited you became, urging me to let you do it, now, at once, the less I wanted to see it there. And the more sceptical became the quarryman's smile at the way you warmed to this stone rose, lying there on the ground, so pathetically amputated, till it stiffened in a grimace. And his panting old mongrel bitch, sniffing at our ankles, put paid to your loquacity by squatting down and pissing on it. All round us the chill mist of a damp English autumn quivered in the sunset; and in the smile the old man threw me, putative owner of a stone rose, was a strange compassion, as if he knew how much more I, who am already turned to stone, would have appreciated a bouquet of living roses, deep red as menstrual blood, quivering with love, aflame with a man's desire . . .

Through the dusk so hastily come in from the sea he led us past the stone block to his shed. And gave us each a stained brown mug of hot tea, splashing in milk from a bottle on his rickety table, sugar from a half-open packet. And you, still so boyish and vital, said, 'I'll fetch it the day after tomorrow!' And hurried out into the dark to the car.

'Very good, sir,' the old man said, satisfied. But I, Jenny, lingered on a minute, two minutes, in his shed with the tea mug, its warmth giving my hands new strength as the stonemason observed me in the dim electric light. The look in those eyes could have been Mother's. I stroked the mongrel's shaggy fur and she pressed herself up against me. Then we went off. Away. Home. Anywhere. Nowadays it's all one. In his shack under the night sky, for a few moments as long as years, I'd felt at home.

The fog thickened. Ahead of us, me and you, Jean-Paul, whom I believe I love but who seems nowadays to be more in love with stone roses, cat's-eyes gleamed between the hedges floating by under trees that reached up old hands towards the sky's blackness. And I remember thinking, Tonight stars must fall!

The older children are at school. The little ones down at the swings with Rita. Jean-Paul, at his typewriter, no longer belongs among the yawning umbrella men. Nowadays he works at home, mostly to be near me in the days, as at night. The sound of his electric typewriter clatters through the old house. Consoles. A split psyche demands support, love, analysis. His efforts are sublime. But can only momentarily conquer death – the death that's been lurking inside me ever since I was born, an unwanted girl-child in a Strindbergian vicarage in a land of ice, far from this Sussex, so mild, so verdant. But I suppose I'll never escape and am doomed to carry its ice floes that, forever inside me, invisible to others, are slowly slicing me up. There are moments when Jean-Paul's omnipotence seems able to exorcise both God and the devil, liquidate my debt of sin, this punishing superego that like a querulous ghost lives on in our white Swedish furniture. Then, for a few hours, I'm a soft, warm, happy woman and mother, loved, loving, close and physical. The children's bodies, their curly tousled hair, their hungry mouths redolent of apples, their mental curiosity, come flooding in over me – ah yes! – all my desire is to live, in them, through them, content to see in the clear flower-like blue of their eyes the *joie de vivre* that I have always taken for granted grows only in other people's gardens. Then I see it. Light green, as pellucid as a leaf, it is a jewel worn as of right by everyone – rich or poor – who lives out his or her days free from an Old Testament superego. Not forever being jabbed at, in a state of nervous anxiety.

Then I, wicked, sinful Jenny, know I am capable of love. Beyond words, laws, prohibitions. In such moments I no longer feel I'm carrying the cross that, too heavy for themselves, my parents off-loaded on to me when they rested, each in their own ditch beside their *via dolorosa*, little knowing that each time they took it up again and struggled onward their child, pale-faced and droopy, back aching and sweat running down her forehead, was tagging along behind towards a Golgotha she could make no sense of.

At such moments I, even in dank midwinter, pluck wild Swedish summer strawberries, thread them gleaming red on blades of wet English grass. Then I, Jenny, discover in my own meagre being oasis after oasis; gushing fountains; palaces set in exquisite mosaics; fruits hitherto unknown. Then I, in this earthly desert where we all grope and fumble, find I can tell stories without end or beginning. Then I can venture down into this vale of tears and with my glittering green gem of happiness dazzle all who sit there; the depressed, the apathetic, the drop-outs; the suicides. Dazzle them so they're ready to get up and flee this dreadful place, leaving it the desert it should always have been.

In such moments I can take you into myself, Jean-Paul. And you sink inside me, falling deep into the innermost depths of voluptuous oblivion and for a few blissful moments forget all about this other Jenny who, miserable and alone, strays about in this old house. Then I'm the fair-haired, weightless Botticelli angel that you, one hot August day, first saw on Dartington's lawns and in whom you at once recognized the vision – smiling, beckoning, unattainable – that you'd dreamt of in German air raids, torpedo attacks. Then I am again for you the fairest of women, flaxen haired, smiling my dreamy smile. You don't see the greying hairs, do you, my slack belly, flabby after so many pregnancies? Thirsty, with closed eyes you taste my inner core, as if sipping an exquisite wine, touch my swelling clitoris, until I cry out for you, for you . . . Then you, Jean-Paul, and your Jenny unite, become one. Are one body, one soul, soaring bird-like upward with hard, strong wing-beats, through the thick clouds, up, up towards the light.

Yet our happiness, translucent, sea-green, is only momentary: the deeper it pierces ecstasy's flame the more vertiginous our plunge downwards through the English oaks' myriad branches. Scorched, extinct, mere children of the flesh, we fall like ripe red fruit to the ground, bruise ourselves; resume our everyday existence in this stone house of ours that looks like a church; turn ugly and worm-eaten.

The Bird of Happiness – the one Jenny's mother gave her when she visited England for the last time; a visit we shall be describing in some detail. Happy and touched by her mother's gesture, her children around her, Jenny had taken it out of its box marked Genuine Swedish Handicraft, unwrapped it from its tissue paper and immediately hung it up, a brilliant red spot in the rather murky sitting-room. 'Oh, thank you ever so much, Mother , dear,' she had said, hugging and kissing this little greying woman that was her mother.

'It will bring you luck, Jenny. Take care of it'

'But of course, Mother,' Jenny had answered, a trifle taken aback by her mother's serious, even ominous, tone of voice.

'Human happiness is so frail, and mostly it is we ourselves who break it to pieces, cling to it as we may. Anyway, that has always been *my* experience . . .'

ACT I

The Mother's Visit

It was a fine afternoon in early October. In an Indian summer still lavish with perfumes and colours, the pink roses stood out wide-eyed against the house's greyish sandstone. The children, thrilled to bits at their grandmother's arrival, bubbling over with excitement, ran happily in and out of the French windows, wide open on to the garden. Jean-Paul and Jenny had fetched her from Tilbury that same morning and now she was going to stay with them for three whole weeks. At long last mother and daughter, grandmother and grandchildren, would have any amount of time for each other. It isn't so often nowadays that Jenny can visit her old parents in Stockholm, nor is it easy for her mother to tear herself away from her life partner, so pathetically dependent as he has become with the years, less and less able to cope. But now, boarded out with the sisters at the Ersta nursing home, he will just have to do without having her at his beck and call.

Even at Tilbury Jenny noticed the change. Her mother had grown old. It wasn't just that her back had become hunched and rounded; there was something sad, old and fragile about her whole being, a hint of suffering that must soon strike her down. Her features hid a kind of certainty. The joy of reunion, all the smiles, an appetite for life that still hadn't quite left her – nothing of this could hide the dark shadows under her eyes or the downcast, almost bitter lines around her mouth. The insight had clouded their reunion, thrown a flitting shadow across the unnaturally warm and spring-like sunshine and darkened the defiant splendour of trees and autumn flowers.

Spring-cleaned from end to end, its windows polished, bedecked with blossoms, Jenny's and Jean-Paul's house receives this ageing Swedish woman. A traditional English roast beef sizzles in the oven and a home-baked apple pie with Swedish vanilla sauce fills the house with a faint odour of cinnamon. The mother's nostrils quiver and a touch of saliva appears at the corners of her mouth. Just for a few moments she looks completely happy – as yet the bird of happiness has no speck of dust on its wings, and hers is unmarred. For she loves good food.

'Oh, Jenny,' she says, almost tenderly. 'All this, *for me!* What an effort you must have made!'

Jenny smiles. It has always been her self-imposed role to be her mother's comforter; to try to make her happy; to listen to her lamentations about her hypersensitive, even at times downright difficult, husband, her two 'unfeeling' sons, their coldness towards her – her laments about life in general. For some reason all manner of injustices, large and small, have a way of falling on this dark little woman, either drop by drop, like rain, or in heartless hailstorms. And to feel sorry for her, to fall into genuine grief and sympathy, has often been Jenny's masochistic manoeuvre, her ingratiating way of making herself real to her mother.

That this mother of hers is a ruler among women, a sensuous force of nature, a will that only God can tame and which in the end He must tragically destroy, is something Jenny doesn't quite grasp. By Jenny she is adored, worshipped, mysterious and out of reach. It is as if she were shut off by a pane of glass that Jenny must shatter if she is to get through to her heart, cut and bleeding. No glass needs be broken this luminous autumn day, however. The laughing children fling themselves straight at their grandmother's heart, cling to her and are overwhelmed with presents. In return the grandmother is heaped with more or less precocious drawings and other odds and ends of their own devising.

Pipe in mouth, Jean-Paul observes his Jenny. Sees she is the only one of them still outside the glass. Knows that behind her smiles of motherly delight lurk grief, envy and despair. Something tells him that the older woman, all unawares, is in danger of being attacked and penetrated, summoned to yield a love whose pale fronds press like eternelles against that frosty window; a love never quite given and for which she is now too old.

At the same time he cannot help being fascinated by this mother–daughter drama, as yet only in its idyllic first act. People's behaviour patterns, their everlasting theatricals and compulsively repeated blunders have become Jean-Paul's great if tormenting interest in life. And in Jenny's family he has found drama enough to make up for dramas that otherwise, perhaps, have been lacking in his own. Only when people attack his Jenny does he leave his observation post, rush on to the stage, intervene and do his best to sort things out: attempts that usually only succeed in still further confusing the scenario and calling down on him the actors' curses as he tries to break off the performance and drag the heroine away back to his own reality, to this stone house . . .

Not that Jean-Paul needs to hoist any storm signals just now, for in the same instant – inexplicably, everything else being so very calm – a strange gust of wind whirls round the house. He casts a troubled glance out into the garden. No quiver, not even a tremor, goes through those branches whose leaves, otherwise so sensitive to the slightest trembling of the air, gleam gold in the afternoon sun. Silent, majestic, they stand there enjoying this last respite of mild autumn sunshine before winter rains and storms. It's as if they're unaware of this wind that now, a second time, as if panting for breath, chases round the house. Neither Jenny's mother nor the children seem to have noticed anything. Calm and benevolent, the grandmother's eyes, radiant under bushy dark eyebrows, rest on her grandchildren. Only Jenny has turned pale. Gives a slight start, as if chilled. Looks questioningly at Jean-Paul.

'Did you hear that?' she whispers. And in her eyes is something forlorn, as if the wind had grabbed her with invisible hands and already thrust her outside the others' circle.

Jean-Paul nods. Unnoticed, their glances meet. Then he remembers his role as the one who must always calm the other; yes, all the roles he has to play in his wife's fragile existence. Always he must hide his own fear.

He puts his pipe back into the corner of his mouth.

'I'll go and see . . .' he says quietly.

But when the wind whines a third time he sees the colour has drained from her face. Her hands clutch the arms of her chair; she makes to get up. Her glance fastens on her mother, then settles distantly on him as she mumbles something inaudible. When he touches Jenny she is as stiff and cold as one of her own antique china dolls, packed away up in the attic.

'. . . whether the boiler's gone out.' This he says in a special tone of voice only she understands – an inflection of the language they have worked out together during years of mutual adaptation, passions, torments and happiness.

Reassured a little, her grip on the chair relaxes.

'More apple pie, lovies?' he hears her say. 'More vanilla sauce, Mother , dear?'

Jean-Paul goes out through the French windows and down the steps to the boiler room. Among the black heaps of coke, illumined only by a few slanting sunbeams, gleam a pair of green cat eyes. This ancient boiler house, lavishly overgrown with pale pink rambler roses and moss, is the cats' favourite hide-out. Here they make love, fight, doze off to sleep and in its darkness lie in wait for any mouse that may scuttle by. Shovelling in some coke among dying embers that he erotically associates with post-coital exhaustion, he sees in front of him her face, frozen with terror, as white as china. Her doll-blue eyes.

'Who are you, Jenny?' The question aches through him. '*Where* are you?'

The pang lasts only a few seconds. Flinging the shovel aside, Jean-Paul emerges from the boiler house into the Sussex afternoon sunshine, sinking now against deep blue shadows and no longer quite so warm.

Jean-Paul's journal, 6 October 1963, a bar in Dublin

I am still tired and dizzy after yesterday and last night, a restless one. Though I have smartened myself up more than usual for this conference, I still feel only half-awake, unshaven and shabby. I must force myself to attend the sessions, which at the same time are an escape from the goings-on at home, which are becoming increasingly bizarre, less and less explicable. My mother-in-law's arrival seems to have brought to a head the unnatural situation I have so long been living with but which I have learnt to accept as normal – as our only way of surviving, Jenny's, mine and the children's.

My hand shakes so much I can hardly write. My thoughts dart about. I realize I am frightened, very. Am beginning to be infected by my wife's anxiety, now almost chronic. It is only here, on my own, among strangers in strange surroundings, that I am forced to look this fear of mine in the eye – the fear I almost always manage to suppress when I am with Jenny and the kids.

Jean-Paul, *calme-toi, mon vieux!*. Try to regain your mental equilibrium, tedious though it is. In this corner of the hotel bar, dark but somehow reassuring, with a glass of cassis in front of me, perhaps I'll be able to stop worrying if I write down what is on my mind.

The fact is, Jenny isn't only my wife and mother of our four children; she is also the strangest, most captivatingly ambiguous – well, grotesque – creature I have ever come across. Closed in on herself, either apathetic or overwhelmed with panic, she can infuriate me – a fury I am obliged to change into either pity or mere intellectual curiosity. Against my own will I am forced down murky psychological jungle paths that, had I chosen an extroverted and above all sane life companion, it would never have crossed my mind to explore. It seems I am not alone in this. Many others, far more cunning and knowledgeable, are said to be trying to find a way through the mazes of split personality. Sad to say, it is *à la mode*. So I am not quite as alone in this as I often feel I am, particularly at night in the silence of my study. Behind me stands Uncle Siegmund. How well you knew your age's hysterical female psyche, as fostered by upper-middle-class Viennese homes – not all that different from the one Jenny grew up in, in Stockholm's Östermalm district. What you had no experience of, however, was that icy northern country I have never felt at home in; the melancholy of its dark winters, and least of all its people's morbid longings to 'rest for ever under a cross' (as Jenny's father so elegaically puts it) in a snow-laden churchyard.

So far I can go in Freud's company, no further. Nor with Satre, my illustrious compatriot and namesake. Neither of them, it seems to me, can throw more than an occasional gleam of light on Jenny's and my complex existence. What if we are just a couple of blinded moths, helplessly fluttering about, drawn to the deadly lamplight? Two lunatics without either the sense or the courage to *choose*, once and for all? To free ourselves from all these double exposures, the whole sorry mess?

That Scottish psychiatrist, now – what was his name, Lane, Lamb, Laing? – anyway, the one they interviewed on television the other evening about how the schizophrenic's home relates to his or her role as a sacrificial lamb incarnating all the other family members' latent insanity? As if I haven't long ago tumbled on it myself – all that stuff about the 'double-bind'! Haven't seen for myself how the lamb becomes the visible boil squirting out the crazed family's accumulated pus!

When I have a spare moment I must try to get hold of his book;

take a closer look at all this, which right now is so pertinent. In fact I would like to have a chat with him. Before it is too late. Before Jenny goes to pieces altogether, perhaps, and I am left alone with the children – and myself.

My mother-in-law, yes. Cropping up again just now in our lives, seemingly so innocent! For a few hours that last evening, our situation became suddenly quite delightful, exalted even, but also turned so dark, it brought me, desperately in need of help as I am, to the point of despair where I now find myself.

Or am I exaggerating? Seeing ghosts in broad daylight? Making out our situation to be worse, more entangled, than it really is? Jenny has been longing to see her mother again, imagining and dreaming of it! How can she unleash so much anguish, such shocking personality splits? True, I admit, we are a couple of cliff-hangers over an abyss. My concern, which will always be there because she is so unstable, easily punctures the dream of domestic bliss that life in Sussex lulls us into. I'm always trying to give some direction to our lives – to Jenny's, the children's and even my own, which just now seems to have disappeared over the horizon. Seems to be bleeding away into a receptacle – into Jenny. And I just let it happen – oddly enough without, I think, becoming embittered, or notably aggressive . . . Well, is that quite true? Mostly I am aware of a half-suppressed anguish, a kind of boredom; and at the outset of each new day a sort of melancholy that makes it hard to get through it. And when evening comes and I have been able to chuck away another day into time's maelstrom: relief.

Mais merde alors! Ce n'est pas moi, en fin de compte! The egocentric Parisian chatterbox, full of *joie de vivre*, who, even if ironed out by an English education, I admit, was ready for anything; keen to take on board whatever life might offer, emotional or intellectual!

Though now I doubt it. Can it be that from the outset there

was an emotional vacuum, due to my parents' stinginess with their love, reduced to a minimum, like a gas flame? A black pit of emptiness, only too ready to let someone like Jenny fill it, to accept her in sickness or in health, never closing my eyes to the exceptional difficulties I saw in her, almost from the moment we met? Just now my life seems to be being swallowed up by someone else's. Jenny's.

Our welcoming dinner over at last, I suggested a stroll in the fading autumn sunset. Victoria, Michael and Rosalind rushed on ahead with a tail-wagging Tittine barking her head off. My mother-in-law, tired, I thought, and a trifle short of breath, threw Jenny a questioning glance where she sat with little Jojo asleep in her arms.

'What a lovely idea, Mother!' she said, tired too. 'And you can take another look at your beloved English trees!'

'But . . . aren't you coming?' Charlotte's voice sounded disappointed. Wondering. A shade suspicious.

'Another time, Mother, dear. I must put Jojo to bed.' Jenny sounded more cheerful than she probably felt. Her voice faded away into the drumming of the dishwasher. (It was Rita's day off, as usual.)

I wasn't deceived. As soon as we had gone ten yards I knew Jenny would dump Josephine in her cot, shut herself in our bedroom, swallow a Valium, put on a record, lie down on our double bed, close her eyes, listen to Bach, Handel or Vivaldi and drift off into a dream. Where to? If for an instant I could hope some line of an unwritten poem, like a caged bird, was fluttering about somewhere inside her mind, I certainly would not begrudge her a moment to herself. But it is ages since any firebird like her brother's took wing inside her. Instead, it sits huddled in some dark corner of her soul, daren't take flight. I have never doubted that Jenny is a poet – too many fragments, chaotic, unthought out, lie in her desk drawer. Why has her strength abandoned her? Don't know. Surely a single nasty review can't destroy someone's

whole gift? The flight, the leap through soft, cloudy obstacles, is
still there in her lyrical fragments . . . yet something is missing.

Sometimes my wife seems boundless. A mystery. And it both
delights and terrifies me. Perhaps that is why I, this Indian-
summer evening, was taking the children and my mother-in-law
out for a walk while hearing Handel's jubilant Water Music, it
seemed, resounding through the sun-drenched mist and the
meadows' opulent verdure.

Later, evening, 6 October

I have been interrupted. It is difficult to be the overwrought,
troubled man I actually am and at the same time play the interested participant in this conference, join in the heated discussions,
drink cocktails, make small talk and eat futurological dinners.
Admittedly, the pressure lightens somewhat among my extroverted colleagues, who at least seem cheerful enough and aren't
peering into themselves all the time or trying to delve into intri-
cate psychological problems. Yet I am constantly aware of my
Jenny and feel guilty for having had to tear myself away from her
this morning and leave her, despite her night of fierce anxiety
attacks and nightmares. I couldn't stand between them. Mother
and daughter will just have to sort out their relationship.

Where was I? Oh yes. Charlotte and I were just going out for our
evening stroll. We walked quietly along the treacherous muddy
path behind the house, leading across the fields and meadows
down to the farm and into the woods.

The children had run on far ahead; only their voices rang out
like cheerful English church bells through the thickening twilight.
For a while Charlotte said nothing. Then, coming to a halt, she
gazed out a trifle nostalgically over the misty landscape towards
Paxhill's towers, silhouetted against the sky's pale golden pink on
the western horizon.

'How lovely it is here,' she remarked quietly. 'So soft, so restful, so old-fashioned and idyllic! It's as if the modern world has never touched this landscape. Here you know nothing of the stress and worry that torments us all in Sweden! I can't say how grateful we are, Henrik and I, that our Jenny has at last found a safe harbour. Surely such calm, safe surroundings must suit her? Until she met you, Jean-Paul, it was as if she had no goal in life – except her poetry of course. She was just fluttering about. But now she seems to have found herself, as wife and mother.'

She threw me an appealing, penetrating glance, as if wishing at all costs to hear the whole truth about her daughter and against her own will hoping to hear me contradict her. Though the evening was mild I shivered; I felt myself turn pale, my mouth become dry, and I went weak at the knees. Stricken suddenly by the apprehensiveness that Jenny's family – particularly her mother and Leo – always inspires in me, I avoided her inquisitorial glance. In their presence one shrinks, dwindles in some way; finds oneself suddenly in a field of high tension, fenced in by electric barbed wire. Small though she is, my mother-in-law – in stature I mean – there are moments when she seems frighteningly large – as big to me in my overwrought state, anyway, as that medieval castle on the skyline! Up until then I had been fooling myself into thinking that I could avoid those intimacies with her that always turn into confrontations. But now there I was, trapped like a silly little mouse in a mousetrap

'Why don't you answer me, Jean-Paul?' I heard her complain in a tone of faint reproach. 'Is there something wrong between you and Jenny? You needn't be afraid to confide in me, There is *nothing* I'm not used to hearing! Nothing in this life surprises me any longer. As for Jenny . . . I really don't find her as blooming as I'd hoped. She seems worn. Nervous. Tense in some way. Like just now at table, when that gust of wind . . . or whatever it was . . . threw her into a panic.'

I tried to gather my wits together. Slip out of the trap. So, she had noticed it, had she? Does nothing escape this extraordinary little woman, escape her intuition?

'*Tout va bien, Tante Charlotte*,' I heard myself reply with false heartiness. 'Things are fine between us. Jenny loves living in the country. She has never been better!'

Her eyebrows darkened, turned even blacker, as if drawn with charcoal. Everything else around us darkens also. A breeze had begun swaying the tree-tops and from somewhere beyond the blackberry thickets down by the farm the children's voices, so cheerful a moment ago, were reaching us in gusts like cries for help.

'There is something you are *hiding* from me, Jean-Paul,' she went on, looking straight through me. 'As soon as I try to be help-ful, probe the depths, you become nonchalant, evasive. Why are you always so frightened of realities? If only you knew how my days and nights are filled with worry on Jenny's account! You're play-acting. Just pretending to be brave – courageous, I admit. But also tilting quixotically at windmills, don't you see that? And if you aren't careful they will crush you! You think you can save your charming Dulcinea just because you love her – and Henrik and I appreciate what you are doing for her, more deeply than you per-haps suppose. But the fact is that Jenny, although she has managed to give herself a lot of children, is nothing but a neurotic child; weak through and through and utterly dependent. The truth is, I'm afraid she is not long for this life unless with God's help your love for her – which frankly is beyond me – can save her. The fact is, my dear Jean-Paul, I have given up hoping. Yet I never cease praying for our poor Jenny; for Leo, who is having far too much success for his own good; for my poor Fredrik, so cynical, so embit-tered. I'm more worried for our children, with their terrible heredity, than I can say!'

Inside me I felt a violent rage welling up. *Coûte que coûte*, I was seized with a basic desire to be rid of this mother-in-law of mine, standing there in the twilight, roaring out these horrors about this enigma, her own offspring, the wild passionate creature whom fate, one blazing hot August day in 1947, flung into my arms on Dartington's lawns! At the same time I couldn't help admiring this primitive force that, briefly let out of its parochial cage, was flinging itself at me; the same force, at once destructive and creative, as my illustrious brother-in-law's. For a few moments I just stood there, paralysed. These people always contrive in some way to make my own little world look like a chipped mug, stained with English tea. Hardly strange if I give Jenny's family a wide berth! But in the same instant my own mood changed. I hope I'm not becoming like them: forever oscillating between blackest despair and moments of brittle happiness, between fury over someone they regard as immoral, or even criminal, and deep sympathy, insight, Christian forgiveness?

I buried my defence of poor Jenny: that it is they – her own family – who have made her the way she is, inocculated her with these dreadful anxiety attacks, so that without my everlasting support she couldn't cope with life. Touched by the expression on Charlotte's face – so world-weary, so affecting in its sadness and despondency – I said nothing. After all, I couldn't hurt the feelings of someone so exposed, so fragile, so obviously weary to death? Here was no lioness. Just a very sad, old woman who, for obscure reasons I can't hope to plumb, is grossly disappointed in life, badly let down. Beyond and beneath her lament lay some real unspoken suffering that all her life has been cutting into her flesh and that she'll soon be taking with her into old age and death. For a moment my sympathy for her threatened to swallow even my everlasting sympathy for Jenny. But I could only stand it for a moment:

'You say you are worried about your children,' I replied, my faintly ironical overtone pricking our almost sacral mood. 'But surely you have no reason to worry, at least not for Fredrik, who is carving himself out such a brilliant diplomatic career; and still less for Leo, who is off like a rocket to the stars! Whereas Jenny . . . it's not easy for her to be the younger sister to two such . . .'

'And what do you mean by *that*, Jean-Paul?' She sounded tense. If I hadn't caught her by the arm she would have slipped and fallen in the mud, perhaps hurt herself on the barbed-wire fence. 'Are you making fun of me? Leo? Jenny? They are worlds apart, not to be spoken of in the same breath! *Of course* I'm worried about Leo. He is burning his candle at both ends. But he is a *man* and a *genius*! Whereas Jenny . . .'

'Is a mere nothing! Didn't you nickname her *Nitti* when she was small? And what does that mean if not a blank lot in the lottery? *Un petit rien du tout?* A disastrous nickname, if you ask me! Your family, if I may say so, distributes its roles all too drastically!'

'My dear Jean-Paul, now you are going too far,' she flared up. 'How *can* you say such a thing? Upset me so? If you only knew how such nasty little insinuations hurt my feelings! And I, who have always taken you for a gentleman!'

Angry, she shook herself loose from me and plodded stubbornly on in the direction of some lights still falling from our open windows. We were almost home now. Suddenly, quite out of breath, she turns. Looks at me imploringly, almost tearfully. Says almost in a whisper: 'But tell me, Jean-Paul, before we go in. How do things *really* stand with Jenny?'

By now I had almost had enough of her, her dominating ways and her everlasting worries, no matter how touching or hurtful to others. It is all too much for me and there is a point where I no longer give a damn about any of them. She puts me out of touch with myself, as it were. Sets my own identity in question. How long had we been out walking? She had even confused my sense of time. Over our driveway – the tip of our wretched, ill-grown wellingtonia was as usual waving tragically as usual in the wind – darkness had begun to fall and stars were appearing in a black sky.

I lit my pipe to calm down.

'Surely that's something you can ask yourself?' I said morosely.

'But why won't she *talk* to me?' Charlotte complained in a low voice. 'Why is she running away from me? Behaving so distantly?'

'On the contrary. She wants nothing better than to be with you in peace and quiet. If you only knew how she has been longing to see you, looking forward to your visit! And how dreadfully she misses Sweden. I doubt whether she will ever settle down here in England.'

'But my *dear* Jean-Paul! For us it is a blessing from heaven her being here! Tired out as we are, she would be altogether too much for Henrik and me. I can't say how grateful we are that she is out here, our little Magdalena . . .'

Suddenly she sounded quite tender. Her lips seemed to caress this odd name. We were just going in through the porch door. Confused, I took my pipe out of my mouth and knocked it out against the stone buttress.

'*Magdalena?*' I said bewildered. 'Who's she?'

A cunning little smile in the dusk.

'Why, Jenny, of course! It was another of her nicknames when she was small. Surely you've realized by now that there is more than one Jenny?'

I was left standing there in a world gone mad. Even as I write this down I feel terrified. In the chill of the autumn evening my house, my trees, my children that I love so and above all my Jenny all seemed to be jumping about wildly under the stars, mocking me for my stupidity in taking them to myself and loving them. Was it my mother-in-law's parting shot that set the make-believe round-about spinning? The one I'm still riding on?

My pipe struck the wall like an angry woodpecker. Is my whole life made up of nothing but sandstone? In this compact, stony sur-face on which we live out our lives is there no crack to let through the light of human kindness, of freedom? Not the tiniest little avenue of escape? I groan at the thought. Rather take refuge in lies, in fantasies, in soft half-truths and make-believe love, than stand here marking time forever, wide awake on the stony surface of our existence!

Gradually I regained my balance, calmed down. The church clock struck nine and still my house stood there, embedded in its garden, still redolent of its roses, and my relit pipe glowing like a glow-worm! *At least I was myself.* And Jenny? She's mine. No such woman as Magdalena existed – other than as a warning shot, a monstrous invention of my mother-in-law's crazed imagination. Soon the children would be sound asleep in their beds, and out here in the dark no one would be fluttering about, accusing me of having chosen a wrong life, of having let myself be fooled . . .

What am I? A tormented intellectual, a half-French Englishman, not yet forty, educated at a famous school, and whose mother, even if her ideas are a bit mouldy and Victorian and altogether too close at hand to suit my wife, is 100 per cent English! Father a hyperactive, ambitious, razor-sharp French liberal, killed before his time by a German torpedo in the Atlantic. I have his sharp brain, muted by my mother's English common-sense, sometimes dull, sometimes biting. Neither I nor, I think I can say, any of my forebears have ever been afflicted by any serious mental illness – except for my overworked father's paranoia and my mother's no longer justifiable vanity. And of course, my own ruthless passion for my blonde Scandinavian wife.

I know that her otherwise so desirable person hides one or another *fleur du mal*. But not, as far as I know, a half-witted Magdalena. *Mon Dieu* – if You exist – to hell both with that wretched Magdalena creature and with my mother-in-law, with her genius for stirring up trouble! Amen.

One more whisky from the bar to calm down. Then I'll drop off to sleep as sweetly as one of my own children. And tomorrow, maybe, for my own edification, jot down the sequel . . .

Jenny

They have been out quite a while now, Mother and Jean-Paul. Like a transparent glass of red wine from which I'd like to drink the juice of oblivion, the sunset is sinking behind the dusk's grey, velvet curtain. The English haze comes stealing into our rooms, bringing with it anxiety and desolation. I can see them coming towards me up our gravel drive: two hunched cripples. Hand in hand, faceless, they float forward over the damp lawn. Silent but assured they grope their way into the house, up the carpeted staircase. Suddenly they are standing in the room, staring eyeless at me. Like two beggars needing food, money and somewhere to spend the night, they wait patiently. And I feel their icy chill. Even though my body, still quite young and healthy, puts up a resistance, I am not able to stop them gliding into me. Their greedy blue fingers seize on my heart, sate their hunger on my guts; then they try to settle down inside me, and their rest becomes my unrest. My growing unrest.

Why am I so frightened always? After all, I am surrounded by people, big and small, who love me – or at least I assume so. Even after all these years Jean-Paul still adores me, won't let me go. So why am I standing here in the dusk, panic-stricken, alone, my pulse beating wildly? Why don't I scream at these two beggars to clear out?

Urgently, I turn on all the lights. Today, at least, my mother-in-law can't come rushing in and turn them all off again, because she has gone away. Electricity is expensive in this country and she is worried about her son's economy. She thinks I am extravagant with all these lights. I switch them on. She switches them off. And she hates my Swedish candles! Sometimes even blows them out. Somehow our Swedish custom of sitting around lit candles upsets her. She says it is morbid.

Jean-Paul is all she has left. All that matters. For her, I and my children are irrelevant, a net that her Jean-Paul has managed to get entangled in while outside her field of influence. As for what is left of my life-flame, she would like to blow that out, too. If she could . . .

It can't have been like that to begin with. To begin with there was nothing. Fancy abandoning Jean-Paul, handing him over on Paddington Station, only seven weeks old, into the care of a nanny and then pushing off with her tyrant of a husband to some mouldy old Venetian palazzo and floating idly about for a whole year in gondolas instead of looking after her new-born son! I know. I have seen them. The photos. Dressed in white, indolent, sensual, unspeakably vain, she lolls against her lord and master while their offspring, far from Venice's filthy canals, smiles up at another woman.

To begin with, yes! But no sooner did she get home than she woke from her trance and dismissed the nanny! Well, she is not dismissing me. Ever since the children and I moved down here from London her stifled love for Jean-Paul has flared up with dreadful ferocity. We are outsiders. Don't belong here. If she had her own way it would be she who was living here with Jean-Paul, in some kind of mother–son symbiosis. That is why she switches out the lights and I switch them on again. She wants to snuff out our love, darken my life and the children's. Sometimes I dream about her long hat-pins.

Jenny shivers. Everywhere some enemy is lying in wait for her. Everyone wants to hurt her, everyone except Jean-Paul and the children is spying on her, laughing up their sleeves at her, criticizing her for being so impractical: not daring to learn to drive, not being up to cocktail parties, refusing to play bridge, join the golf club, or go to flower shows, coffee mornings and garden parties. They all want to attack her, the odd one out. A wanderer. An introvert among extroverts who listens to classical recordings, preferably Leo's. To Jean-Paul's secret irritation a whole pile of them lies on her bedside table, staring up at her from their glossy sleeves, with Leo's dark, sternly concentrated features cruel evidence of an unjust fate.

Even that sullen, greedy Rita, who has come home from her day off, despises me, Jenny thinks; regards me as a useless, incompetent, lazy, no-good mother who sometimes even avoids her own children because she doesn't want them to see into her dreadful state of mind. Rita has just given the little ones their bath and put them to bed. Now, down in the kitchen, I can hear her laughing and joking with Vicky and Michael. Just back from their walk, I suppose? Walk! What walk? Oh yes, with Jean-Paul and Mother. Where are they? Where is my Jean-Paul? Love him, don't love him, love him? Doesn't Jenny love her Jean-Paul? Can't she love anyone any more? Come on, Jenny, answer!

But just now, hanging here crucified in this bedroom between her two beggars, Jenny can't answer any questions.

Mother. Inconceivable, in this day and age, that neither Fredrik, nor Leo nor Jenny-Nitti have ever been allowed to call her Mummy! Will Jenny, this time, dare smash her way through that glass wall, get close to you, Mother? Surely there must be some last lingering glow? Jenny – I, that is – sees . . . see how you have aged, Mother , dear. Jenny may be paralysed, but she isn't blind; she who is perpetually observing everyone around her. Observing you. But now she is tired of observing, all she wants is to snuggle up to you, hear your voice say, as it used to when she was little and ran a high temperature, 'What's the matter, Nitti? Why is Nitti crying? Doesn't she feel well? Has she got a pain somewhere?' And my tears would splash over your chubby warm hands and you would hear me wail, 'Help me! Jenny can't go on, can't stand any more of this. Jenny can't stand being Jenny any longer. She's got a pain in her soul, a terrible pain!' Surely you, if anyone, must know where this pain comes from, a pain that can suddenly throw itself over someone, turn them into a stranger, *someone who isn't there*? Oh, Mother, don't let your Jenny be torn to pieces! Don't let this horror wind her round and round its cruel fingers like a worn-out handkerchief and then throw her into the dark . . .

Why don't you say something? Why don't you help me? Turn me away this time, and I'll let you know all about the real me! I'll show you another Jenny, a wicked nasty one, who will bite your hands instead of kissing them; a Jenny who knows how to drive a ruthless steel drill into your stony old heart! And whose only longing is to smash this glass wall that's always stood between us. Oh yes, you know very well what I mean! You who love opera. Who never turn down one of Leo's free tickets. The fact is, you are having a lot more fun than Jenny, bored to death among the roses in this foreign evergreen country; Jenny, who never sees anything but the garden's stone walls, same wall, same ivy, always and forever the same; same house, same children, same husband! Day after day, night after night! Surely you realize that she's a Stockholm girl, a *poet*, a creature of town apartments, who will be driven infallibly insane, bleed to death inwardly here in this *vie de campagne*? Doesn't it terrify you that her music is dying inside her, that all her dreamy visions are fading away as she lives an endless chain of grey Mondays? Don't you realize she is one of your three terrified kids, the ones that Krabataska, the Estonian storybook witch, used to fly up and down our vicarage's white stairs with, dragging them out of their beds in the dead of night, whisking them away under her cloak to her forest hut to torture them with life in an institution? Or, if they escaped from her clutches, leaving them pale-faced and mentally disturbed for ever? But she has taken the wrong child, Mother, the wrong child! Jenny has never been naughty – only mad. Threatened by anxiety, petrified, that's what she is! Threatened by these two wretched beggars that I am imploring to leave me, at least for a little while, until I can pull myself together, so that I can seem calm and collected when you and Jean-Paul get back from your walk. Don't you see how terrified I am of the trolls' mountain they'll shut me up in if this goes on? How envious

I am of everyone who is alive and can create, while huge, jagged rocks, impossible to shift, block me on all sides, obstructing the path I once wanted to follow and which Leo is speeding down like an express train? If only I could find it, follow it, perhaps I could find myself. But now it is too late . . . Forgive me, I must make Jenny calm down, give her a couple of Valium . . . There now, that's better. Calmer now.

Mother, I love you so much. I ask for so little! Only for you to caress me . . . let me be near you. Forget Father, Fredrik, Leo, forget them all. And be with me. I need you. Surely you remember Nitti, she who used to sit and sulk on the kitchen steps outside our house among the blue hills, rocking a log, instead of a doll, wrapped in an old shawl? Why did you all laugh at her? Didn't you realize there was something very, very wrong with such a little girl? '*Bist du bei mir*', how I love that little love-song; I can hear it over and over again. I know you aren't God, but I don't know where He is – if He is anywhere.

Oh well, never mind. Don't overstrain yourself for my sake! Neither you nor Jean-Paul can follow me into the trolls' mountain. It is only natural that I *cling* to him and the children, even though it is just a matter of time; of how much longer Jenny can force herself to go on living in other people's worlds, pretend to be an upper-middle-class wife, mother and housewife. The trolls' mountain beckons, whispering that once inside it you live in a wild-grown garden, timeless, clockless. All pain numbed by drugs and injections.

Right now you are out taking an evening stroll with my Jean-Paul. I can just see how you fasten your sad brown eyes on him, like two stars, as you cross-examine him about me. And how embarrassed and divided he, whom I love so much, feels. He both wants to confide in you and doesn't. The tension between you grows. You forget the children. You, Jean-Paul, are feeling more and more nervous, pressured by her brown inquisitive eyes to pour out your worries into her ears, always avid for some tragedy. And you, in spite of everything, yield to Mother's curiosity, no less razor-edged than Leo's. Her eyes drive you on from one admission to another – about our home, our children, our sex life. Well, not that – she is much too prudish, too touchy about sexual matters! Even so, you are certainly talking about me; how I'm cutting myself off; how labile and easily shattered, nowadays, all my relationships are with others, with your old witch of a mother, with the nymphomaniac Rita.

Oh dear, Jean-Paul, how I let my manic thoughts run away with me! You are not that stupid. You are the only fly who never lets itself be caught in Mother's spider's webs. You wouldn't betray me, even under torture. Would you?

No, Jenny isn't evil, she wishes no one any harm.

And look! They are tiptoeing away, the grey beggars are leaving me. And I sink back on to the bed, exhausted.

Footsteps down there on the gravel. She hears Jean-Paul's voice: 'Magdalena? Who's she?' To Jenny it sounds like a cry of dismay, of suppressed pain. Her mother must have shot an arrow straight at its target. She starts up from the bed, listens tensely. Her heart thumps. What now? Again her nerves panic, take flight like a flock of startled birds. All her family are expert throwers of poisoned, double-meaning, darts.

No more crunch of footsteps on gravel. Now they must be standing in the doorway, motionless in the light cast by the crescent moon as it flits between night's indigo clouds. Cut to shreds like old curtains or ragged dresses, they chase each other high above the house, the garden, the sleeping village.

'Why, Jenny, of course!' Her mother's voice snaps through the air as if beheading a rose.

In her mind's eye Jenny envisages the strange half-smile playing on her mother's lips – nothing of its feline satisfaction eludes her. She gives a start. Tenses up. Grasps the import of her mother's parting shot: '*Surely you've realized by now that there is more than one Jenny?*'

It's as though her mother has tossed a key in through the open bedroom window. The key to her heart. Jenny darts over to her wardrobe, hunts through it. Trembles in every limb. Goes hot and cold. Her shaking hands know what it is they are looking for: her black velvet dress with its white lace collar. For a few seconds as she flings aside Jenny's clothes and changes into it she is in an agonized vacuum, as if her own self had flown out of the window, become one of the ragged clouds, up there in the night sky.

Somewhere in the house the cry of a small child. Child? She has no child she must run to and console. She is on her way towards death, must stand and weep at the foot of the cross. Why must that child start crying, just now of all times? Just when she is gliding into the Magdalena her parents, in that other country, wanted her to resemble? It only irritates her. Only her faith could lead them to the Resurrection and life eternal. Only on her could they hitch a ride to heaven. That's why they'd loved her so, playing this game . . .

Why won't the child inside her stop crying as she stands there staring at her own pale features in the bathroom mirror? Its whimpering, reiterated lament hurts like a rough-hewn cross being nailed together inside her as the child writhes on it. But in her lace-collared black dress Magdalena, she of the transparent face, goes downstairs, enters the sitting-room.

Jean-Paul, October 7

A night of unruly dreams. Is it due to the whisky or my bad conscience, for leaving them alone together, if only for a couple of days? Don't know. Away from Jenny I feel more and more fragile, both in mind and body. It gets worse hour by hour, until finally it brings on a migraine. Above all I feel utterly bored with everything and everyone. Compared with Jenny and the children everyone around me seems dreary, colourless, wearisomely pushy or else mere shadows. Most boring of all is their everlasting attempt to organize so-called reality, as if forever chewing on the same piece of gum.

Jenny and I – we are in danger of becoming a *folie à deux*! Jenny dearest, no matter how odd, capricious, you are, for me you are the only person in the world. Sometimes you can seem happier, more in love with life than anyone I know. When we make love I am abolished and made new. In your arms, in your body, I no longer know what is you, what is me . . . Together we die a little while and together come back to life.

Dear love, dear Jenny, in your dark background, your obscure and muddled past I am only too happy to explore all those difficult, oppressive things that torment you so much. I will follow, led by the little light in my soul, even back to the very beginning if you like. Because I am sure that is where the trouble lies. Impervious to my love, deaf to all analysing, consoling words, it compels me to hazard guesses that can't be put into words . . .

But Jenny, darling, we must hurry! We may not have much time left. Though your mother's power, her brilliance, has become subdued, soon to burn out, in my eyes she is lethal. Her effect on you, her hypnotic effect – like yesterday evening – scares me. I don't doubt that you love her. Yet no matter how tenderly you embrace one another, each of you is struggling to cut the umbilical cord that still binds you. Isn't that so?

How long-winded and verbose I become, here on my own, while the others are enjoying themselves dancing, or over there at the bar! All I really meant to do was write down what happened next . . .

Where was I? Oh, yes, your mother's strange power over you.

Letting her go on ahead into the house, I hung about in the garden to relax, shake off the tingling apprehensive feeling, the field of tension that your mother – well, your whole family – always creates. Woe to any poor devil, any non-genius, who happens to come fluttering into it!

Calmed by our rose garden's tranquil perfume, pipe in mouth like a baby's pacifier, I went indoors. Our spacious and, as far as we have been able to afford it, rather pleasant sitting-room – a fusion or, perhaps one should say, symbiosis of Swedish and English manor-house styles – lay in semi-darkness. Silent, as if ashamed of itself, your old square piano you used to love to play seemed to hide its walnut face; similarly the huge painting of the Holy Family with John the Baptist as a child, a premature heirloom. The whole room, where we used to make music, seemed half-asleep in the dark. Only a log or two snapped and crackled anxiously in our Scandinavian-style fireplace, while on the mantelpiece two candles like wise but nervous virgins fluttered in their brass candlesticks as they watched over you and your mother seated in front of the fire. Now and again one tremulous candle flame would signal to the other: 'Not for an instant, sister dear, must we weary, doze off or fail to keep an eye on this mother, this daughter. In this room there is danger in the air. Powers incomprehensible to mere mortals are at work!'

And so they were. Something odd, inexplicable, was going on. It was as if the reredos picture from some Italian church had unhooked itself from its usual place above the white-gilt Gustavian settee and seated itself in front of the fire – but with a faintly pathological change of dramatis personae. In lieu of the Madonna, looking mildly if absent-mindedly down at her son, fruit of so mysterious a liaison, it was your mother's sallow countenance that was gazing quizzically, mournfully down at you. And you, Jenny, were sitting snuggled up to her swollen knees. Wordless, you looked up at her in masochistic adoration that both disgusted and paralysed me.

Nothing is so painful, so utterly bewildering, as seeing someone one loves estranged, beyond one's reach, transformed. This woman, her long tresses combed out straight and with a little silver crucifix dangling down her black velvet dress – she was no longer you, my troublesome, neurotic darling; you of the worn-out jeans and flowery skirts, with hair carelessly but charmingly pinned up. No longer my wife, sometimes wildly funny or temperamental, sometimes deeply sensitive, but nowadays, sad to say, all too often depressed. Whom I, in spite of everything, can usually get through to. I certainly couldn't get through to this dumb-struck, adoring creature who, crouched there in front of her mother, had dressed herself up as Mary Magdalene. Just then I could have hit her, shaken her out of her soppy religiosity, her dream. Anything to awaken this sleep-walker! A split-personality act so well staged that it could have been pure theatre. But wasn't.

Confused, I tried to recall what I dimly remembered about Mary Magdalene but had long ago dumped in my unconscious. Who was she, really, this woman who had suddenly put in an appearance by the dying embers of my sitting-room fire? Passive, soulful, probably rather plain and unattractive, wasn't she the opposite of the Mary who had 'chosen the better part'? A listener, forever cringing at the Master's feet, guzzling his words? Anyway, that was about all I could fish out of the dusty nooks and crannies of old scripture lessons.

But enough of biblical ponderings. Something was going on here that I couldn't grasp but each moment found more and more upsetting. A kind of hypnosis; something I have never experienced, only read about in Freud's account of Charcot's clinic in Paris. Can it really be that this dynamic little woman, this mother, possesses powers quite beyond either my understanding or my experience? That she is able to shatter Jenny's and my life together? In that moment some dark, evil power seemed to be wrenching my Eurydice off to a forbidden underworld. Oh, Jenny,

Jenny, come back to your Jean-Paul! Don't let those amber eyes seduce you into the nothingness of an eternal life beyond anything I can imagine! Oh, Jenny, Jenny, come back to me and the children! You are no half-witted Magdalene listening at Jesus' feet – no, what am I saying, at your mother's! She is not Christ; just a power-greedy, ageing woman who has come to visit us and whom, if she persists in conjuring you away like this, I will send packing tomorrow! Stop your play-acting, Jenny! You are no actress. Just mentally confused, a bit disturbed, not surprisingly, in view of your background up there in that horrible northern country where the sun either shines twenty-four hours a day or it is as dark as midnight! You have the children and me to help you get through our one-and-only life. Eternal lives don't exist, Jenny. They are clergyman's chatter. It is this life right now that we must live.

My silent appeal made no impression. Apathetic, I sat down facing these two, this mother, this daughter, in my high-backed leather chair. Wordless, like two deep-sea divers tempted to tear off their oxygen masks and perish in a life–death ecstasy, they seemed bent on plumbing the depths of each other's soul.

No longer able to bear my spectator role, I closed my eyes but contemplated behind my fingers this witch of a mother-in-law and Jenny, who had let herself be torn away from me, the only person who has ever loved her, passionately, for her own sake. Jealous and bitter I observed them. Does Jenny love her mother more than me? Is she a grown woman, or quite simply a babe-in-arms, greedily suckling breast milk that any normal adult would find disgusting? Is that all she really longs for? Peace at the maternal breast? And the woman I have married, is she completely infantile, only pretending to have grown up?

And I remembered that time when we were making love and she, in the moment of orgasm, cried out, 'Mam . . . mam . . . mamma . . .'

At that moment Victoria, in her muddy riding boots, burst in.

Stinking of horse dung and playing tough as only a fourteen-year-old can, she had obviously been out for an evening ride with the stable boys.

'What the *hell's* going on in here?' she cried, her riding boots coming to a halt in front of her mother and grandmother. Shrouded in the fire's gloom, neither of them seemed to pay her the least attention.

'Daddy! Why is Mum looking so daft?'

As she turned sharply towards me I saw how her lively teenage features had turned pale; how shaken she was. Scornful, with a despair verging on fury, she went on: 'Daddy, what are they *doing?* She isn't even my mum, I don't recognize her. Are they acting some play, or what? Mummy, Mormor . . . Hello there! It's me, Vicky!'

Crouching down beside Jenny she touched her hand. Exclaimed, 'But, Mum, you're icy cold!' Her anxious questions and exclamations still tumbled over each other as little Rosalind came running in her nightie. Halting in her tracks, she too stared a moment at Jenny. Then began whimpering: 'Mummy, Mummy, I've had such a horrid dream. I'm so frightened!' And flung herself on her. Only then did Jenny – but even then only slowly, reluctantly, as if returning from some distant country unknown to the rest of us – come to her senses. Stare dreamy-eyed around her. Her natural pallor returned. Drawing our sobbing little girl to her she said in a low voice: 'Forgive me. It must be late. Are you all hungry?'

'Yes, we are,' replied Victoria. '*Madly!*'

Suddenly all the lights went up and in came Michael, carrying little Josephine and her teddy bear. With a sleepy smile Jojo stretched out her chubby little arms to Jenny, who took her into hers. At which Michael, throwing his mother and grandmother keen if not very interested glances, switched on the television and flung himself down on the sofa. And abruptly the room, so deathly quiet a moment ago, was invaded by a Wild West shoot-out, whose bullets whizzed and whined through the whole house.

My account of this sudden scene change gives no real idea perhaps of how the children's interruption had shattered an atmosphere, doubtless fascinating to a theatre-goer or a psychiatrist but which I had found utterly horrible. And not only I but Victoria too, I'm sure. For a brief moment she, too, had known all the horrors of exclusion.

A moment more and we were all going about our business: Jenny upstairs with her two sleepy little girls; I, taking over Martha's role, to the kitchen, to try and find my ever-hungry teenage daughter something to eat. Between chews at a peanut-butter sandwich she threw me a questioning glance. 'Why's Mum dressed up like that? Why were they sitting there staring at each other like a couple of corpses?'

I fumbled for an answer. Couldn't find one. How to explain to a teenager a relationship so deep and complicated as Jenny's and Charlotte's, which even I couldn't make head or tail of? But Victoria, determined to have one, fastened her gaze on me like a searchlight. At a loss, I shut it off.

'Just now I really don't know, Vicky dear,' I mumbled evasively. 'Some other time. We'll talk about it some other time '

Just then my mother-in-law, smiling a gentle, wistful smile, appeared in the kitchen. There were shadows under her eyes. A harmless, ageing woman, for whom the hour was too late and whose own end was approaching.

'Good night, my dears,' she said. 'Now I'll go up and say prayers with the little ones.'

' "God who loveth tiny children".' Vicky quoted the Swedish children's prayer. A shade ironically, a shade envious.

'Precisely, my big girl,' Charlotte said and left us.

'Mummy isn't going round the bend, is she, Dad?' Vicky asked me in a low voice. 'Sometimes she seems so . . . odd. Not really with it any longer . . .'

In my daughter's clear, searching eyes I saw a precocious wisdom, a dawning awareness of how painful it always is to grow up, cross the threshold to adulthood. A girl-woman, Victoria was insisting she be told the truth – a truth the child in her still wasn't up to bearing. A step she daren't take.

'Of course not, darling,' I said, with exaggerated self-assurance. 'She just put on that black dress for Mormor's sake. They were enjoying a solemn moment together by the fireside, that's all. You know, like when Mum was a child.'

This half-truth had hardly left my lips when Vicky, bursting into tears, threw herself in my arms – something she hadn't done since she was little and had fallen over and hurt her knees. Nowadays it was rare for her to show any feelings, not to me anyway, or to Jenny. And now . . . this explosion.

'Daddy, Daddy,' she sobbed, 'I got so frightened. Don't go to Dublin tomorrow! They'll only spoil my birthday, carrying on like that – Mummy and Mormor!'

Before I went in to Jenny, I took a look at Michael in the sitting-room. Snuggled up in one corner of the old blue sofa with his thumb in his mouth, he was staring at some programme that couldn't interest him in the least. The same sense of threat, which each of our children was reacting to in one way or another – either violently, like Vicky just then, or dumbly, shut up in himself, like Michael – passed through me. And again I felt helpless and alone. If it were only a question of Jenny and myself! If only I had to cope with her odd behaviour! But how am I to help our children to skirt her neurosis and not be damaged for life? It is impossible. I'm not omnipotent. Both Vicky and Michael (Rosalind too) are already showing signs of insecurity. Are gradually being thrust out of their childhood garden, walled in by our love and happiness.

'Come on now, Michael,' I said. 'It's late. And do switch off that television.'

'Where's Mum?' he asked, grumpy, slowly getting off the sofa. 'Since Mormor came she hasn't given us a thought. And she promised to help me with my homework.'

'Which means you haven't done it?'

His feelings hurt, he shrugged nonchalantly.

'But you could have asked me to help you, couldn't you?' I joked. 'I'm quite good at writing essays, you know. After all, I write them all day long!'

'But Mum *promised* . . .'

Turning a disappointed little back on me, he wandered off up to his room. An abandoned nine-year-old.

Dreams in a Mirror

Clad only in her night-dress and with her hair down, Jenny is sitting in front of her bedroom mirror. The windows are open on to the garden.

She is wholly absorbed in her own mirrored image. Mirrors fascinate her. She hates them. They terrify her. On several occasions during her anxiety attacks she has begged Jean-Paul to get rid of every mirror in the house. 'They are dangerous,' she explains afterwards. 'I sink into them like deep waters. Or feel I'm going to pieces and want to smash them! We weren't allowed to have any at home, you see. It was forbidden. Sinful. Like wanting oneself. Loving oneself. So I used to pinch little bits of the maid's or the cook's, bits that had got broken. Locked myself into the loo and stared at myself. It was strange: one moment I looked like a bloated toad, the next like a fairy-tale princess. And no matter how I tried to make out what the real Jenny looked like, those bits of mirror always told lies! Only Mother had one in her bedroom. It hung over her chest of drawers. And still does. One day I will inherit it. It has a gilded neo-rococo frame, with chubby cherubs blowing trumpets. But it was so high I couldn't reach it. And anyway Mother didn't bother with mirrors! She was far above such earthly conceits. Never used any makeup, only a little powder on her nose. 'God cares nothing for our outward appearance,' she used to say. 'He looks straight into our souls.' And at other times: 'The eyes, Jenny, are the mirrors to the soul.' I firmly believed that if I climbed up and took a look at myself God would punish me! Squash me between His thumb and forefingers, like an insect, and throw me out of the window.'

Sometimes Jenny tells Jean-Paul her dreams. One recurring dream is of being locked up in a palace where ceiling-high mirrors reach to the ceiling between the wall panels. Dustless, with never a scratch, they gleam and shimmer, as if for the queens of some bygone court. She is alone. No one disturbs her. No man lusts after her, no children are crying for their mummy. No one is demanding instant obedience. In this merciful silence she can now calmly admire her own beauty, criticize her own faults, her physical short-comings, form some idea of what she is really like. Even more urgent: in this castle of mirrors she is free to find herself, the one who strangely, long ago, ran way. Now she is calling to herself, this shy, timid creature, being reunited with her as if with a twin sister, deeply loved, long missed. Full of wonder, calm yet exalted, she sees in her dream her outward appearance. She is so beautiful! She is tempted to caress her own body, touch her skin with her finger-tips, touch her hair, her life-giving body, still shell-like and closed in on itself, despite four childbirths.

But then something happens. An opaque film obscures the mirror; then a mist, a fog. And Jenny's eyesight, too, dims, isn't able any longer to make out her own shape, only a moment ago so clear and brilliant. She fumbles her way blindly through the palace's darkening halls. Her wish-dream of solitude and free self-contemplation turns into panicky isolation, and she tries to cry out for Mother, Father, for her brothers, friends, children. For Jean-Paul . . . But no matter how she struggles, her scream stifles to a cramped howl. Everything around her grows light and she can see again; but no longer her own image. In the giant mirrors, which somehow seem to have turned greener, more transparent, like french windows opening out on to the park, she glimpses familiar faces. Her father's; solemn, ceremonious, high above her as if in a pulpit. Instead of noticing this young woman and her mirror gaz-ings, his pale-blue absent eyes look into another world, into that life of the hereafter that she is out of touch with, fixated as she is on mirrors. 'Forgive me! Forgive Jenny, she'll never do it again!' she calls up to him. In vain. Her father's face, childlike, blissful, illuminated as if by some celestial searchlight, fades; and underneath him the grandiose baroque pulpit, with its golden, overfed cherubs awakened from their ecclesiastical slumbers, sails away. They fly straight up into the clouds above the park's trees, towards a welcoming night sky. Touched to the heart by this ascension, Jenny falls to her knees. And in the same instant her mother's face appears, clear and close in the mirror:

'Mother,' she wails, 'help me! Don't leave me, I'm so frightened! Always, always frightened.' But her mother's eyes are sad and distant. She is suffering. Demanding sympathy? Though longing to reach Jenny, for some reason she can't. And her own struggles are no less futile. Between them is an implacable wall of mirrors. In her mother's veiled, sad glance, heavy with an inscrutable suffering, there is no smile a small child can mirror and smile back to. Here, Jenny is close to her life's enigma. Her insoluble enigma.

Yet after all it is only a dream, and as in a film its cuts are swift, traumatic. Abruptly her two brothers' faces pop up. Right through the mirrors Fredrik's prematurely balding pate shines like a new moon, imperative. And his black pebbly eyes, like cut gems in a jeweller's window, gleam ironically at his sister, eight years younger, whom he doesn't even know, hasn't ever tried to. Since he hardly opens his mouth as he speaks, his words, supposed to be funny, are indistinct, almost incomprehensible as he addresses this desperate, unknown woman, his little sister; this altogether temperamental, excessively illogical and hysterical creature. Something about not 'sinking' (or does he mean 'thinking'? He affects an old-fashioned aristocratic lisp and his words, despite their possible profundity, are indecipherable). Quickly she turns away. To Leo. Whispers: 'Oh, Leo, I'm so lonely! Neither Father, Mother nor Fredrik care about us! We've been abandoned, we don't even *exist!*' But Leo just screws up his heavy-lidded eyes in that critical, quizzical way of his. Asks crudely: 'Haven't you had just about enough of fucking on Sussex dunghills with that little French jerk of yours?' She shivers in the icy air of his brotherly scorn. 'What the hell have you done with your life, sister dear?' he goes on. 'Why did you have to leave me, leave Sweden, leave us all for that shit Jean-Paul? Why don't you work regular hours, write your poetry, create? You who were so damn talented! Surely you can't be content to fritter away your life producing a bunch of screaming brats!' Wrath cuts through his voice. He has been deeply hurt. And he gives vent to one of his famous guffaws, bois-terous, unmotivated, joyless; just a diabolical bray, blurted out by a soul in torment.

At this, for Jenny, the dreamer, everything goes to pieces. His laugh shatters all her mirrors. Her dream palace hails down over her in a myriad tiny, razor-sharp splinters, cutting her crouching body to shreds. Sliced through and through, no more than a bleed-ing shred of herself, she makes a last effort, reaches out for a frag-ment to mirror herself in.

But the face she sees is monstrous. Bleeding. Disfigured. No skin specialist, no cosmetic surgery, no makeup will ever be able to do anything about it. Like a leper or a nuclear survivor, anyone with such a face can only hide it from others' eyes.

Or die.

Jean-Paul's journal

Why did my wife's horrible mirror-dream cross my mind just as I entered our bedroom, so pink, so conservative, so English? Perhaps it was because Jenny looked so lovely in front of her dressing-table mirror? I don't know. Maybe my mother is right, grievously jealous though she is? That Jenny has bewitched me; trapped me in her tangled skein, spun up there in the primitive Nordic forests? Turned me into a worker ant, day in, day out, dragging impossibly heavy burdens to her anthill, while its queen just lies there and enjoys herself? She has turned you into one of those hairs of hers she is always brushing and brushing, I thought to myself, calming down. Maybe it is about time you tried to remember your own dreams, instead of forever trying to interpret hers, especially as more often than not they seem to be figments of her poetic imagination . . .

In an egoistic outburst of tedium and weariness I tactlessly interrupt her session at the mirror. For once I ignore her feelings, her nerves.

'What kind of a bloody-fool farce were you and your mother staging this evening? Don't you realize it scares the wits out of the children?'

She jumps. Throws me a look as sad and reproachful as her mother's.

'No need to be crude, Jean-Paul! Swearing doesn't suit you.'

I grasp her shoulders. A grip unnecessarily hard, wrathful, full of suppressed aggressions.

'Why do you have to suddenly turn into someone neither I nor the children recognize? How do you think it feels for us? Didn't you see how it upset Vicky, and Michael, too, though he didn't let on. *Qu'est-ce que tout celà veut dire, Jenny?*'

Her hair brushing ceases. She lays down the brush I gave her in Paris, the one with the silver monogram. Now she is no longer looking at herself in the mirror but down at her hands, nervously pressed together like two slim white paper-knives. Yes, I see it now. I have been trying to turn a stub-nailed daughter of a Swedish clergyman into a well-manicured Anglo-French *dame du monde*, her dressing-table littered with Lancôme's sophisticated face-creams and Dior perfumes! How much of the housework, really, is she dumping on Rita, on Mother's Violet? And the children – does she even look after them properly when I'm away? The fact is, I have spoilt her.

She stares at me, amazed. Doesn't even seem angry. Just astonished at my outburst.

'Staging? What do you mean? What have I done? Frightened you and the children? I'd never frighten them, as you know very well.'

Her gentle smile calms me. She is so lovely, my Jenny, so caressable. How can anyone with her fine, clear complexion dream that her face has been ravaged, cut to pieces? Has she already forgotten that nasty Magdalena episode or is she just pretending? Oh, Jenny, behind your soft exterior why are you so full of contradictions?

But I insist. She and her mother were definitely playing theatre, down there in the sitting-room! For a while, long enough to scare first me then the kids, they shut us out.

Half embarrassed, half excited, she gives a tense, brittle laugh:

'Oh, you mean our *tableau vivant*. It was just make-believe – a kind of charade we used to play at home! Theatricals weren't like cards or sex. It was about the only thing that wasn't forbidden.' Another small nervous laugh. 'And anyway, where's the harm in the children – or you – seeing some theatre for once in a while, here in this dump? At least it's a change from donkeys and flowers, birds and bees.'

'*Je n'y comprends rien!*'

'Idiot. Surely you realize I did it to please Mother? She likes me when I'm Magdalena.' Adds with wry charm: 'Even *loves* me a bit, in a way she definitely doesn't love Jenny.'

'Well, I do! I love her however she is . . .'

'Do you? But what about Magdalena? You don't even know her. You had better take out your Bible. Then you will see what a goody she was, asking nothing for herself. Unlike your Jenny, who can hardly put a foot right.'

As she says this, her voice quivers and the faint greenish tinge, which I have noticed both in her and in our two little girls when something scares them appears at the corners of her mouth and nostrils.

51

'She was a whore, wasn't she, a fallen woman?' I say cynically. 'Maybe all she wanted of Jesus was to seduce him?'

Her plucked blonde eyebrows narrow, become almost black like her mother's.

'Ssh, Jean-Paul, you don't know what you are saying! You are blaspheming! Why must you always spoil anything that's holy?'

I yawn. Fed up and mad at myself. At my far too complicated wife. At all sacred things!

'Jenny,' I say, laying an uxorious hand on her shoulder. 'I don't give a damn for the Bible, or for your mother, and still less for your amateur theatricals. Why can't you just be *yourself?*'

Suddenly Jenny looks frail, tormented, as if by a pain inside her. A wraith blown in through the window by the misty autumn night. At once I take her in my arms. Try to caress, console and kiss her.

'*Mais chérie*, you are *mine* after all!'

My words just throw her into a rage. Wrenching herself out of my embrace she gasps that I am a fool, a male chauvinist French pig, determined to over-protect her, make her feel like a sexually abused child. I haven't a clue about her Swedish need for female autonomy. I *hate* her lovely old mother just as I hate the whole remarkable family I have so ruthlessly cut her off from! With malice aforethought I have dumped her in this draughty, spooky old house here in England, where she is pining away like a prisoner next door to my insufferable old termagant of a mother, whose tongue is as sharp as a saw-edged cactus and who spreads nasty lies about Jenny over the whole village; yes, and even about the children whom she, my monstrous mother, doesn't even regard as grandchildren, just a brood of snotty-nosed foreign urchins, insatiable cuckoo eggs on whose account her son, like a caged starling, is destroying his brilliant career! My lady-mother doesn't remotely care that Jenny is the daughter of a dean, a court chaplain – not to mention the sister of a world-famous conductor! *Simply because they aren't British . . .* In my mother's mind Jenny is just a voluptuous whore, whose only talent is to lie on her back, put her legs in the air and seduce her alas all too-oversexed son, over and over, leaving him, exhausted and sallow, to stagger off to his next futurological congress! His virility, his will-power and – not least – the genius he is supposed to have inherited from my mother's retrospectively canonized husband, all this is gradually being destroyed in Jenny's unmentionable little hole.

Yes, that (more or less) was how my mother's tongue was poisoning family life in this rain-sodden village, in whose high street Jenny soon won't dare show her face. Oh, how Jenny *hates* her mother-in-law! How can a woman like that know what it is like, having four children! All she can do is run off to cocktail parties and coffee mornings and bridge parties, rubbing shoulders with the local upper-class money-bags! Oh, Jenny could *kill* her! Either that or pack her bags and leave this green country, as stagnant and unchanging as the village pond. This wasn't where she and her children belonged! *Home, home* to Stockholm, to the pine forests, the spruces, the lakes, the white snow, and the blue summer skies that she, languishing away in this stone house under its diseased elms, longs for so much she could *die* . . .

She broke down, shaken with sobs. And I, afraid each moment she would start screaming and wake the children, put my arms round her, pressed her to myself, assured her I understood that her little biblical scene was nothing but a harmless charade, a way of getting close to her mother, and that it was I who had wholly misunderstood the situation and was causing all this noise in the night. Sobbing in my arms, she seemed to calm down, relax, pressing herself against me and – to my embarrassment – slobbering wet doggy kisses on my hands. Cold insight crept over me: that she is no longer responsible for her behaviour; is hardly aware of her personality splits, which to her are tragic realities. Or that she is mentally disturbed and needs expert help if she isn't soon to go to pieces altogether . . .

My total helplessness horrifies me; and it is in an attempt to get some mental grip on the situation that I'm writing all this down. In this cruel dilemma neither my so-called intellect nor my obsessive love for Jenny are of any help. Only professional psychiatry can cope with cases like Jenny. Sooner or later I will be forced to send her away, like a broken clock. Risk the clock mender's diagnosis: 'Hopeless case. Works damaged beyond repair.'

My revulsion and terror at this thought were so strong that I too began trembling all over, clinging to Jenny as if it were I who were ill, not her. And in that terrified embrace, in the misery of our threatened love, we met and made love more stubbornly, wildly and painfully than ever before, until Jenny's cry tore through the bedroom, penetrating the mild darkness of the Sussex night, soon followed by my own ecstatic groans. I was flung like an ocean wave, a great breaker, on to the shore of her moist, soft body.

After she had dropped off I just lay there, relishing the peace of the night; this brief respite, when for a moment no one stirred up any trouble, demanded my attention, nagged or wept. Though I was drowsy after our *amour*, I tried to stay awake a little longer, ponder things in peace and quiet, undisturbed in my own solitary world, before the morning circus started up: the stony-hearted alarm clock, the little girls' morning rush for our bed, Vicky splashing about in the shower, the toilet's flushings and Rita's angry banging and rattling down in the kitchen.

Jenny, too, seemed far away from the sense of anxiety that can attack her even in her happiest moments: first with its warning signals of inexplicable sadness and restlessness; then with a kind of wordless unrest that she tries in vain to ward off, defy and deny and does everything she can to shake off. Her sleep seemed deep and tranquil. Gently, not to wake her, I smoothed away the long, damp tresses from her sleeping face, just then so young and girlish again, and yet, on closer inspection, already scored with suffering.

Tenderly I kissed her naked breasts and again, as I did so, the vision of her mind and body as a kind of unexplored but endlessly beautiful landscape flitted through my mind; the same image that I had seen so clearly that first night we ever made love. Of an immense land, boundless, enigmatic, exquisite yet deadly. And I remembered how, almost like a hallucination, it had seemed to be a warning against involving myself with her. Yet how avid I had become to possess her the more terrified I had become of this foreigner's youthful attraction, her power; to live *through* her, even if the journey cost me my life.

Though frightened and wary, I chose Jenny. A fated decision. With idiotic, youthful heroism I was sure I could orient myself along those dark, uncharted paths and down this fascinating landscape's perilous steeps, into this female body that sometimes blends so swiftly and fierily with mine; at other times receives me with reluctant distaste or frigidly rejects me altogether. Jenny, with her clitoral excitements, her snail-like slowness or else, caught in sudden short-circuits, her tendency to break off our intercourse. Jenny, with her puritanical ennui or insatiable desire for repeated orgasm, is certainly a most demanding partner. An enigma. More and more my lust has had to learn to restrain itself when she has none. Nothing – least of all intercourse – can force itself on her. Her will, so fundamentally enormous, rules both our lives and our love life. As I have come to realize.

There, my mother is right.

Why, oh why, can't I set her free? I love her so much.

Soon after midnight Jean-Paul is woken by his wife's cry. Although he is tired and sleepy, he takes her into his arms, tries to calm her. Her cries are small, strained, come in little spasms that turn into whimperings. Her eyes are still closed, her forehead still moist with sweat.

'What is it, *chérie*? Do try and calm down – there now! I'll get you a glass of water.'

It is not water she wants. He mustn't leave her, not for a moment. Hot and chilled at the same time, she stares wide-eyed past him, out into the bedroom; seems neither to see him nor anything else. But there is something else she sees. A vision of terror. An evil dream she is still in, can't drag herself free from.

'I was dreaming . . .' she gabbles, her pupils unnaturally large and her body in his arms stiff and hard. 'Oh, it was horrible, horrible . . .'

'Dreamt? Tell me.'

Now he feels cold as well. Though damp night air is coming in through the open window, it is her terror, her inner icy chill that is infecting him. He wraps the blankets more closely around them.

'OK, *ta rêve*. You know it won't be so horrible once you've told me about it,' he encourages. Switches on the light. His patience is sorely tried. Soon a new day must begin. In a few hours he must be off to that conference in Dublin. But he forgets himself, as he always does for Jenny. It is in her white face, with the shadows under its eyes, worn but now radiant, that he exists.

Stammering to begin with, then coherently, she tells him her dream. And Jean-Paul listens, acutely. Pays attention to each detail, as he has taught himself to do this last year as her anxiety has grown manifestly worse. As yet he is hardly aware of the effects that his intuitive insights into the neurotic depths are having on himself.

'We were in a big forest – Mother, you and I and little Josephine,' she whispers into the shadows. 'It must have been in Sweden, it was so dreadfully cold. We were high up, in a mountain pasture . . . with its empty, grey timber shacks . . . snowed in. Snow – stretching away in all directions. All of a sudden the whole sky was on fire. You looked so small and scared. But Mother just stood there in her galoshes, deep in a snow-drift, fascinated by the landscape and the hues in the sky.'

Whenever Jenny is excited she slips back into her native

tongue and Jean-Paul has some difficulty in following, at points doesn't get it all. Half sitting up in the bed she stares, as if a thousand miles away in the Scandinavian forests, out into the grey misty sky not yet pierced by any streak of dawn.

'And then?' he yawns, wishing she would get on with it. 'What happened then?' Soon it will be morning. They have so little time. She loses herself so easily in digressions, *la petite Jenny*. As is only natural. After all, by nature she is an artist. A story-teller, a sort of Scheherazade who, when describing a face, a flower, can't help seeking artistic detachment from her story's framework by losing its thread. A tormented expression comes into her features and she struggles on:

'Well, you were clapping your arms and saying we must get away as soon as possible from these icy heights. So we slipped quickly into a sleigh, you, Jojo and I on the front seat and Mother reluctantly behind us. We all snuggled down under thick furs as we went whirling across the snow and through the forests. Suddenly we heard horrible howls. Looking back over my shoulder I saw a pack of Alsatians coming after us, their red tongues hanging out. Though we were going fast, they were getting closer and closer, and at any moment they would fling themselves at us and eat us whole.'

'And then?'

Jean-Paul seems to recall faintly having heard all this before, in a bad translation of a romantic Swedish novel he had once read in Paris.

'Then – then I . . . I did something dreadful, *horrible* . . .' she forces herself to say. Jumping out of bed she goes over to the window, where she stands with her face in her hands like a child that has been stood in the corner.

'*I flung out Mother to the dogs* . . . She had dwindled to a little bundle, didn't even resist. Suddenly I felt so big, so strong! Immense, capable of anything . . . But it had given us a respite, a

chance to get ahead . . . while the wolves, no, the Alsatians, I
mean, were tearing her to pieces! Oh, how dreadful, dreadful! To
save our lives I'd thrown a poor, sick old woman out into the snow,
where she became a mass of bleeding strips of flesh – she who had
just been gazing at the sunset!'

She sobs, trembling. 'I *murdered* Mother, don't you understand?
Oh, how could I, how could I dream such a thing? I love her so
much . . .'

Against his better knowledge Jean-Paul points out that it was
only a dream, after all. And here in Sussex there may be Alsatians
but no wolves. A nasty, cruel dream, it is true; but one that shows
how strong her will is to survive and save herself and Josephine –
and him. (That her dream also more obviously reveals a wish to
get shot of her mother is a point he keeps to himself.)

At this Jenny throws him a strange look. And in the light from
the bedside lamp her eyes, usually so blue and naive, seem to turn
an indeterminate dark green, like Leo's. And her lips momentarily as scornful as his when he laughs. Or is Jean-Paul mistaken?
Seeing devilish things? Suddenly he feels utterly alien, unwanted
and in some peculiar way threatened. And for a second or two she,
that pale, naked woman over there by the window, is not his helpless Jenny but a creature capable of anything.

'As for you . . . you vanished,' she adds slowly. 'At my dream's
end you were no longer there . . .'

Jean-Paul, by now wide awake, takes cover behind a jest.

'You don't mean to say you'd thrown me to the wolves too?'

He feels faintly sick. For the first time in their life together he
is really frightened of her, normally the sole object of his concern.
And a seed of doubt sows itself in the silence between them as to
how much they really love each other.

Jenny doesn't answer. The first rays of sunrise play on her shivering body. On the window sill, pearly and pink, slightly ruffled,
lies a climber rose, still a trifle pale after the night, yet glowing with

pride at having survived it and thrust its way in. From outside comes a bird's faint twitter and a cock crows down at the farm. Yet another autumn day, bewitching in its deceptive beauty, is beginning.

'I don't know, Jean-Paul,' she says in a low, pathetic voice . . . 'I was just standing there with a dead child in my arms. Not Jojo. She seemed more like myself . . . Behind me was a long hospital corridor, and in front of me a sliding door opened noiselessly. Beyond it was *nothing*, nothing at all. Just darkness, drawing me into it. And the air so black I couldn't breathe. Oh, Jean-Paul, I'm so scared, so *frightened*. Please, please don't leave me! Not today! Not all alone with Mother! Don't go away!'

And she throws herself down on the bed beside him, clings to him with a strength he would never have believed she possessed. Which he must break away from. With a promise to ring home the moment he gets to Dublin, he gets up, shaves hurriedly and dresses. Swallows a cup of black coffee dumped down in front of him by a yawning, hollow-eyed Rita. Quickly checks through his briefcase to see that all his papers are there. And plunges out to the car, whose engine, of course, is so soaked in mist that it won't start; he has to ring for a taxi to take him to Gatwick. As he gets in to it he turns, and at the open bedroom window sees Jenny standing stiff and pale; a stone virgin who can't even lift her hand to wave to him or blow him a human kiss.

As in her dream she is standing on the brink of nothingness, filled with black air.

Nicole

Jean-Paul's journal, midnight, 8 October
Well, here I am again, sitting in this hotel room. It is late, but I can't sleep. I am worrying now about Jenny, now the children, now my mother-in-law. I am even beginning to feel a bit sorry for her, being flung to the wolves out of that sleigh in Jenny's dream; understand her better. She must have had one hell of a life with that melancholy husband of hers. Divinely inspired in the pulpit he may be, but at home a neurotic. And with her gifted but ruthless sons. And a frail daughter nipped in the bud by early frosts. I seem to be commuting to and fro between feelings of guilt and worry at having left them, and a strange indifference. In fact relieved at being able for a few days to be away from the whole bunch of them. It's absurd, I know, but perhaps a way of getting my breath back? How would I react if mother and daughter really went berserk and killed each other? Can't say. I'm too tired even to imagine it.

Mostly it is the children I worry about. I often see Vicky's greedy eyes on me, longing for me to give her some of the love and attention I lavish on her mother. Hear her snap at Jenny or defy her with her silent defiance. Her 'Why do you *coddle* Mum so all the time?' In a word, her jealousy is beginning to be a problem. Of course I ought to give the girl more of my time, but Jenny seems to have more and more need of me, and my work demands more than I am really up to. If only I had someone to confide in! On the other hand I am afraid to expose Jenny, her inferno, to an outsider's ears . . .

Not too happy either about Michael's defensive attitude,

which seems to express itself in politely sending the whole lot of us and everything else to the devil and sucking his thumb as he drugs himself on television. Though he is nearly ten now he is already becoming reserved, wrapped up in himself and in technology. A future engineer perhaps? He already knows much more about some things than I do. He used to adore Jenny, was always clinging to her skirts, kissing and hugging her. Nowadays I am afraid her odd ways are scaring him off. Probably it would be best if he could get away from home. I shall have to see if I can afford a good boarding school. I am no longer enough of a chum for him . . .

And then there is Rosalind, so ethereal, so imaginative, a Jenny in miniature; a child who goes her own way, always thinking imaginatively in symbols, fairy-tales and, now and then, in dreams that are frighteningly vivid. And, lastly, our little Jojo, so dependent on mother-love and care that I am afraid she is beginning to be Jenny's pretext for opting out . . . a bolt-hole . . . Aren't we all dependent on each other, over-sensitive, greedy for security! How can Jenny, who never seems to have really known any, pass it on to her children? She lavishes love spasmodically on us but often, all too often, she withdraws, shuts her door, hands over responsibility for bringing up the children to me and Rita who, I suspect, is beginning to be pretty well fed up with all of us.

Odd, that business with Gilbaud – just when I am beginning to need a confidant! Most unpleasant too. This evening, after all the insufferable speechifyings at dinner, all the toasts to futurology's future – if it has one – he broke into my solitude. In many ways he is brilliant, even eminent. Yet Monsieur G isn't popular with our little lot, who finds his gloom, punctuated by double-edged, sometimes hurtful sarcasm, oppressive. Respected he may be, even feared. But we tend instinctively to avoid his company. In the bar he came over, asked if I minded if he sat beside me. Impossible to escape. I was delighted, I lied. He sat down heavily, facing me, with his brandy and a cigar. And there we sat for quite a while, the two of us, cut off from all the noisy post-dinner laughter and babble, without a word to say to each other. And I could feel myself getting soaked through by his gloom, his life-weariness, breaking over me like a wave. Gilbaud is a big man, a voluminous paunch balanced on top of two long, spindly legs.

When he still didn't say anything, just went on contemplating me from under his bushy eyebrows, I began to feel rather scared and in nervous, jumpy French launched into what in my opinion is the proper way of writing scenarios, etc. But I saw he wasn't listening. Was far away in his own thoughts. My voice trailed away and I looked at him. His eyes were half closed, as if listening to very serious, sad music, and tears were running down the deep folds and wrinkles of his pale, pudgy face.

Abruptly he began:

'You are the only one I can talk to, *mon vieux. Tous ces gens-là ne sont que des marionettes.* Forgive me for buttonholing you like this. *Mais on ne se comprend qu'entre compatriotes, quoi?* And I have a notion you are not feeling too bright, either, *hein?'*

I felt unpleasantly exposed, cornered, seen through, but accepted a cigar. So – everyone can see it then, that I am in the dumps, despite all my efforts to skip about with the other 'marionettes'? Being picked out by this melancholy Dostoevsky figure doesn't exactly help matters.

'This is certainly the last time I can go through with one of these circuses,' he went on. 'Not after what I have just been through . . . All these extroverts . . . trying so hard, yet it all means nothing . . . all so meaningless . . . You understand, Didier,' his dulled, booming voice went on as he gulped down another cognac. 'I can't go on pretending. Have to speak to someone . . . if everything's not to go to pieces. She has taken everything I had . . .'

'She – who?' I asked, confused. The noise from all the others came in a great wave between us.

'Nicole – my wife.'

Just those words. No more.

Suddenly it seemed as if this tragic man and I, sitting there on our own, were on an island; my own worries drifted away, detached themselves, became a small cloud on the horizon. Time and space shifted. Only Gilbaud and his grief, yet to be explained, existed.

'I wanted to give her everything, create a paradise for us all – her, the children, myself – beyond all evil, suffering, ugliness, everything that is wrong with this world of ours. Particularly as she had never known her parents or had a home; grown up in convent schools, well, you know, brought up by nuns. Though lately she had given it all up: not gone to mass or confession, even mislaid her rosary and crucifix. Since she had never had any of the good things of life I poured them over her, spoilt her. Naturally I took it for granted she loved me no less passionately, no less ecstatically. At first she hadn't wanted anything, was dreadfully religious, scared of a world she didn't dare live in. But gradually that all changed. She broke all of her ties with the nuns, no longer gave a damn about the poor that she had always been so indignant about and began buying herself expensive dresses from the Rue St Honoré, perfumes, all that. Took up with the wrong sort of people, too, you know, rich, superficial types. Threw parties for them. All that. And became more and more demanding. Had to have a flat in Paris, a country château with a tennis court and swimming-pool – *tout ça* – particularly that infernal swimming-pool.'

Again he fell silent, stared empty eyed into me, without seeing me.

'She went on and on about it, said she couldn't live except in the water – she was dotty about goldfish, believe it or not – and pedigree dogs. Well, I could understand that, herself being illegitimate. I have been her daddy, her mummy, her lover, the lot.'

'What about the children?'

'Two,' came his reply, almost as if it hardly mattered. 'A boy and a girl. She has taken them too.'

Still understanding nothing I just sat there, staring back at him.

'Took? What do you mean?'

He drew a deep breath.

'I had been away too often, on business. Well, you know how it is . . . After our second child was born she got depressed, confused in her mind. I paid for an expensive but unfortunately unsuccessful analysis. Got her a nanny – a cook and a gardener were already part of the establishment. So she really didn't have to lift a finger. But whatever it was that had gone wrong inside got rapidly worse. She became bad-tempered, quarrelsome and, above all, dreadfully demanding. Wanted more and more of me. But when I got her a new car, she just crashed it. Yes, Didier, the fact is, the girl I'd married and whom I loved because she had felt for everything and everyone had turned into a destructive egoist. A little terrorist, living only for her own convenience, her own sexual and materialistic satisfaction. As for me, I found myself written off, replaced by a lover. She never stopped eating and drinking, particularly drinking; and taking tranquillizers and sleeping tablets.'

Silence again. By now the bar had closed and we were alone. It was nearly midnight.

'But how? I mean . . . what happened?' I asked bewildered.

He choked down his tears.

'The end came on the eleventh – can it really be less than a month ago? It's beyond me. I wasn't at home. But the nanny told me. That morning she, Nicole, was in high spirits. Gave the staff a day off, saying she would look after the children herself. It was a brilliant autumn day, you know, the park's colours already turning red. No one suspected anything – except the nanny, but Nicole told her sharply to go out and enjoy herself with her boyfriend and not come back before the children's bedtime. So, much against her own better judgement Michèle – the nanny, that is – pushed off.

Not that she enjoyed her free day. By half-past five she was back. Found the house strangely silent, empty. No sign either of Nicole or the children. But the television was on. The first thing the girl saw was what looked like the remains of a children's party – cake crumbs all over the place and ice cream dripping from the table. Then, to her horror, she saw the budgerigars were lying dead on the floor of their cage – someone had wrung their necks! The goldfish had been taken out of the aquarium and lay scattered about the floor . . . Going out into the garden she almost fell over Nicole's favourite dog. Shot.'

He swallowed.

'And on the bottom of the swimming-pool . . . Nicole. And the children. Both of them. Drowned. She had clutched them to her. Her grip was so strong that the rigor mortis made it almost impossible to separate them. It appears she had taken an overdose . . . extraordinary. Ice-cream, tablets, alcohol. *Michèle, la pauvre fille, a presque voulu se suicider, elle aussi!* After she had fetched the police she broke down completely. And I have had to pay for a mental hospital, where she is still resting, accusing herself of not staying at home that day . . . Says it is all her fault, which of course it isn't.'

Another deep sigh. Closing his eyes he added:

'Nicole had burnt all our love letters. The photos of us and the children, of her favourite dog Mon Roi, all relics of our first happy years. She had only left one photo intact: of herself at her confirmation, a ten-year-old angel. *Ah mon Dieu, quelle histoire!*'

Gilbaud took out a brittle yellowing photo out of his wallet and handed it to me. Looking out at me I saw a ten-year-old angel, a little bride of God in a white dress and veil, with a look *de otro mondo*. My thoughts flew involuntarily to our Rosalind, on whose little face I have sometimes seen that same painfully soulful look.

'Read what she wrote on the back of it,' Gilbaud said in a broken voice.

I turned it over. In a refined, wispy handwriting was written

'*C'est encore moi. Toute ma vie depuis ce jour-là n'a été qu'une longue erreur.*' Still me. My entire life since this day here has been nothing but a big mistake.

Gilbaud and I went our separate ways in the same silence that earlier had brought us together. Lifting himself heavily out of his leather armchair he walked away across the hotel's threadbare carpeting, back into his grief.

The image of his Nicole, a childlike Swedenborgian angel for whom life had been too much, won't leave me. Can too much love have muddled and destroyed her? Made her destroy everything else? Or was she still just the little confirmation pupil who had stagnated in some great disappointment? And her swimming pool's chlorine waters, what did they signify? The amniotic water, the life source – where her childish self finally sought out its death?

Before switching out my bedside light my thoughts go to you, Jenny. Do I love you too much?

Dublin, 9 October, lunch break

All cut up by Gilbaud's story. Couldn't help ringing home again early this morning. To hear Jenny's voice. Not very considerate of me perhaps, ringing her so early. After a while she answered. Sleepy. Astonished.

'But, Jean-Paul, it isn't even six o'clock!'

And when I asked her how she was, told her how worried I had been:

'Worried? What about? Everything's OK. Mother and the children are doing fine. It's today Victoria's having her donkey party, remember?'

'But you, Jenny? Yourself? It's only you I've been thinking of.'

The phone went silent.

'Jenny?'

Yes.'

'Aren't you feeling too good? Has it been hard having your mother around?'

Her voice came back like a slap in the face.

'Stop interrogating me, Jean-Paul! Didn't I say everything's fine? Mother's happy, so are the kids. Rita's nicer now.'

'But you – yourself?'

No reply.

My anxiety grew.

'Jenny, are you crying?'

'No of course not! Why are you trying to upset me? Everything's lovely here at home.'

A big yawn.

'Jenny, I love you! I'll be home as soon as I can.'

'I love you too, Jean-Paul.'

Her words came quietly, as from a distance. But quite clearly.

Later in the day
I'll stay till the conference is over.

Charlotte's Troubled Soul

Lindfield, 7 October 1963

My dear old clergyman,

At long last I have time to write you a proper letter; I hope you've had my brief epistles from the boat and on arrival. I don't need to tell you that my thoughts always go (or fly) to you. It is strange, is it not, how though we old people, who have shared all the troubles of a lifetime, wear each other out when we are together and often can't stand each other another moment, belong together even so; I would almost go so far as to say are 'in love with' each other! Of course, being parted for a while does us both good and it is nice to see and experience new people and places, as I am now seeing and experiencing England. Yet at the same time the thought of you lost and helpless, without me to look after you, all on your own, cuts me to the quick. And, old woman though I am, I can't say I don't at times miss your morning and evening kiss, the way you put your arm around me, though I – forgive your Lotta – often dismiss you so coldly and gruffly, being always so terribly busy and caught up in my own life rhythm, still so energetic compared to yours. Don't misunderstand me. I'm not saying anything against *your* life rhythm, my dear old clergyman, you who most of all enjoy the calm days when nothing happens and no one comes to see us. You are like a candle whose flame burns ever more calmly, whereas mine still gasps and sputters in all these cross-draughts.

It was a wise decision you made not to come with me and see Jenny, Jean-Paul and the children and their home here. It is set in exquisitely beautiful surroundings amid a landscape opulent with ivy and other climbing plants that to us northerners seems positively luxuriant and where (believe it or not!) the roses are still in bloom. As yet no frost has dared touch these Indian summer days, streaked with its coppery reds, where the damp morning mists and an occasional chilly evening give a foretaste of autumn's melancholy or winter's gloom. Sitting wrapped up in blankets and shawls in Jenny's garden with a pale but welcome sunlight warming my old body I am enjoying a kind of illusory summer. Beneath these trees, perhaps a century old (one has just died and points its leafless branches stiffly up at the sky), Bonny (the donkey I have given Victoria for her fourteenth birthday) wanders about. Sometimes he comes trotting up to me, thrusts his affectionate muzzle quite shamelessly into my needlework, knocks Poul Bjerre's *Death and Resurrection* down on to the grass. (Sad to say, Victoria seems *afraid* of her donkey, and my gift seems more of a burden to her than a source of joy. When the animal happened to nip her arm in a show of high spirits, she got quite hysterical. I bandaged it up for her and tried to calm her down, but the girl is all shaken up and won't see reason. What a disappointment!) The children's good-natured mongrel Tittine is a most peculiar blend of every thinkable breed. She frolics about me too, licks me and watches me out of wise, wondering eyes. A most intuitive animal, almost like a human being. It is almost as if only she understands my situation here in Jenny's home and silently knows what I am feeling and thinking but daren't show . . . But, my dearest life-companion, how I do ramble on! I will try to unburden my overloaded heart in an epistle to you, always so sensitive and brooding and whom I have always as far as possible shielded from my worries . . . But now the truth presses too hard upon me and I must yield to the temptation to tell you all about it (I can always censor anything that might upset you). You see, old friend, not to speak in riddles, 'as in a glass darkly', it would all have been quite simply too much for you, though you love her deeply, seeing Jenny again.

It is true I am enjoying the sunshine, the wealth of trees and flowers, this slightly old-fashioned English atmosphere, so much gentler and friendlier than our Stockholm stress! And anyway, the joy of seeing Jenny, her fine, lovable Jean-Paul and our grand-children – so delightful on the day I got here – was undiluted, boundless! My old heart warmed to them when I saw how happy Jenny is as a wife and mother in this large, and, as it first seemed to me, 'homely' house, a mixture of light Swedish Carl Larsson style, sunshine-yellow Elsa Gullberg curtains and – to my taste – rather heavy English antique furniture. Jenny received me with open arms. It was obvious she had been longing to see me. Thanks to this Jean-Paul who, if you recall, we were at first so wary of, the frozen, evasive part of her nature seems altogether gone. He is a *wonderful* person, secure in himself, warm and manly, a singular combination of French intellect and easy-going English tolerance; a real gentleman and a good father. No question that he adores our Jenny!

Dare I continue, or do I weary you, so that you lay this letter aside with a sigh and, knowing what is coming, light one of your cigarillos? You see, even on the very first day, right in the middle of the splendid dinner they welcomed me with, I noticed a sudden change. It was, how shall I say, as if a cold wind swept through the room, making the little ornamental bird quiver – the one, you remember, I bought for her at the craft shop, and which Jenny had already hung up. She turned pale, became all tense. And Jean-Paul, too, became anxious. And even the little girls, who only a moment before had been sitting there like dolls at the table, seemed troubled. This peculiar disturbance, this foreboding, last-ed only a moment, it is true, and I did my best to convince myself there was nothing supernatural about it or my sudden feeling of alarm; that it was just a last tremor of all the tension before leav-ing Sweden or due to the fatigues of the long journey.

Upon Jean-Paul suggesting a walk in the evening sun, I jumped at the idea. Actually I would really rather have rested a while in the room they have prepared for me – most delightful, with creamy white and rosy curtains and bedspread to match. Through its quaint little windows and the trees' dense foliage I have a view of Lindfield's ancient church and churchyard, full of ancient gravestones leaning this way and that. The children ran on ahead, but Jenny, much to my disappointment, said she would have to stay at home to put little Josephine to bed (which wasn't necessary at all, as Rita, though off duty, was only sitting reading in her room). Neither did the furtive exchange of glances between her and Jean-Paul escape me. It struck me as strange that our daughter, so soon after my arrival, should try to find a pretext for avoiding me, after we have been apart so long . . .

Well, I will not be long-winded. Our walk into a glowing sunset, along pot-holed muddy paths between gigantic stinging nettles and barbed wire but with a splendid view out across misty green fields to the dark silhouette of a venerable seventeenth-century castle, went quite smoothly. Yet at the same time I couldn't rid myself of a feeling that Jean-Paul was just making conversation; trying to avoid more personal matters. This put a certain distance, a coldness, between us. To my natural if perhaps slightly over-anxious inquiries about Jenny's health, physical and mental – and God only knows we've had worries enough on her account! – his only reply was a laconic: 'Jenny? Oh, she's fine, never been better. She is very happy here in England, and so are the kids.' And so forth. Yet the tense, weary expression on his face filled me with obscure misgivings. For some minutes, as we stood waiting for the children who had run off and were playing with the dog beyond some bramble bushes, the thought struck me that he was *afraid* of me – though why anyone should be afraid of *me* is more than I can imagine! That you, my dear old friend, sometimes – and our sons *often* – can scare other people in a way they don't understand, I perfectly realize. But how can anyone be afraid of me, a tired old woman, humbled by having all the rough edges knocked off her, more and more aware of her own exhaustion? Suddenly his worried, fearful look turned into one of sympathy, of piety almost, and he gave me his arm, supporting me homeward along the darkening path almost as if I were his own mother. When I think how atrociously our two sons carry on and how cruel they can be at times, both to themselves and others, I find Jean-Paul's refined sensitivity and consideration for me most touching.

As for the three children, charging on ahead like little savages in the gathering dusk, he didn't seem troubled in the least; only intent on getting back to Jenny as quickly as possible, as if she were in some kind of danger. Whereas in my opinion it was the children who needed attending to and putting to bed. Especially little Rosalind, who is only five and seems fragile in some way. Believe it or not, she is already starting school and a Catholic one at that (the Sacred Heart). English children start school too early!

Only then did I notice how unbelievably boisterous these children are, particularly Victoria and Mikael – a couple of untamed animals really, products of a so-called free upbringing. As if they live in a world of their own, a kind of zoo, where their parents neither know nor care what is going on or what they are up to. Utter chaos, really, no rules or boundaries.

It pains me to have to tell you what happened afterwards that evening. It was all so *absurd*, so unreal, bizarre, unnatural; anyone who didn't know our poor Jenny and her odd ways would think I was making it all up, or that it wasn't she but I who was half out of my mind. Coming into their huge and, as I say, rather over-furnished sitting-room (I was alone, Jean-Paul had stayed outside to finish his pipe and wait for the children), what do I see in the murk, illumined only by the glow of the fire and a couple of candles? Not our Jenny who, if Jean-Paul is to be believed, is so delighted with her life as a deeply loved wife and mother of four.

But Magdalena! You remember how as a child she used to dress up in a long dress and make a perfect fright of herself pretending to be that holy woman, sitting with hanging hair at the Master's feet as she listened to the Sermon on the Mount – which she had learnt by heart and used to quote, in and out of season?

Shocked, exhausted from my walk, I got as far as an armchair by the fireside. And what does she do, if not kiss – well, no, that is the wrong word – *lick* my hands, mumbling over and over through her tears: 'Mother, Mother . . .' and stare up at me (almost as if I were the Saviour Himself), half *hypnotizing* me! I was completely paralysed, couldn't think of a word to say! It wasn't merely distressing, it was outright *mad!* I just had to go along with her macabre game, if that was what it was, her piece of sick and stilted play-acting. The imploring, deeply tragic gaze in that death-mask of a face froze me to my chair. I could neither stir nor react. It was as if I were one of the logs in the fire; old, charred, burnt out. Fortunately the children came storming in and put an abrupt end to it. If Vicky hadn't given a little scream and Jean-Paul obliged Jenny to take little Rosalind in her arms, I would quite simply have collapsed, had to be taken off to hospital, my overstrained heart was beating so hard! Woken from her sickly role-playing, Jenny became herself again and took Rosalind upstairs to put her to bed, whilst Mikael, poor little lad, quite *unnaturally* unemotional and unaffected – at least to all outward appearances (but I'm sure appearances aren't to be trusted!) – slumped down in front of the television. From the kitchen I could hear Victoria's insistent questions and panicky appeals to Jean-Paul as he tried to calm her down. Poor, poor children!

So my earlier misgivings, that everything is *not* as it should be in this apparently happy home, hadn't been unjustified. Jenny, our beloved child, is suffering from some kind of personality split, in other words has only apparently recovered from all those dreadful breakdowns in her girlhood. So much is obvious.

Feeling utterly alone and dejected, I went upstairs and withdrew to my charming but draughty English bedroom, where I tried to calm down by staring out through the window. But its little diamond-leaded panes were all misted over and all I could see was a frigid new moon shining over the graveyard, reminding me all too tangibly of 'death's pale minute'. So, slipping in between the clammy sheets, I tried to pray for us all, especially for our poor grandchildren and their sick mother, who is certainly on the verge of a nervous breakdown at least. But I was trembling with cold and my prayers bounced back at me from heaven like a rain of tennis balls. After a while I heard Jean-Paul's weary footsteps coming up the stairs. Plucked up my courage and called out to him. Ever the gentleman, he came in and asked whether there was anything he could do for me. And when I told him I was cold, hurried back downstairs and in no time at all returned with a couple of hot-water bottles, which he put in my bed. But when he tried to fob me off again with a *C'est bien, Tante Charlotte, c'est tout?'* I could no longer contain myself. And without considering his feelings, burst out:

'No, Jean-Paul, it isn't *bien*! I really must have a serious talk with you about Jenny and the children.' At which he looked awfully depressed, sighed and mumbled: 'When I get back from Dublin, Aunt Charlotte. Please, not just now. Good night!' And in fact I had forgotten he was leaving early next morning for some conference in Ireland. Poor boy, he is so overworked!

For a long while I couldn't get to sleep. First I heard raised voices between father and son, probably about the boy's beloved rabbit, which, it seems, is normally allowed to scuttle about indoors and even do its business on the sitting-room carpet – ugh! – followed by Mikael's dragging footsteps as he came upstairs, far too late a bedtime for a schoolboy of hardly ten! Then there were little cries, tired grunts of protest from the little girls' nursery; obviously Jean-Paul had gone in to settle them. How can they

Act I

sleep with that spotty red and white night-light, like a poisonous
mushroom? But Jenny says they are afraid of the dark – can you
imagine *us* ever pampering *our* three children like that? Some kind
of argument followed from Jean-Paul's and Jenny's room. For once
Jean-Paul sounded really *cross*, almost aggressive. He was speaking
in French, I think, quick and staccato, and suddenly she gave such
a loud cry I almost flew out of my bed. Silence ensued – it must
have been quiet in there for quite some time because I remember
settling down among the hot-water bottles and wondering why
they can't make proper blinds here in England. The moonlight was
shining in through the chintz curtains; it was all very romantic,
but the moon in some way was too intrusive and inquisitive. All of
a sudden I was startled from my drowsy state (I had taken my
sleeping pills) by groans, excited cries of pleasure (from Jenny) and
a long-drawn-out overly expressive one (from our son-in-law).
They were making love! How I wished I had brought my ear plugs
with me! On the other hand, how could I know that life in the
English countryside wouldn't be quiet and peaceful?

After *that*, as you can imagine, I couldn't get a wink of sleep.
My heart was palpitating most dreadfully and in the end I was
forced to switch on the bedside light and take a digitalis.

I was well aware of what I had done. You can't fool your own
conscience, Charlotte, I told myself. In some mysterious way it
must have been *I* who, from inside Jenny, had conjured up that
Magdalena creature; waved my conductor's wand and (as Leo
likes to put it when he talks about his musicians) 'brought it out'
in her! I had noticed Jenny's bedroom window was wide open and
had more than an inkling she was standing there behind the curtains, spying down on us. Must have heard me telling Jean-Paul
about the 'Magdalena' business. What can have got into me?
Surely I can't have been avenging myself on Jean-Paul for his
refusal to confide in me, expose his own and Jenny's situation and
these children's who, truth to tell, are much too much for them?

75

Can I have acted on so wicked an impulse? If so, may God forgive me! Jean-Paul is the last person in the world I would want to hurt. He is an over-burdened mule and I certainly don't want to add to his burdens! If only he would realize how much *I* have been through in life, how accustomed I am to listening and helping others! But he is different. And I will have to be patient. One thing, though, really gets on my nerves: and that is his obstinate way of maintaining that Jenny is in perfect health, happy and able to cope, when she obviously *isn't*; never has been and never (short of a miracle) will be.

I shouldn't have said that about Jenny being split – being not only Jenny, but several different people. I saw how deeply it affected him.

No, my dear old clergyman, I shan't be sending off this letter to you – at least not uncensored – in your idyll among all those adoring women out at the Ersta Rest Home! Some things I have always had to keep to myself and always shall. In order to spare you.

My long-dead ma once said to me: 'Charlotte, my girl, you have a dangerous power over other people. You are by nature a ruler, something that in a man is an asset, but in a woman hazardous, even disastrous!'

Leo, of course, has inherited it.

The Red Lion, Lindfield, 9 October

My dear old friend,

Thank you for your letter, I'm so pleased to hear you are in good hands and have begun cultivating some acquaintances! You so badly need to. I know how strongly inclined you are to isolate yourself, how you like to lie for hours on that sofa of yours, sink into melancholia and cut yourself off from a life that, God knows, deals us some nasty blows. I hope you have had my little greetings and postcards? What I have really been trying to do has been to write you a longer, more detailed letter, but life here is so hectic, never lets up for a moment, and I am forever being interrupted. In order to get a little time for myself – particularly in the mornings when the children are at school, or during the afternoons or evenings when they are all at home and their boundless vitality is quite simply too much for me – I have moved down to the Red Lion, a so-called pub, or inn, where a kind Scottish landlady and her blind husband have let me have a large, comfortable upstairs room. For Jenny, too, it is a relief not to have me on top of her and the others all the time.

It is raining heavily. Charlotte, losing the thread of her letterwriting, has a good mind to crumple up what she has just written for the second time and drop it into the waste-paper basket and, instead of empty, hypocritical phrases, write her husband the undisguised truth. She would like to give vent to her inner rage, her feelings of helplessness and ambivalence; for the whole tormented state of mind she is having to put up with but that she has stubbornly made up her mind to endure, day after day, during her so-called holiday. Actually there are moments when she would much rather pack her bags and clear out, go back to the routine, hectic yet somehow secure, of her tedious Stockholm life with her husband. Since he has been pensioned off he sees less and less of other people, isolates himself in his study with his Latin and Greek schoolbooks. She would also like to confess to Henrik how dissatisfied she is with herself, her self-reproaches and nagging feelings of guilt, how lonely she feels. But it is out of the question. Unthinkable.

She closes her eyes to shut out the view from her room over the high street, where wellington boots under colourful umbrellas are hurrying from shop to shop and the traffic swishes by if as in a doll's Stockholm. Even so, all this is preferable to strident voices and howling children. Above all she is secure from her daughter's unremitting gaze, tormenting and persecuting. What is it that Jenny wants? What is it that she is demanding of her ageing mother? Why do her eyes eat her up, focus on her in this unnatural, painful way? It feels as if her daughter were sucking and sucking all her life's juices, all her strength, with a long straw; wanting to establish some kind of a – what was that word she had read in Poul Bjerre's book that she couldn't make head or tail of? – symbiosis. As if Jenny wanted to get inside her, into her most secret thoughts and feelings, explore, chart out her being. Knock at the door of her exhausted heart, ask over and over: 'Do you love me, Mother? You do, don't you? But when I was tiny? Are you sure you don't love Fredrik and Leo more than me?' – *ad infinitum*!

There is something sick, unnatural, about this. Something she isn't used to. For such a long time now Charlotte has buttoned up her innermost self with hard studs. Neither Henrik, Fredrik nor Leo are in the least interested in her feelings. For them she is a function. A buttress for their problematic existence.

Charlotte gets up from the rickety little desk. Her legs, numbed by the raw English climate, have swollen up. She pours herself a drop of brandy in the tumbler on the washstand; in the mirror above it finds herself confronted with a face, haggard, ashen pale, yet enlivened by a pair of eyes remarkably sharp and clear, despite so many sufferings, that shine with youthful intensity and a lust for life that, still intact , to Charlotte is not a little troublesome.

Odd, she reflects. The lines around the mouth and on the forehead, the streaks of white in the grey hair, prove that I am old – and ill. Yet those eyes could be a young girl's. They have more life in them than Jenny's and are almost like the children's . . . they contradict the overall impression of a decrepit old woman. My word, it will be a long time before those eyes want to close their lids in death's everlasting sleep. And that's for sure.

At the thought of death Charlotte takes another sip of her

cognac, feels its warmth rise inside her, listens to the rain as it falls on the window, no longer a dreary patter but like the rain that must have fallen on the Ark. Just now she is in her own cosy ark, warmed by the sighing gas fire's bluish-pink flame; yet instead of an Old Testament prophet or a swarm of wild animals, her own invaluable thoughts for company.

Suddenly elated, a trifle tipsy from her drink, she sits down again at the desk. Picks up her fountain pen. And writes:

My dear old husband,

Why must I *always* spare you? As if you were made of glass or china? Isn't it about time you had a real shock, a real 'knock' as they call it in this country, something to shake you up? Don't you think I have had just about enough of pampering your delicate nerves (so like Jenny's, the apple certainly doesn't fall far from the tree!)? Of forever being considerate, all too considerate, towards your everlasting hypochondria? You will survive me anyway. After my last heart attack Professor S. told me I can only count on a few more years. Of course I was, as usual, too considerate to tell you. *But now you know!* And when I get home – that is if I ever get out of here alive! – I suggest we swap roles. It can be your turn to shield *me*; you can take all the knocks from the outside world. Read for yourself Fredrik's ominous reports from his disastrous marriage, hear about the growing pain in his heels, how fast he is becoming paralysed, turned into a cripple, tormented by a dipsomaniac wife. Why on can't you from now on be on the receiving end of Leo's temperamental outbursts; hear him sing the praises of some new and wonderfully beautiful young woman and how his latest mistress is better than the one he has just down graded, humiliated and sent packing! Why can't you get up out of your armchair, take the trouble to come all this way to Sussex and try to clear up this insanely disorganized and neurotic home? In this old stone house, ruled by four children who tyrannize their exhausted father with their 'free' upbringing as he in his stupid generosity and out of sheer escapism (he loves pink spectacles, this son-in-law of ours!) never stops lavishing sweets and pocket money on them. To say nothing of a singularly lax, introverted and apathetic mother who, it is true, loves them by fits and starts, even worships them, but is utterly unable to discipline them or bring them up as a mother should! What is needed here is a little of your clerical authority. Only your wrath, which can so suddenly explode and frighten people to death, could clear up all this mess, instill in these children God-fearing obedience and order. Alas, you have simply *no idea* how our religion, our old-fashioned piety, is being trodden in the dust here, like their plastic toys! Oh, these poor children, sprouting like weeds, without higher values or any of the older generations' morals! Jenny would never *dare* scrutinize you as she does me; she would give in to your iron will, respect you and, knowing full well your attitude towards 'pseudology', stuff her neurosis away in one of her hopelessly chaotic chests of drawers, and wake up to her own life, her duties to her husband and children – and to me, her ageing mother! But oh dear, no, not even you, my dear old husband, could cope with this merry-go-round! How angry, how outraged you'd be, how red you'd go in the face, how grumpy you'd become; and what fearful judgements you'd pass! After which you would simply go to pieces and, like a sick child with high blood pressure, come home again and for months on end go on and on about your own inability to cope with life, your distaste for everything, your bad conscience. How well I know you, my – in spite of everything – dear, old, life companion.

Some dead leaves have flattened themselves against the window, try though the rain may to wash them off. Fascinated, Charlotte stares at the tree outside, at its fluttering, wet little leaves, so near her as they fight for the last seconds of their brief lives. Then her pen scratches on, in a final crescendo:

It ended in a scene, yes, almost in an end to our relations! After we had avoided each other for several days without a word spoken and getting on each other's nerves, almost hacking each other to pieces, it came to an outburst. Jean-Paul's absence, of course, had a lot to do with it; had left us at each other's mercy. Just like in the old days . . . Determined not to criticize, not find fault, not *interfere*, and yet above all try and get some kind of order into all that lawless muddle, I gritted my teeth, struggled with might and main to behave myself in my role of a polite lady's companion, so estranged we had become! But in the end Jenny's eyes on me day and night – like a cat intent on some wretched little mouse – so grated on my nerves that the dam burst. And I exploded. Told her angrily, *ruthlessly*, what I think of her.

Naturally, as usual, the whole scene was sparked off by a mere nothing that had been irritating us both. During these years in England Jenny has turned into a sloppy, not to say sluttish, house-wife, dragging about in slippers all day, dressing in some kind of a smock – apparently the 'in' thing, as they say here – and reviving her drooping spirits by chain-smoking (at least twenty a day I should think!) and countless cups of tea. It wasn't the right moment for the truth to come out, I admit, *but when is it, ever?* It was Rita's (the au pair girl's) day off. Out in the kitchen the washing machine never stopped buzzing, like an irritated insect; wet socks, soiled nappies and gentlemen's unmentionables lay scattered about everywhere, to say nothing of Mikael's indescribably muddy cast-offs after his 'cross-country runs'. The dishwasher had gone wrong and since in this – as I see it – altogether too phlegmatic country it is impossible to get anything repaired on a Wednesday afternoon (half-day closing), unwashed plates, mugs, cups and glasses overflowed in the sink. And as Jenny never seems really to get anything *done*, but flaps about from one thing to the other like a brainless hen, the vacuum cleaner stood idle in the middle of the sitting-room carpet amid great fluffs of grey dust.

With the Rita girl 'off' as usual, Jojo, perched on one of Jenny's hips, clung to her like a baby. Both the little girls had frightful colds – small wonder, with the draughts whirling madly in through the old house's doors and windows and out again into the pouring autumn rain! Little Rosalind seemed feverish and droopy and Jojo was whimpering in Jenny's arms.

Suddenly *I'd had enough*. Couldn't stand it a moment longer! My feelings, which I had being trying to keep down, shot up to forty degrees, like mercury in a thermometer. And banging my finger down on the table top (yes, Henrik, I know how you hate this little habit of mine), I shouted: 'Oh, for goodness sake, Jenny, do put out that disgusting cigarette and blow the child's nose! Can't you see how runny it is? If *you* don't do it, I shall!'

And what do you think happened? Jenny just gave a strange fleeting smile, wiped the snotty little snout with a corner of her so-called maternity dress – all the fashion here just now – and, burying her pale face in the child's hair, peered out at me with a timid, fearful look. You know what I am like at such moments: once I have started there is no stopping me, I boil over like a saucepan. Yes, I gave her a piece of my mind, told her exactly what I thought of their – to our way of thinking – apathetic *laissez-aller* way of bringing up their children and of their whole chaotic household, which had thrown me into complete confusion, house-proud old housewife that I am! The tension had been too much. I was at the end of my tether, simply couldn't hold my tongue another moment, watching this fashionable farce of the 1960s, of so-called modern life, and all the time yearning to *intervene*, even if it hurt her feelings and upset dear, kind Jean-Paul, who is simply *working himself to death* to make ends meet, always bending over backwards to do his best for everybody – so much so that he obviously doesn't have a moment to spare *even to discuss his problems with his mother-in-law!* My longing to be with her and her children, I told her bluntly, had turned into bitter disappointment, yes, a *nightmare . . .*

At that Jenny let out a scream – a cry so awful I can still hear it – like a wounded animal or someone being operated on without anaesthetic:

'Oh, Mother! You don't know what you are doing! I have been longing and longing for you, done everything to make you happy, as we all have, because we love you – all of us, Jean-Paul, the children and me! And now you have to go and *ruin* it all with your harsh, critical words . . . You are *cutting me to pieces* . . . like you always did at home . . . I'm back in that ditch in the woods – bleeding, in my fine, white coat of rabbit fur . . . and Grandmother, Fredrik, Leo and Lill-Nisse are standing there scoffing at me. Oh, Mother, Mother . . .'

Beside herself, shuddering, deathly pale, she clung for dear life to little Jojo, whose chubby little arms were round her and who burst out howling at me as if I were an evil spirit. I have never, *ever* seen Jenny in such a bad way! She seemed to be half in another world, in some hideous dream-world of her own. Ditch? What ditch? Faces? Surely not my ma's, her brothers' and her little cousin's? Certainly not! Never! There is no longer any doubt in my mind: the dividing line between our daughter's normal and sick self is as thin as spring ice! What figments of a sick mind!

'Well, Mikael,' I said as calmly as I could, 'Mormor realizes it is best she leaves.' The little chap, who had just come back from school, had been a silent witness to the whole horrible spectacle. I got up to up to my room and pack.

But then something incredible happened. Little Rosalind flung her arms round me, made me sit down again, climbed up into my lap and hugged and kissed me with a passion I would never have thought possible in a five-year-old.

'Don't go, Mormor!' she whispered, over and over again. 'You must stay and help us with Mummy – you were going to plant those bulbs with me, read me all those goodnight stories and say my prayers with me!' And Mikael, too, put a calm comforting arm around me:

'Don't go back to Sverige yet, Mormor, please! Mum will be ever so sorry, and we are all so fond of you! Wait, I have an idea.'

Sitting there with Rosalind in my arms, I felt utterly powerless, overwhelmed by our grandchildren's love – something I had never dreamt of. How wrong I had been, how cruelly I had misjudged them! For the first time since I had got here I felt truly close to them, a real, deep affinity; and in the midst of all this misery a great happiness sprouted in my old heart.

But Jenny, she just sat there as before, huddled with her youngest, who had dropped off to sleep, as if the two of them had melted into one. Said nothing, didn't even look at me; perhaps no longer even knew where she was; seemed to be on a level where I couldn't reach her.

In the background I heard Mikael's cocky schoolboy voice speaking on the phone: 'This is Mr Didier Junior speaking. Could you please sort out a room for my grandmother? The fact is, we are a bit cramped here just now.'

At that moment, covered in mud and stinking of horse dung, Vicky came bursting in. As usual she had forgotten to shut the front door and a gust of cold autumn air swept into the room behind her. 'What's going on here?' she shouted. 'Has someone kicked the bucket? Have Mum and Mormor put paid to each other or what?' Oh, this girl, this incredibly difficult teenager, marching insensitively on through life, trampling everyone else underfoot – her mother, her father, her brother, her sisters . . . and now me! She, Jenny's first-born that we adored so much, the prettiest, most endearing child imaginable – now a teenager in filthy riding breeches, a grubby school blouse and her hair all unwashed.

Showing no compassion for her broken-hearted mother or her tired old grandmother or even her frightened younger sisters, she charged out into the kitchen, made herself a couple of gigantic peanut-butter sandwiches, opened the fridge and gulped down half a litre of milk straight out of the bottle! But then, surprisingly, declared:

'Poor Mormor, not much fun for you here, is it?' I could hardly believe my ears. 'You'll see, Mum'll be OK as soon as Dad gets home.'

Then came in and sat down beside me. Said as she chewed: 'It's all right, Mormor. Me and the donkey are getting on fine now. Jolly nice of you to give him to me. Thanks ever so! I'm ever so fond of him now he's stopped biting me!'

The whole girl was radiant with warmth and gratitude. Gone was the cold, off-handed manner I had found so hurtful ever since I got here. Now we are 'chums' again – isn't that the word? – and her eyes sparkled at me like they used to when she was little.

After that everything happened very quickly. With friendly male authority Mikael explained he had arranged with his blind friend at the Red Lion to give me a nice quiet room and helped me pack a few necessities. Rosalind clung to me, didn't want me to go, but he calmed her down, assured her Mormor would soon be back. 'And you, Vicky,' he said firmly, 'you look after Mum and the little ones.' And went out with me into the rain.

Quite a sight we must have been as we trudged down Lindfield High Street under my black umbrella. Mikael lugging my suitcase, his school cap askew on his blond hair and his socks hanging half-way down his legs under a pair of strong boyish knees. Schoolboy he may be but a real little gentleman, not at all the insensitive delinquent I had taken him for . . . And I was sorry, deeply sorry for losing patience and being too upset to hide my feelings from my poor daughter who, in some way, I can't deny, is mentally deranged. God grant she doesn't become *schizophrenic!*

Old people must have the sense to keep their loneliness and sorrows to themselves. God had made trial of me in our daughter's home and I failed miserably! Could this be His final attempt to curb my rebellious will, my explosive temper? If so He has failed. Close to tears at this piteous exit from our daughter's home, I restrained myself in the presence of our brave young grandson. But my grief, probably God's punishment on me, went on rattling inside me like a coin in an empty bottle. Out of this disaster, even so, a fragile joy has sprung up. This unsuspected sense of harmony with the grandchildren.

It is late in the afternoon. Once again, Charlotte has penned a letter that will never reach her husband. Already it has gone to its home amid the contents of the waste-paper basket, shortly to be taken downstairs and cremated in the lounge-bar fire by the Scottish landlady.

A bluish-red flame flickers from Charlotte's gas fire in the dusk. Charlotte lies down on the bed, rolls herself up in the blanket. It is so peaceful and quiet in here. Out in the passage the Red Lion's blind landlord is talking in undertones with his wife. Before Charlotte drops off her thoughts go to reincarnation, a topic she has read a great deal about of late. This life of hers, is it really the only one she will ever have? Despite her Christian faith she is drawn to Buddhism, its doctrine of suffering and ultimate nirvana. Not that she dares broach the topic with her Lutheran husband. Already she has begun to catch glimpses of a great light at the end of life's tunnel, so often unbearably dark and a struggle to get through. She is not afraid. Actually she doesn't believe in death as the end of everything, doesn't want to. Instead she sees a light. And wonders curiously what God may still have in store for her. On the whole I have been a good, conscientious girl, she thinks. So please, God, let my next life be just a little bit easier! she prays, in a touching blend of Christian piety and somewhat naive Buddhism.

But Charlotte has hardly dozed off when footsteps are heard coming up the carpeted staircase, followed by discreet but urgent taps at her door. Half asleep she drags herself out of bed and opens up. In front of her stands a new, attractive young woman whom in her confusion she doesn't immediately recognize; her daughter, and at her side Jean-Paul, just back from Ireland. Taking her into a perfumed embrace and kissing her, this unknown other Jenny says gaily: 'This is no place for you, Mother, it's too depressing. Tomorrow you are coming home to us! Rita and I have tidied everything up. It looks lovely. The kids have been out picking flowers and Michael has fixed two electric fires in your room! Right now he and Rosalind are making a blind for your window! Rita is baby-sitting tonight – so let's go out and have a good time, all three of us.'

Jean-Paul, too, plants a chivalrous kiss on her hand and a more affectionate one on her cheek. Neither of them wants to listen when Charlotte protests that she is perfectly content to be on her own here, doesn't want to intrude on their family life, etc. etc. But no, they insist, her place is with them. That is obvious. Never mind about silly little tiffs. Misunderstandings are only to be expected in view of the 'generation gap'. But now they are all going to out and have some fun, celebrate Jean-Paul's home-coming.

His car is parked down in the high street and soon they are in Brighton, seated in a cosy corner of a nice French restaurant, enjoying supper and sips of red wine. Charlotte, exhausted, has been taken completely by surprise. Feels all upside down. The more wine she drinks (and Jean-Paul keeps refilling her glass) the less her problems weigh on her. A few more glasses and she has almost forgotten the contretemps between herself and her daughter. All nasty, tragic matters dwindle till they are no bigger than currants in a bun, and even her own heart condition and imminent demise, as prophesied by Professor S. in Stockholm, no longer exist. She, Charlotte, is as full of life and as young in spirit as this couple sitting there in front of her, who, to her embarrassment, keep throwing each other such amorous looks, an infatuation, rather like a cosy eiderdown. All her little efforts to make serious discussion blow away like thistle-down or are waved aside by Jean-Paul.

'There, there,' he says. 'Don't you worry your head about the children's morals. They are stuffed with religion at the convent school without us taking them to church and, as for Vicky, the grammar school is as strict as can be. Much stricter than in Sweden. No, my dear Charlotte, the children are *not* being brought up as Catholics, but some of the nuns are good teachers. And at least they teach them some French!'

For his part Jean-Paul says he is an existentialist, a word he explains at some length, but of which Charlotte understands very little.

'And, Charlotte, you really mustn't worry about Victoria. She is just a typical teenager, a bit precocious perhaps and naturally a wee bit jealous of her madly attractive mother! *Voilà tout!*'

And Jean-Paul and Jenny look at each other with such desire and obvious sensuality that Charlotte again feels suddenly old and lonely and left out. The memory of a long since faded love, a passion strangled by the strict Protestant God and middle-class morals, wells up inside her so strongly that for a moment she almost collapses under the impact of violent feelings that she has always believed she has locked safely away, like pressed flowers in some dusty old herbarium. Poor little Vicky, she thinks, immediately identifying herself with the unruly, lovelorn, jealous teenager who is doing her best to grow up in this atmosphere of sensual passion and desire. How is she going to develop, in a home dominated by such an obviously over-erotic mother and a loving but, well, in some ways rather weak father who thinks he can dismiss everything with a *c'est bien?* Just now it is more than she can grasp that this young woman opposite her, all smiles, is her own nervously unbalanced daughter. Nerves don't kill you, she thinks cynically. Not like heart attacks . . .

So when they suddenly bring up the topic of their big 'surprise', a trip to Paris they have been planning for her – Paris, which she has been longing to see all her life! – she just smiles a melancholy, preoccupied smile. Says of course it would be lovely but right now she is far too tired even to consider it. For at that very moment the thought of death has cast its sudden shadow over her, darkening her path. And Jean-Paul, intuiting this change of mood in his ageing mother-in-law, suggests it is time they break up their little party and make for home.

As they drive along the sea front at midnight, Charlotte asks Jean-Paul to pull in a moment to the pavement. And though she can clearly hear Death's slippery footsteps following her over the shingle, she, leaning on her son-in-law's arm, goes down towards the ocean, rhythmically flinging its dark breakers towards them, then seething, falling back. Something inside her ebbs and flows with those waves, is no less eternal than them and, like everything's relentless end, beyond its reach.

Charlotte's diary, 9 November
Well, it looks as if Jenny and I are off to Paris tomorrow after all, but somehow I just can't feel *happy* about it. There has been another scene with Vicky, who is being very difficult. This time it was about the donkey. The simple fact is, the girl is too lazy to take the poor animal food and water after she has got home from school, so he is left standing in a little field all on his own.

'You can go and feed him yourself, Mormor,' she flings back at me. 'After all, it was a kind of present to yourself, wasn't it?' What an absurd accusation! I was *most* upset and, worn out by the children and the whole atmosphere, reacted strongly. Whereupon Jenny got cross at me and I went out for a walk on my own, wishing I was *far* away. Jean-Paul was as calm and impartial as usual and it has all been cleared up, but this evening I am *exhausted* and would just like to go home! Oh, how I hope everything will be all right between us in Paris now that Jean-Paul can't come. Jenny is a bundle of nerves, up in the air one minute, down in the dumps the next, and can't bear to hear any home truths about herself, her children or her, to my mind, sloppy home. God help us all! How I have always longed to see Paris, and it *mustn't* be a fiasco, not after all my ma's rapturous accounts of her time there as a young *étudiante*. Even after all the things that went so wrong for her, as well as her tragic loss of Joakim, she always used to brighten up when she remembered her time in Paris – the only respite she would ever have before marrying an older widower with three sons (one of them becoming schizophrenic) plus two of their own children, Joakim and me, that is. Not until we've been severely tested by life do we understand our mothers. Only now, already in the valley of the shadow of death, when I am about to flutter like a butterfly for a few fleeting days and nights in Paris, do I feel close to you, Ma, in spite of everything . . . for you never loved me like you did Joakim; and inside me I was burning with envy! You *couldn't* love little girls, or understand them; the truth is you despised them. Femininity, for you, was an unexplored mystery. Dear little Ma, I have forgiven you. But you didn't give me much of a start in life, did you, as a mother for my own daughter? I didn't feel any happiness when she was born. All I felt when she was laid in my arms after a difficult labour was distaste for life and – I confess it – aversion towards this little girl who, through no fault of her own, wasn't another son. As for Henrik's ecstasy, it was unbearable. He was so deliriously happy that he went to the market and bought enough salt herrings for all the cats in Uppsala to feast on in our back yard! His adoration and worship of his Jenny Henrietta was a scourge that separated me from my last-born and left me in a wasteland of depression. My breasts, which had overflown with milk for Fredrik and Leo, dried up like two hard pears; and I was at a loss to see in my little girl any of the charms that Henrik was always going on about. For me she was just a failure, an ugly, wet little lump of spiritless flesh (though of course I didn't say so). But when Fredrik and Leo got Henrik's enthusiastic letter telling them they had a little sister, they reacted like I had – just tore it up and threw it into the fire. My heart was like a stone. In my despair I called to God for help; yes, even begged him to take this cup from me! Which God promptly and terrifyingly did by making the poor mite very ill indeed – from an unsterilized feeding-bottle that caused colic and vomiting. At only two months, she had to be rushed off to hospital, where she almost died. Forced to stay with her day and night, seeing her wither away, I felt I was in prison – outside the hospital window Uppsala was aglow with September colours. My strange insensitivity thrust the little creature who had inhabited my body for nine months even further from me; the little creature who was being swept downstream in the great river that flows out into the ocean of eternity – so, anyway, I hoped in my heart of hearts. Henrik, distraught with grief, unshaven, pale, tearful and sweating with anxiety, stubbornly stood watch over us both. Neither eating nor drinking, it was as if he were ready to follow his little darling one into the last darkness. Seeing his parched lips move in prayer, I worried more for him than for this unknown child, fast fading away. I kept my feelings to myself, no one saw through me – except perhaps Ma, as she peered in through the incubator's glass and saw the tiny body gasping for breath. Many conflicting emotions flowed in that look. I could see she was thinking of me and of Joakim. 'Poor little mite,' she whispered, with tears in her eyes, blowing her nose so loud that it echoed down the corridors. 'Perhaps it would be better if . . . After all, you do have two strong healthy boys . . .'

But the miracle occurred. Jenny recovered. Smiling in spite of myself, I carried her out of the hospital and into life where afterwards, with utmost self-control, I did my best to be as good a mother to her as to the boys. But love is not to be forced and as little as you, Ma, loved me, could I love this clumsy little girl, so like Henrik, with her thin, flaxen almost-white hair and protruding ears that no sticking plaster seemed to help and her pale-blue watery eyes that on the least provocation would fill with tears.

Why were her feelings always so easily hurt? Our Jenny has always been over-sensitive, touchy, introverted, like a flower that prefers the shade and turns its face away from the sunlight. An everlasting reminder of my long-extinct love for Henrik, a fragile egg hatched in less and less of a love-nest but where the male still passionately insisted on his 'rights' that the hen, concealing her anger, found no pleasure in yielding to. What would have become of her if poor Henrik hadn't loved her to distraction? A star that had dropped out of the sky into his arms! Thank goodness successive cooks and nursemaids – particularly Maja and Yvonne – took her to their hearts as a surrogate for the children they never had. Sometimes I wonder if Jenny weren't a bit retarded, autistic even, isn't that the word? Things are bad enough as they are and for the most part her childhood was a sorry story. No, I shan't dwell any more on all that – after all, it is all so long ago, what is the use? Best forgotten. But at least she is attractive to men. And smart enough, above all, to get herself a husband like Jean-Paul – so sensible, patient and filled with a miraculous love for her! Henrik has never lavished such devotion on *me*! I have just been his mule, staggering under burdens. Maybe Vicky wasn't quite wrong, accusing me of giving the donkey to myself. Because I *understand* donkeys! Poor wretches, so apparently compliant and stupid, yet apt to lash out all of a sudden and bite when they have had *enough* of submissive suffering! Their souls (if they have one) are savage, rebellious. Abused as they are by people who misunderstand and maltreat them just as they have misunderstood and maltreated me!

Basta! Enough! Early tomorrow I am off to Paris, firmly intent on having a good time for once in my life – for the first and probably last time I am going to experience the city of my dreams. *And nothing and no one* is going to stop me!

PS. On reading through what I have written (about Jenny's and my earliest relationship) I am struck by how cold and unloving it all sounds. Though the hour is late, I must put these jottings straight, so that no one reading this after my death shall form the wrong idea about me. Though my feelings for Jenny, if the truth be told, aren't as irresistible as they are for my sons, I am deeply fond of her and love her much as my Ma came to love me at the end of her life, when in her loneliness and distress of mind needed a daughter's love to console her. I am no longer the person I was; I have become resigned. True, Jenny isn't the person I would have wished her to be (and very far indeed from the support I was to Ma!). But I accept her *as she is:* weak, impulsive, dependent. Not at all untalented, she is a clinging vine, with none of Fredrik's ambition and capacity for hard work, utterly without Leo's vitality and genius – yet at the same time soulful, touchingly generous, threatened as she is, having inherited Henrik's melancholia, his anxiety and nerve sickness that infests his blood like a parasite and that has obviously been passed on to her. This is why I am so dreadfully sorry for them both and include them now in my evening prayers, asking God to protect poor Henrik, *but especially Jenny and her little ones.*

So writes Grandmother Charlotte in her diary, and – to make doubly sure – underlining the last few words twice.

Thoughts in the Night

Vicky

This evening I'm dreadfully upset. Nothing is any fun. Don't feel like doing my homework or watching television. I have put my little sisters to bed and read them a goodnight story. Funny how I can make them drop off without any fuss – with Mum they are hopeless and she just gives in to them. Really I ought to turn in too but just sit here on the edge of my bed, biting my nails and thinking. It is stormy outside, rustling the leaves round the house. Autumn has really come now and everything is being torn to pieces, swept away and changing from lovely reds and yellows to dark brown. What fun it would be to be an artist when I grow up! Well, perhaps . . . I'm happiest when I'm out riding on my own, looking at the countryside: the bare branches, heaps of rotting leaves, the smell of bonfires in people's gardens. Here in Sussex it is mostly damp with a purple-grey mist, though the sun can break through and make the dull, sleepy landscape all golden again. Best of all is riding on the Downs, beyond Ditchling, where Angela Holmes lives. She is horribly rich with two ponies but is nice to me anyway. Often she lends me one. Bonny could never go that far. From up there you can see the sea and the beech woods. The landscape unfolds like one of Granny Mildred's patchwork quilts. There is a path that goes along under the hillside that the pilgrims took one way to Canterbury, the other to Winchester, where Dad went to school and where they prayed to St Swithun for rain. Being miles from home and looking out over those fantastic views feels great. Then all the grown-ups' rows and the silly things they say, even the houses we live in, look tiny, kind of don't mean any thing anymore. I suppose that is what I need just now. Peace and quiet to get some perspective on what the grown-ups have been saying.

This evening I'm so unhappy and lonely I could hug myself. They, Mum and Mormor, are in Paris. Good thing Dad couldn't go at the last moment. Something to do with a job he is doing. Mum and Mormor went half out of their minds, Mum screamed hysterically that she would rather not go at all than go alone with Mormor. Poor Mormor! She just sank down on a chair and mumbled: 'Oh, dear God, that's all we needed! *Without you, Jean-Paul!* How can Jenny and I manage?' In the end, after a lot of fuss, they got going, probably too late to catch the Newhaven train. Almost forgot to say goodbye to us, they were so *echaufferad* – that's Mormor's word, means 'heated up' – or anyway used to. Shouldn't be surprised if in the end Dad didn't have to drive them to Newhaven.

It's so empty here in the house, desolate sort of. Cold too. The boiler must have gone on strike again. Downstairs Michael is sitting in front of the television with his thumb in his mouth and I can't get a word out of him as he sits watching his beloved 'Saint' squirt nails at his pursuers from behind his white Volvo sports car. Lady, his rabbit, has come indoors again, dropping her pellets of shit all over the place as she dances round in figures of eight on the carpet. Well, 'they' aren't here so it doesn't matter and anyway I agree with Michael – animals have as much right to be indoors as we have. If I could I'd let my donkey lie on the sofa! The little ones are asleep and Rita's 'gone to her English course' – I don't think! She is with that man she met at the Red Lion. And it'll be ages before Dad gets home from London.

In a way I think he is pleased to be rid of Mormor and Mum for a while. How can there be so much high tension between those two? It's not as if they weren't fond of each other. The air seems to *shudder* between them. It is a war of nerves, worse than school. It makes me feel so horribly anxious, I want to run as far away as I can and hide! Why are they like that? I'm so sorry for them, I wish I could protect them from each other.

Maybe it will be like that one day between me and Mum? Is it always like that between mothers and daughters? It's difficult enough as it is between me and Mum. After all I'm not a child any-more, I'm a *woman*, the same as she is – as she knows, though she doesn't treat me like one. Instead of a chum she treats me as if I were some kind of enemy . . . I love Mum and I need her . . . I want to talk to her about a lot of problems but have fun together, too. Like we used to in the old days, when she was such a lot of fun, playing with me and Michael when we were little. Is it being here in Lindfield that has changed her? Of course anyone would go round the bend, having Granny next door. But it's not just that either. All round Mum there is a kind of shadow. She just drifts about alone all the time nowadays, as if there were a screen in front of her, the kind we used to have round our beds when we were small . . . She only lets in Dad and Jojo. Sometimes not even them. Dad says she is OK. Says it to protect us. But it's not true. Mum feels awful, utterly awful, and I would like to help her, take away that shadow, that screen . . . But how? You can't get through to her.

Of course Mormor's terribly critical of Mum, of us all. She can't understand that in this family we like to improvise and be a bit bohemian – Mormor and Morfar *live* by the clock: the times they must take their pills, the news on the television. Mormor thinks we are just lazy, sloppy, badly brought up English slobs who are not being properly looked after! It's practically killing her, having to bottle up all her criticisms. All her perfectionistic Swedish house-wife eyes can see are untidy drawers and rooms all in a mess. And Mum can't stand being criticized. She is so touchy, so *moody*. Can't fight back, stand up for herself. Is sure everybody is against her, gossiping about her behind her back. And it frightens her more and more. Soon she will be too scared to face anyone. If anyone gets aggressive and criticizes her (like Mormor did the other day) she goes bright red, then turns deadly pale and confused and says something odd that has nothing to do with anything. It's dreadfully scary. As if she had gone off and left us and locked herself up in an imaginary room of her own.

I see into Mormor too. I know how hard it is for her not to intervene. She almost explodes if she can't have a free hand to 'help' in her own way. It's more than she can do not to stick her nose into it all, control and fix everything in *her* way. In the end people get so exhausted they just give in and *let* her dominate them. Only then does she calm down. It's Dad's little joke that she is like Napoleon, who was forever going to war to rule every country in Europe.

In a way I understand her. Things at home here are in a hopeless muddle. It's just that Mum hasn't got the energy to cope or make us do as we are told and bring us up properly, 'lay down the law', as Mormor calls it. It's all too much for her. Mormor loves drawing boundaries. 'If one doesn't, and just lets life take over,' she says, 'we all get out of hand and make ourselves unhappy. Grownups are like children, need a firm hand to draw boundaries.' Well, I agree. How nice it would be if Mum and Dad were just a bit firmer, tougher! It's as if they don't care enough about us and find it easiest to let us have our own way. Sometimes it's almost as if they were just playing mummies and daddies . . . Though I wonder . . . sometimes it seems as if Mormor has always had to draw up boundary lines for herself. She is *tremendously* temperamental. She would probably like nothing better than to break out, blow everything sky-high that gets in the way of that will of hers!

But why do we have to let someone else rule us all our lives? A strict God who will never leave us in peace? Mum has told me how they – she and her brothers, that is – went in terror of Him, always lurking about their home and waiting to punish them. Like an unwanted lodger! Surely one can manage oneself? Without an invisible Somebody breathing down one's neck?

The nuns in that school Dad sent us to when we first got here – what a mistake that was! – used to carry on about God all the time. Not like grammar school. Grammar school is OK, not at all claustrophobic. Not that He was supposed to be all that strict; more loving really, always ready to forgive. Poor little brides of Jesus, those nuns, poor, chaste and obedient, every last one of them. So I suppose God is their father-in-law . . . I feel so sorry for Jesus, having a flock of wives like that lot at the Sacred Heart trailing after him, all either too fat or too thin, wizened and bony, either sensuous or spiritual looking, Though a couple of them were ever so beautiful. Sister Gabrielle, for example, who looked after the five- and six-year-olds. Every time I go to pick up Rosie, Sister's beauty takes my breath away and I feel quite calm inside. She makes me almost believe a shy angel has come down to earth a while to share our earthly lives with us and love us without keeping us within bounds all the time. Never goes on about God, either, or purgatory or Jesus' horrible death on the cross. Never forces any of that disgusting crap about the suffering saints and martyrs down your throat. She is spiritual, sees right through you. Despite her boring, closed-in life – imagine! no boyfriends, sex, fun or pretty clothes – she never seems sad or down in the dumps, as I am this evening. I wouldn't mind having her here so I could give her a big hug. Though then she would break in two – or else be scared of me and all my sinful, earthly desires and fly out of the window and back up to heaven.

Stop it, Victoria! You are getting to be as cynical as your dad is sometimes. Poking fun at things that really are special and lovely.

Muriel

I couldn't have stood her another moment, or those snuffling little dogs of hers, almost as demanding and disgusting as babies they are. She gets my goat more and more nowadays, my youngest sister. Always was the odd one out. That time outside the house in Dawlish – how long ago can it be now, fifty, sixty years? – sitting there on the front-door step – incredible, us being so old . . . well, anyway her, even though she is almost ten years younger – with her tears splashing down on to a picture book called *Odd*. Obviously, Midgo came into the world far too late, shouldn't really have been there at all, Mother being well over forty and already having seven of us to cope with – far too many girls – and only two boys, Mervyn and Charlie. Oh God, what a tragedy, Charlie being killed in the war, *our* war, that is. The first one. Though the eldest, he had always been the icing on the cake. Such men don't exist nowadays. Weaklings, the whole lot of them, with their hair hanging down their necks! Imagine, the other day Jean-Paul saw one in the City, with a bowler on top of his goldilocks! Sometimes one wonders where it has all gone, anything that meant anything. I suppose I was a bit gone on Charlie. No man has ever been as wonderful as him in my eyes. He always rises to the surface above all the other corpses. Of course it was wrong of me to let Midgo drive off in her Rolls-Royce, dead drunk and with those little snuffling horrors in the back seat. In a state like that she is a macabre menace, to herself and everyone else. But I couldn't stand her another moment, and she'll drop dead one of these days anyway, drinking like that . . .

I used to enjoy my home here, a little place of my own at last – after all the troubles, the wars. Paris. And now, not least, after all those rows when I was staying with her in her Hampshire manor-house. The truth is, it is icy cold in here! Unhomely. Run to seed in some way – I see it clearly now, after being away for a week. Even Midgo, drink-sodden though she is, seemed to notice it – that is, if it weren't just one more of her devilish little manoeuvres, one more way of getting at me after our rows last week? Why otherwise did she pass a triumphant scarlet-manicured Pekinese claw over the tea table to show it needed dusting? Say ironically, 'Your dear little Violet doesn't seem to have *worked* very hard while you've been away, does she? Can't think why you keep her on! Servants are such a *nuisance* nowadays. Lazy liars, the whole lot of them. And thieves too. Tell her to go. Do as I do. Manage on your own. A good thing I have my Barney to give me a hand. Men are so much more useful, in so many ways. You need one, my dear Muriel. At our age they are like vitamin injections.' Her age. My age. Age . . . And from the dust she went on to Barney, that big lout, stable-hand he was or something, whom she has been having an affair with all these years. At her age! It is horrible when people of our class lose our dignity, sink into the mob. The general decay. But that is how it is. On the way down, everything. I'm even becoming resigned to Jean-Paul not coming to anything now. And of course it is all *her* fault, in there. Destroyed everything, she has, with her seductive ways, though I'll never understand what he sees in her. Certainly she isn't beautiful. He, who could have married anyone! There is a weak streak, Mother used to say, that runs through the men in our family. Can't keep their women in order. Not like Jean did. He was a real man, even if he was French. You had to hand it him. Not that I ever really understood all those strange ideas of his . . . Well, I suppose I'll have to tighten the reins with Violet, have a word with her. No doubt about it, there is something dreary about everything in here since *they* came, a vague air of melancholy. In my little house, which used to be so elegant. My pride and joy. Not a proper frame for me – what that can be good for, such a lot is *passé.*

Muriel Didier heats water for her hot-water bottle and makes herself some Ovaltine. The chill in her kitchen tonight is so piercing that the floor of worn tiles sends icy shivers right through her slippers, bought at Liberty's, they too no longer in their first youth. It is blowing hard outside and beyond the Gothic windows of her house the moon, like a restless ghost, is being chased in and out of driving clouds. The house was once a chapel but was converted by her ten years ago, furnished with thirties' relics that have survived the war years, from hers and Jean Didier's Paris flat. Through her kitchen's rusting window frame she can see a light still on in Victoria's bedroom. Really, she ought to go over and shout up to her to put it out. A schoolgirl, at this hour, with her light on! Listening probably to those detestable, caterwauling Beatles. Or that horrible little song 'What Are We Living For?' forever floating faintly in from next door the moment Vicky comes home. Good question. What *are* we living for, Muriel wonders, quickly snatching up her milk pan off the gas before it bubbles over. Those long, furbelow skirts, for instance, that her daughter-in-law goes swishing about in whenever they – more and more rarely – have to receive some visitor from Sweden; they are a caricature, they insult her almost more than Vicky's tarty miniskirts! They do just as they like, those kids in there. No discipline, no manners, no regular hours! Was it Michael or Vicky who smuggled in that horrible little grass snake into my downstairs loo? Neither admits to it, just titters. They *know* I loathe snakes, worms, spiders. Parrots are different; they are fun, especially the one we had in Dawlish when we were small, who used to squawk 'Shut up, Muriel! Shut up!' That time I had garland of flowers in my hair and was walking in the garden in my long white lace dress, pretending I was the Duchess of Devonshire, the most beautiful, richest little girl in the world . . . Well, I was, for a while . . .

But those poor children, what is to become of them, Muriel mumbles piously, turning the gas off and extinguishing her kitchen's dim forty-watt light. With a mother like that, that cross I'm carrying for my sins. I simply can't imagine how my son, who is 'normal' at least, can love such a spaghetti-like creature! 'The truth is, *Maman*,' he'd said ironically that day they'd had a row, 'you're jealous of her!' There was a time when I could take it as a joke; but in some way even joking has become dangerous, so none of us dares to, for fear of *her* taking it seriously and it all leading to tears and hysteria and I don't know what else! If one daren't joke, what else can one say? She has absolutely no sense of humour that Swedish woman; accuses me of being tactless, letting my tongue wag. How can I be jealous of a prig? Of course I have my short-comings, who hasn't, but jealousy – how could Midgo in her underhand way accuse me of it, too? – jealousy isn't one of them. It's enough to make one livid. Here I go and in my despair confide in her – all I have to put up with from Jenny and her brood that Jean-Paul has hung round his neck, try to lighten my heart, ask for a little sympathy and consolation – and all she can find to say is: 'What a shame! Poor Jenny, poor kids!'

'What do you mean, poor?' I said. 'Not for anything would I be in their shoes or have you for a mother-in-law, you, *who have always been so jealous!*'

No, no, Midgo has got it all wrong. She has always been neu-rotic. It's that Jenny creature who's jealous – of me. Of my good taste. My easy way with people, of my gifts as a hostess, my finesse, intelligence and knowledge of the world. Otherwise why does she always grab hold of Jean-Paul, tired out from his long day in London, the moment he steps inside the door? Never even let him relax over a sherry with his mother? Well, I'm above such passions, my whole life-style is on another level. Jean was a brilliant man. 'Muriel, dear,' he used to say, 'jealousy is one of the most humili-ating states a human being can sink to!' And now that trouble-maker Midgo has the nerve to fling at me: 'Truth to tell, you wish you were married to your own son!' Words so bizarre that they sent a chill of horror through me. Only an alcoholic, tippling in secret from morning to night, can come out with such lunacies. And it will certainly be the last time I ever open my heart to *her*! Only to hear I haven't a streak of motherliness in me, couldn't even bring up a litter of Pekineses: 'you who went off and left him to a nurse when he was only six weeks old, your Jean-Paul! Don't you think it's a bit late in the day for mother-love?'

No, no, all those poisonous things she spat out, it's best to forget her, and Jenny. Not to mention that Vicky girl, running around in riding breeches with village boys, like a mongrel bitch on heat, down at the riding stables. Anyway it's something to be grateful for, that Jean-Paul hasn't gone off to Paris with Jenny and her black little witch of a mother. Wonder if he'll be home soon? Isn't that his car I can hear through the bedroom window? thinks Muriel and on her way through her sitting-room, with its green Venetian rococo furniture painted with pink roses, gathers up a biography of Madame de Maintenon to take up to bed. Identifying with celebrities of bygone days is one of her few remaining pleasures. It is like reading about herself.

A few purplish flames left over from her tea-time fire with Midgo are gasping their last in the grate. No, Muriel, don't think of all that . . . Instead it occurs to her that most of the heat actually goes up the chimney, snoring like a drunk this windy night. Afraid of setting the house on fire even so, she screens it off with her antique fire-guard with its portrait of an eighteenth-century woman on it, hair piled up and a coldly observant expression on her face. To her bridge friends Muriel insists it's a genuine Gainsborough, unsigned, alas. Maybe Jean-Paul is right. Maybe she ought to put in double glazing and central heating. She is frozen through. Chilled to the bone. But central heating is so expensive. And unhealthy. And she is saving every penny for Jean-Paul. Who will soon certainly be needing it . . .

Vicky

No, if I'm going to hug anyone it will be Roy, down at the stables. God, how good-looking he is! What if he is working class and Granny says he can't speak 'properly' – with that nasal, upper-class twang she means. I don't give a damn. Roy turns me on. Only has to touch me, give me a leg up on to the horse or something, to make me go all shaky and sticky between my thighs. I want him to seduce me! Do what Dad does to Mum at night, what makes her scream so that you can hear it all through the house. They say it 's painful the first time they penetrate you and you bleed a bit, but so what? Have to put up with something to get rid of that relic, the ones those nuns are terrified of losing, their shrivelled little rosebud they cling to all their lives till they turn into little frustrated devils or go out of their minds! Roy is dark, strong, not all that tall but with a profile like the nobleman in that old Italian painting I saw. I have tried to draw him, but somehow it always goes wrong. For God's sake, how do you *become* an artist anyway? I can feel he wants to sleep with me, there is this warm feeling between us – this attraction. I wish he were here tonight! Is that how Mum feels for Dad? Is that why she only comes alive when he is around?

That long talk Rita and I had the other evening. About sex, boys and so on. Most of the time she is so grumpy and taciturn. I don't think she likes being with us any more. She has turned against Mum, though she doesn't say so. She used to want to become one of those church workers they have in Sweden, who look after people who are sick or old or dying. Since meeting the Wolf she has changed completely. Become another person. Brutal. Greedy. Selfish. She says she wants to go back to Germany and save her soul, but that man has got his claws in her. She's crazy about him, it shows a mile off. Though he's only a road worker he is terribly attractive, but cruel and ruthless with women, I reckon. But she has got that religious stuff hung round her neck, too. Being a Catholic and having to go to mass and confession. Her Mutti and Vatti would murder her if they knew she had a lover. A real savage he is, too. Bites and pinches her so it leaves fiery scratches and bruises on her skin. You would think he'd have enough of that kind of thing, drilling holes in the streets all day! But when she showed me them she just threw me a daft smile and giggled. I said: 'You ought to pack him in. Can't you see he is dangerous! Could get so excited he killed you!' But all she said was she liked violent men! Idiot. I'm never going to be like her, masochistic. That's for sure!

It's hard being a kind of in-between creature. No longer a child. But not grown-up either. It's frightening having to turn into an adult. Say one thing and mean another. Grown-ups switch faces and masks as if they had a whole cupboardful of them! Most of the time they lie to themselves and each other, I reckon. I don't want to be like that. Who am I – really – turning into? When I take a close look at grown-ups I see nothing but faults and shortcomings. Though not in Dad of course . . .

It'll soon be midnight. Why hasn't Dad come home? I can't go to sleep until he does. Not with all the creaking and groaning in this old house. Specially now in the autumn that there is an invasion of mice and squirrels and other little creatures up in the attic. But it's not just the noises. It's something else . . . Me perhaps? It's as if something dramatic is going to happen to us all. A disaster. Something horrible.

A branch taps and taps against my window. The moon is shining sharp and straight into my little room. I don't mind it at all, that's why I haven't pulled back the curtains. When Mormor came it was just a little slip of a new moon. Oh God, if only Dad would come home! There is something I must tell him about. Something that goes round and round in my head, worries me.

Nothing has turned out the way I thought it would when Mormor came. I had longed for her so much. At least as much as Mum had, because Mormor has always made me feel safe. I realize that now. When I was a little kid I used to spend a lot of time with Mormor and Morfar. Mum was always having miscarriages and babies. Spent half her time in hospital. Didn't have time for me. What fun it was being with them! They forgot about everything else and devoted themselves to me. How lovely it was playing snap and making up games and going for walks in the park. Going to the market-place with Mormor; she would buy me something at the toy shop on Storgatan. Nothing spectacular: a little doll, some crayons, soap bubbles to blow. How lovely it was when they used to read to me in the evenings, chapters from *Heidi* or *A Little Princess* or that old Estonian fairy-tale about Krabataska the witch,who runs off with little children. And afterwards we would say a prayer together at bedtime. Though at times they could get all anxious, particularly after some long, mysterious telephone call from Uncle Leo or Uncle Fredrik. Then Morfar would escape into his study and Mormor would get all silent and start polishing the silver or doing household accounts for hours. Then everything around me became empty and boring and I would start longing to be back with Michael and Mum and Dad. Yet even with the cloud of gloom that sometimes hung over them in their ten-room apart- ment – much too big for them, so big they would sometimes even get lost and wander around calling out for each other – I felt safe. I would sit on a mattress in the drawing-room and play with the antique doll's house furniture that Mormor had inherited from *her* mother's home. As I did with Morfar and his cigar smell in his study with the family Bible, the stained glass window and my 'fairy-tale chair', where I would sit perched on his knee, close to him, listening to *Pelle Svanslös* the tail-less cat or *The Moss Lady*. Same feeling of security as there was in Mormor's room, in her hands as they watered her plants, or as she held me tight, kissed me and whispered: 'Mormor's own sweet little Victoria! Mormor's own little girl!'

That's why I have always thought Mum must be making it all up, all that stuff she tells Dad about her 'anxiety-laden' childhood and how it has damaged her. Mormor and Morfar were my guardian angels. How could they hurt anybody?

So I didn't believe Mum and stuck up for them. Hid in Morfar's old dressing-gown that smelt of his cigars or in Mormor's hugs. Took shelter in their endless love for me.

I suppose that's why Mormor's visit has been such a shock, turning out so differently from what I had expected. Bringing with her all her criticism and worry and anxiety and a strange sense of insecurity. As well as that rubbish about limits, as if people have to be fenced in behind barbed wire. She who never made any limits for me. Even the donkey she gave me – my huge birthday surprise! – has been a disappointment. How I longed to have one! So of course everyone expected me to be thrilled to bits, fall into ecstasies of happiness and gratitude. The truth is, I suddenly realized *it wasn't really a donkey I wanted. It was something else.* What I longed for was for things to change. An end to everything that has gone wrong and is painful here at home. What I wanted was a new kind of life, with an ordinary, happy, healthy mum and a dad who doesn't rush about the place all the time to earn money. A Dad who has time for us. For me . . .

Poor little donkey, he can't do that. So I got scared of him and him of me, I suppose, so he bit me and I started screaming. Screamed out all my despair over Mum and Dad and Michael and my little sisters; at not even knowing who I am, and at life being one long drag, dreary and threatening. Of course they misunderstood me, as always. Thought I was just being silly and hysterical and ungrateful to Mormor and treated me like a little kid, putting me back to where I used to be. And that makes me so wild and cross, like Mormor; makes me spit out my fury like a fairy-tale dragon! But then I hear Mother Agnes's voice from the convent: 'Your temper, Victoria, dear, is your great shortcoming. And you are too impulsive, too stubborn. But that's the way God has made you and I am sure he has done it for a very good reason.'

And Victoria, who is rather a lonely girl, keeps turning over in bed, on her narrow mattress. So many contradictory thoughts and feelings! They're all too much for her to sort out, all by herself.
Muriel

Once in bed, trying to read about Madame de Maintenon's exploits at Versailles, Muriel suddenly sees what is wrong. The fact is, nothing really interests her any longer. She can't concentrate. Not on her book. Not on the decay of her little home that used to be so elegant. Not on anything. It is as if she were paralysed! The thought rushes angrily through her head, wrapped for the night in a pale-mauve mohair shawl. From the raven's – no, cuckoo's – nest next door comes a petrifying *fear*. Something horrible she can't put a name to, can't explain, or get at. Can't *do* anything about. For her, who had coped with so much, even managed to stand up to the brilliant Jean Didier, this awful thing is quite simply too much. It amazes her that her son can – if he can. Yet she sees with painful clarity that every day he continues being exposed to such radiation is gradually dragging him down. It makes her feel so helpless she could weep. 'Sickly women breed like rabbits,' little Violet had said one morning, polishing her silver in the kitchen. How furious Jean-Paul had been when she had jokingly repeated Violet's words! Well, even a blind hen sometimes finds a grain of truth. That Jenny has turned my life upside down – Muriel's thoughts go on, more and more tormented, ever more sleepy – she has made me become all frayed round the edges, like my cyclamen velvet curtains downstairs. Fills me with that strange – what do they call it? – 'anxiety' that Jean-Paul told me she and her whole family suffer from, that time in Stockholm. It sweeps in here like a cold draught.

Muriel remembers how the snow had piled up in great snowdrifts along Jungfrugatan against a black sky, always pitch-black. How suspiciously the Swedish stars had peered down at her as she had struggled on, leaning on Jean-Paul's arm, through ice and snow. The little stars and red lights dangling in dark windows had irritated her as much as the inhabitants of that frozen land. Not a soul had been in sight, that night, with the thermometer down to minus thirty degrees, it had been too cold even for them! Invited by Jenny's parents as their guest but living a little way away in Jean-Paul's lodgings, she had felt completely out of place. After staggering through the frozen snow, sliding hither and thither and almost breaking her neck or legs, they had arrived for dinner six minutes late and been reprimanded by Jenny's mother in her bad English: 'In Sweden we come not late to dinner!' That had been the last straw. They might as well have served up snow as soup. Despite the stuffy central heating, a log fire burning in the grate and their everlasting candlelight, she had felt frozen to the bone, shivering through the evening afterwards as they sat there digesting the food and taking coffee in a peculiar mood of gloomy solemnity. She had felt lost, ill. Even her tongue seemed to have turned into an icicle, as if it had also got stuck. They had seemed like threatening, unreal beings from some distant planet, as if Europe were for ever a million miles away. And she remembers how, with them sitting there all round her in the faint light of their infernal candles, a terror of a kind she had never known before had fastened on her. Only Jean-Paul being in the room had prevented her from losing her self-control and screaming. Now she knows what it was they had exuded, behind all their efforts to be kind and hospitable. That mysterious 'anxiety,' which she hadn't been able to understand, no matter how much Jean-Paul had tried to explain it after they had got back to his rooms.

Faced with that word Muriel's lively mind comes to a standstill. It must be modern, something people have invented since the war. In any case no one, as far as she knows, ever suffered from it in the good old days, back in the twenties and thirties. Must have something to do with the Cold War. To be frightened, she knows what that is! It's the swishing whine of falling bombs that come rushing down at you out of a dully pulsing night sky, howling sirens, the wild ringing of fire-engines, collapsing house façades, the acrid rain-soaked stench next morning as one, in spite of it all, totters into the Merchant Navy censorship office! Fear, ice-cold fear is a telegram: 'His Majesty has the sad duty of informing you . . .' Or, almost worse, no telegram at all – only waiting week after week, month after month, as Mother and Father had done after Paschendael for news of Charlie; being forced each morning to open the big Admiralty envelope and, heart in mouth, run one's eye down the long list of torpedoed ships, panic-stricken that Jean-Paul's may be one of them. Morning after morning, for five years . . . Incomprehensible, that she, who had been through *all that* should afterwards have to put up with something in a way almost worse. Have to stand *this* year after year! And the poor children – Muriel wonders, her heart suddenly softening as she turns over in her warm bed – what will become of them? Her life is in ruins.

Yes, the nasty thing about her daughter-in-law is the vacuum all round her. That sleep-walker face! It is like having to cope with an absence that is always present, an absence and a kind of treacherous nothingness that nevertheless always gets its own way, *her* own way; and makes Muriel, despite all her good intentions, feel utterly powerless. Sometimes she thinks up some way to help. But Jenny always takes it the wrong way, as if her mother-in-law were just trying to interfere or rule her. It is true, she admits, that when they had first come to live next door she had in fact nursed certain plans; thought she would help bring up those children, teach Jenny a smoother, more English way of living and getting on with people. Her good intentions had instantly gone awry. Her plan came to grief. The very first day there had been a row, though she can't recall what it was about. Some silly little words that she had let slip and they had misinterpreted. For several weeks after that they hadn't spoken. An iron curtain had come down between the two houses. Jean-Paul, of course, had tried to make peace. But in some baffling way had never succeeded, not really! It is like always having to talk to someone who isn't there yet who, despite her gentle, ingratiating ways, rules everything.

Things hadn't been too bad to begin with, after they had come to live here – though there had been constant rows, hysteria, childishness and open conflicts. Anyway it had been better than this evasive silence and more or less polite gloom, this deadlock none of us can break, thinks Muriel. Better than not being able to get through at all, which terrifies me! Little by little my *joie de vivre* is draining away, as if I were bleeding to death – Muriel's exhausted thoughts run on as she switches out her bedside light. *She*, over there, just drifts about in her dressing-gown and slippers, smoking cigarettes and lugging that baby about with her . . . wanders about among kids and animals. What does she actually *do*? Does she really listen to that monotonous, tuneless old music – baroque, isn't that what they call it? Is she merely pretending to be ill and helpless, to keep her power over my son, while in reality she is as fit as a fiddle (though it is my firm conviction that all Scandinavians are more or less crazy)? Has something to do with degeneration, thousands of years of inbreeding . . . I'm scared of her. She hates me. In some way wants to harm me. Behind that Madonna-like forehead she is certainly hatching schemes against me; pathologically jealous as she is, she wants to get rid of me. Have him to herself.

If only Jean hadn't died! He would have made her pull herself together. At least Jean was a real man. He would never have *permitted* anyone not to exist! How sad it is, being a widow. I'm all alone, dreadfully alone. No one loves me, or even understands me. Or defends me, or even bothers about me. As for Jean-Paul, he only pretends to . . . Life is just misery. My meaningless days drift by like deaf mutes into dark worried nights – all these thoughts . . . And nowadays I, too, am pretending. I'm just playing at being the woman who used to live in Paris, stuck in this dreary little idyll of an English village, among these dull people, these provincials that everyone on the Avenue Georges V would have laughed at. The truth is, *I'm bored to death*. Would I like to go back to Paris, then?

No, it is too late. Everything is too late. And life there after the war was so tricky, so dreadfully hard. It turned the Parisians into adders. I had to assert myself at all costs to get what I wanted. Then one discovered one *had* a will. Of steel. And *courage*, to save what could be saved – for Jean-Paul. Poor boy, his life and prospects have also been laid waste by the war, by all those years at sea . . .

But coming here, too, was a mistake. Even worse, to let Jean-Paul bring his family here. From that day on life seems to have got stuck in a vicious circle. Why, oh why, has it turned out like this? I can't stand being alone in my house anymore. That is why I doll myself up, deck myself out in the Parisian jewellery Jean once gave me, go rushing out to morning coffees, lunches, teas, and afterwards let my so-called friends bring me back in their cars to more loneliness, to a kind of hatred of myself and others, in an endless *danse macabre*.

Why am I so infernally intelligent, so superior to others? Why can't anyone stand up to me? Jean did. Stopped me dead in my tracks, forced me to submit. All that *faire l'amour*, I didn't get much pleasure out of it; but he gave me the kind of life I needed on a level far above the middle-class circumstances I had been so unfortunate as to be born into. Above the mob. *Au dessus de la mêlée*. To be editor-in-chief of *Le Monde*, that was something! Not like all this abstract stuff my poor boy has to make do with. Futurology, what is that? For us who haven't got a future? Ever-rising GNP, scenario expectations at year 1970, 1980, 1990, 2000 – no matter how often he has tried to explain it all to me, what's meant by these scenarios, what a growth economy is when it's at home – all this dreary stuff that I type out for him, day in and day out, without understanding a single word of it – God, how boring it all is! Though of course if I didn't have it I would have nothing to fill the gaps in my life. He says times will stay good as long as the Vietnam war lasts. But what has the one got to do with the other? Prosperity with war? But he mustn't let on to his clients, who 'don't like to face up to simple facts'. Instead he just goes on drawing his ever-rising curves . . . I can't understand all that. Or his strange abstract ideas. Poor Jean-Paul; by now he should be *known* for something; be famous. After all, anyone who isn't famous, or at least married to someone who is or related to them, isn't really anything, is he? Well, of course, that brother of Jenny's is world-famous, like the people we knew that time in Hollywood, Jean and I – though most of them seem to be forgotten now. The evenings when he pops up on the television waving his conduc-tor's baton, she gets all excited – only to be in the dumps the next day, even more muddle-headed and distant. I can't say I really liked Leo that time in Stockholm when he came to dinner at his parents. Nasty type. Genius. Shrewd, yellowish green eyes, flitting hither and thither, not letting you catch their glance. And that guffaw of his! Though Jean-Paul says it's because he's so hyper-sensitive. A genius. As everyone seems to agree. But Toscanini, he was really something!

How cold it is in here.

Genius, yes. My Jean, now, he was a *real* genius, or at least *tout Paris* regarded him as such. Odd that today no one even remem-bers him. How can one just vanish – without trace? Cease to be even a memory. Who will remember me? Yet Jean had a brain. Looked straight through you with those blue eyes of his! Impossible to lie or have secrets from him. That time when every-thing fell to pieces . . . luckily no one seems to remember that, either! Oh well, perhaps it is best after all that some things fall into everlasting oblivion. He forced me to own up – I who had never confessed to anything – to having gossiped to that curly headed squit from *Le Temps*, who I had thought wouldn't hurt a fly. And next day all Paris knew it – the whole of France. And it brought down the government. The last liberal one, before Daladier started playing at being Mussolini. A shock Jean never got over. Oh God, why can't my tongue ever stop wagging? It just goes on and on, and in those days was at least appreciated as witty. Then, yes. But nowadays – not a smile. She, this Nordic nitwit, takes everything literally. 'Why do you say one thing, Muriel, when you really mean the opposite?' she asked me gently, in her little ingratiating 'do-be-friends-with-me' voice, that time she had threatened to pack her bags and go home to Sweden and I had fallen into a panic and apologized and begged them to stay. 'I don't understand that kind of talk. It confuses me. Don't you understand it can *hurt people's feelings* and makes me feel dreadfully sad?' Never in my life had anyone said such a thing to me before! Oh God, how *boring* they are, these Scandinavians who can't even understand a joke, let alone take one; but have to take everything dead seriously, *au pied de la lettre!* 'Actually you did mean what you said,' she insisted, 'and it wasn't nice of you. It made me feel quite ill.' Well, naturally I had meant it. Though not literally. I would never mean that kind of thing literally . . .

Jean, Jean, why did you take that fatal boat from Tangiers? What odds did it make whether you went on fighting with de Gaulle or stayed in Vichy? Who was going to win didn't depend on you. Wars just happen. And it was obvious we would win, we always do. In the end . . . First Charlie. Then Jean. A bullet through his heart at Paschendael and then a German torpedo somewhere in the Bay of Biscay. What is it like to drown, trapped like a rat as the sea comes rushing in, down the corridors, into the cabins, thousands and thousands of tons of water, down there in the darkness, the whole ocean? Oh, Jean, Jean . . .

Strange, how hard I find it to remember you, Jean, in spite of your silver-framed photo down there in the sitting-room and that portrait of you from 1925 hanging on the stairs. What did you look like? Really? Only one thing I remember. Your eyes, those blue eyes that are always seeing through me, that gleam through time and space. Why didn't I even mourn you? Not really? We had too much to do, you understand, winning the war. Everything hung on us British – after your Frenchmen had run for their lives . . . and the Swedes just wallowed in their neutrality, their so-called anxiety! We felt real fear; it was *about* something. Not nothing. And now the Scandinavians and other foreigners from countries one hardly even knows the names of have the nerve to look down on us, say we've had our day, that everything British is *vieux jeu*, mouldy like my little house, my creation I was so proud of . . .

Suddenly Muriel Didier is back in her big sunlit salon in the apartment on the Avenue Georges V, and the spring sunshine comes pouring in over the tops of the flowering chestnut trees and a scent of *tout Paris* mingles with Chanel's newly launched Number 2, which she has just dabbed behind her ears. Standing at the open window, waiting for her guests, she looks out over the spire of the Russian cathedral. Today Prince Bagration and his witty wife are coming for cocktails, also a lot of other amusing people from among Jean's political and newspaper contacts. Old Madame de Zoubaloff, she too once a princess, but today without a sou, and her handsome, attractive daughter Catherine, who does such elegant needlework; they too must be on their way, together with other Georgian exiles. In the brightly lit room everything is in its place. Mme Muriel Didier adjusts a Lalique mermaid on the marble mantelpiece and looks at herself in the mirror above it. A slender woman, still quite young, with slim sloping shoulders. A triple amethyst necklace dangles down, glittering, on her flattened bosom. And she thinks to herself: How beautiful I am!

And here they come, two by two – like animals into the Ark, she titters inwardly, reminding herself to remember her comical simile for future use. Little Tivolovitch, who after the Reds had once almost shot him instantly became religious, looks like a hypochondriac mouse: 'How are you, dear Tivo?' she asks, knowing he will come back with a detailed account of the state of his failing health. 'Sigguverymuch, my kidney is giving me much trouble,' he says, kissing her hand. Snaps up a cheese straw. He hasn't a penny either. Amidst all her chattering guests she catches a glimpse of Jean, always a trifle distant, always serious, as he looks from one guest to another, noting who has come and who hasn't. A short, square-built man, he gives off a feeling of dynamism. A singular power seems to isolate him among all these people. Just now he is exchanging a few sceptical words with some Frenchman who has the red bud of the Legion of Honour in his buttonhole. The buzz is immense. It is as if the ocean, the whole of humanity – or anyway that part of it which *is* or at least *has been* somebody – has assembled here. The Didiers' Italian chauffeur Vinco, tall and dark, a refugee from Mussolini, is going round serving cocktails on a silver salver, replying with half-disrespectful, half-respectful phrases whenever some guest, struck by his handsome appearance, speaks to him. Vinco, yes, with his shiny, jet-black hair brushed straight back and his soft, sensual lips, she likes Vinco. If only Vinco weren't a servant . . . He comes towards her as she is saying sweet nothings to the Bagrations. What, Vinco? What's that you are saying, I can't hear? So many years have gone by. Weren't you shot by the Germans? Inclining his head slightly towards the open balcony window, overlooking the street, he brings his mouth closer to the amethyst that dangles from her ear. Whispers caressingly '*L'Hispano-Suiza, madame*. There's something wrong with it today. Won't start, *ça ne marche plus, c'est en panne . . .*'

En panne, madame, en panne . . .

Vicky

No sign of Daddy. It's midnight, and there is an owl hooting in the woods behind the garden. No Rita either. Must be lying orgasming with the Wolf. The moonlight, as sharp as a kitchen knife, cuts into Vicky, bringing out truth upon truth.

'Daddy,' she whispers, 'if only you knew how much I love you, how I admire you . . .'

Never be like Mum, she thinks. Never get married and have kids I can't look after! A vet or an artist, that's what I'm going to be, no home either, furniture, duties or babies! Free as the wind – like I'm sure Dad wants to be deep down, if he hadn't met Mum, fallen in love and chucked his freedom away. It's as if Mum has fallen apart, lost herself and gone to pieces. Oh, how I wish she would start writing poetry again like she used to! Why did she give up? Fall silent? And how long is she determined to go on like this? 'It's quite enough your Uncle Leo being so creative,' she said when I asked her about it the other day. And gave a dry painful laugh, more like a cough. 'Compared with him I'm *nothing*. Anyway I *can't*. Since we've moved down here to Lindfield there is no poetry in me.' Why does she always compare herself to him?

My lovely mum – if only she'd start writing her poetry and playing the piano again I'm sure she would stop having her crisis, drooping about after Dad like a lovesick doll and dragging Jojo with her wherever she goes, holding her in front of her like a shield. 'How heavy she is!' she complains, yet carries on just the same. Awfully bad for Jojo too, she will become Mum's little pet, never be able to stand on her own feet. Become part of Mum's anxiety, like she was infected. Because it's Jojo she usually clings to when she gets her anxiety attacks. Like the other day, when Mormor couldn't hold her tongue any longer and all her criticisms came pouring out, and Mum just sat there hunched up round Jojo. Then that strange distant look came into her face and she said something eerie like 'Mother, you are jabbing holes in my soul' and how she was lying in a deep ditch in her nice white fur, with scornful faces laughing down at her! I was out in the lobby, watching them. No one noticed me; it was horrible! At times like that I have to make myself go hard, pretend I'm icy cold, to survive. Dead hungry too, I get, have to rummage in the fridge and breadbin, could eat myself to death for terror. Michael wasn't half smart, sending Mormor off down to the Red Lion!

It hurts so much when Mum is like that. It's as if she weren't alive any more, but had come to a stop; says nothing, and her eyes go dead. Then something inside me stops as well, my life's clock. We are so close, Mum and me . . . almost one person! Same as Mum and Mormor! Stuck to each other, as if their umbilical chord had never been cut.

But I don't want to be another person! Not just part of Mum or of anyone else. I must cut myself off. Live my own life.

Victoria tosses and turns between the sheets. The church clock strikes half-past twelve. She feels she has been abandoned. She is not just upset but sad at heart, as if someone she loves has just died, or is soon going to. Not her, or her brother or sisters; they are all so young, the four of them, and have as yet scarcely begun living. But death is cruel and unjust and can strike without warning. Down in the village a little girl the same age as Rosalind is dying of leukemia; neither medicines, specialists, faith-healers nor her parents' prayers seem to have the least effect. So what about Mum – sometimes she looks so ill, hollowed out, has large, greeny-blue rings under her eyes. Once Victoria heard her telling Dad: 'I'm not afraid of death, not a scrap. I don't even know what you mean by it. To be dead is to be free.' It had upset Jean-Paul dreadfully: 'But, Jenny, that's unnatural, sick! According to Freud, not to be afraid of death is an alarming symptom!'

No, Freud is something Victoria can't make head or tail of. Yet in the same instant she remembers a dream she has often had about her mother. How Jenny wanders off into a fog and leaves them all. Or has fallen headlong from Beachy Head, where people commit suicide, and the police have found her body far below on a rocky ledge, brought her home in little pieces, like one of Rosalind's broken dolls and laid her on the day-room table, staring up at the ceiling out of blue porcelain eyes while they all stand around looking down at her, while Dad and Michael try to glue her together again. 'Tomorrow,' Dad had said in her dream, 'she will rise from the dead. All we have to do now is let the glue dry. Off to bed with you all!' But then everyone around the table had begun to cry, both the children and the animals, her donkey, the dog, the cats, the rabbit, the guinea-pigs and the budgies.

In another dream she is her mother. She sacks Rita and takes over. Alone with her dad she is his 'little woman', his only support in life. Afterwards, in the light of day, she grieves over the first dream, but condemns herself for the second. Vicky is beginning to suspect that she, too, is double, has an evil side to her.

More than anyone else in the family she has a feeling of Charlotte's life being in danger. It has something to do with her not being quite the same person as she used to be. Vicky had spotted it the moment she arrived, and it had scared her. It wasn't just that Charlotte had shrunk, become almost smaller than Vicky herself. There was something in her brown eyes: formerly so vivacious, they seemed to be under sentence of death, showed she knew she was seeing them all – the English trees she loves so, the little girls and, above all, her Vicky – for the last time. For though they haven't hit it off so well this time – quite the contrary – they are still in some strange way inseparable and can read each other's secrets.

Suddenly, in the solitude of this full-moon night, searing and, to a teenage girl, unbearable, Victoria gives a little whimper: 'Mormor, Mormor, don't die. You *mustn't*! I love you so much! I need you. Don't leave me all alone!'

At that moment she hears the front door open and close. It must be Dad! Rushing headlong downstairs her first impulse is to fling herself into his arms, but seeing him standing under the light over the dining table, his glasses on his nose as he leafs through a pile of mail and bills, notes that he is very pale and looks tired and worn out. And a bit bald. He is no longer the spitting image of Jean-Louis Barrault in *Les Enfants du Paradis.*

'Hello, Dad! I thought you'd never come!'

He looks up. Screws up his eyes. Wipes his glasses and kisses her affectionately.

'But, Vicky, sweetheart, are you still up? It's mad! And you've school tomorrow.'

'I don't care. Couldn't sleep. Was just waiting for you. And – it's awfully stormy out . . .'

'What about Rita? Isn't she back yet?'

Vicky hesitates. She knows Rita is living a double life but feels womenfolk should stick together.

'Can't say,' she answers evasively. 'She's probably asleep.'

'What about Granny? Wasn't it today she was supposed to come back from Southampton?'

Vicky turns away from the lamplight. Granny Muriel is another tricky problem; one more of these two-faced adults she is neither experienced nor shrewd enough to understand. A woman of uncertain age, past middle age anyway, who lives much too close to them and who can't stand Mummy. Though she is the widow of Grandpa Didier, who was French, she is an English lady to the bone but at the same time very Parisian and still chic. Unbeknown to the others Vicky admires her English grandmother and would like to like her and be liked by her but in her loyalty to Jenny pretends not to and gives her a wide berth. She scares away Vicky's boyfriends and her manner towards them, in her upper-class impudence, is rude, even downright vulgar, as she always is towards anyone she regards as belonging to what she calls 'the mob'. To Vicky she seems, rightly, to be a horrible snob, an anachronism, an ossified Victorian relic. Even so, this trouble-some grandmother of hers is actually a rather interesting woman of the world, chipped at the edges by all she has been through and consumed by a great passion, a jealousy she can't curb. It burns like an unquenchable fire in her icy cold, rather desolate, yet tastefully furnished wing of this big old house. Not that one understands such matters at Vicky's age. In Muriel's presence she feels unwanted, clumsy, all 'wrong' in some way. In their granny's eyes, they are all of them 'wrong' on account of their Swedish mother, except possibly Michael, because he is a boy! For some reason beyond Vicky's comprehension, her Granny has a deep-rooted fear and detestation of everything Swedish. How this small part of them – after all, they are half-French and half-English too – should be such a thorn in Granny Muriel's flesh is more than Vicky can grasp, and it particularly upsets her, since she loves Sweden and has her roots in her Swedish grandparents. Vicky guesses this is why Granny pushed off before Mormor came, and the true-hearted child in her, as yet untarnished, is saddened by these schisms among grown-ups.

'Granny did look in at tea-time,' Vicky answers. 'She asked kind of in passing where you all were. So I told her Mum and Mormor had gone off to Paris by themselves. And though she said, 'Oh, what a shame!' I could tell how pleased she was you hadn't gone too. Oh yes, and she had Aunty Midgo with her. She had driven Granny back in her Rolls.'

Jean-Paul has been listening with half an ear. Flips a telephone bill over; frowns.

'And at Aunt Midgo's heels five or six of her Pekinese came rushing in, yapping and snuffling as if they had colds. Ran round and round, stood up on their hind legs and pawed at me,' Vicky goes on excitedly. 'They've got such adorable little bulging eyes. But why does she *spoil* them so much, as if they were a cut above any other kind of dog? Granny went out, slamming the door behind her like she always does when she is in a bad mood. But Aunty Midgo hung about quite a while in here and told me a lot of stuff about how sisters can't help loving and hating each other at the same time, and how when she dies she wants to go to the

121

pekes' paradise. And so she probably will, soon – die, I mean – at the rate she drinks and chain-smokes. She simply *stank* of whisky and sherry. She could hardly walk straight! I had to open all the windows when she had gone! Quite gone in the head, she was, even tripped over those dogs of hers and would have gone flying if I hadn't grabbed her. Couldn't help laughing when she called after her, '*Darlings*, come with Mummy!' and they all trooped out after her with their tails wagging like chrysanthemums. Then I heard her and Granny get into a quarrel, it was horrible. It's strange isn't it, Granny always going on about how much those sisters love each other!'

'They probably do, too.' Jean-Paul smiles wearily at his daughter's lively insight into the lives of Pekinese. 'If only Midgo would lay off the booze. It drives my mother up the wall.'

'Poor Aunt Midgo,' Vicky says thoughtfully. 'Perhaps she was damaged as a child.'

Jean-Paul yawns. He doesn't want to hear any more about the unfortunate Aunt Midgo, black sheep of the family. All he wants is a cup of tea and some toast and then to drop into bed. It has been a tiring day that started with his schedule being upset by having to drive Jenny and her mother to Newhaven to catch the ferry. When he had told Jenny he couldn't come too, she had shed bitter tears of disappointment and kept looking herself in that cracked pocket mirror of hers, and her mother had thrown him a look so sombre they might have been going to a funeral instead of Paris.

'Poor them,' Vicky says, quickly making her father a cup of tea and two slices of toast. 'They won't have much fun in Paris. They'll be at each others' throats all the time.'

'Luckily I managed to get hold of Peter Schwarz,' Jean-Paul says. 'He and his Swedish wife, Anne-Marie, you know, they are there on business, staying in a hotel near the Champs-Elysées, and Peter has promised to look after Mormor – in fact he is enthusiastic about them coming.'

'What about Mum, though? She can't look after herself in Paris! She'll be all scared of the noise and bustle, get lost . . .'

It is very late. Jean-Paul, who is a true French connoisseur when it comes to feminine charms, lights a last pipe and contemplates his daughter. She is not going to be as beautiful as her mother. Jenny's beauty when she was young had an aura all its own, of which she herself was oddly unaware. Naturally, Jean-Paul idealizes his wife. That she had once been a plump, near-sighted, daydreaming little girl who had tripped and stumbled over every stone or root that lay in her path and been nicknamed 'Porky', 'Lumpidump' and such by her brothers, is for him a fact as absurd as it is irrelevant. That Jenny nowadays has lost most of her pristine aura and that her beauty is already on the wane is something he prefers not to notice. But Vicky, despite her teenage gawkiness, is already quite pretty and feminine. Under the scruffy fringe a couple of intelligent, eager blue eyes peer inquisitively up at him. And in this late hour he suddenly sees in them Jean Didier's unforgettable look, his challenging intellectual acumen, eyes as brilliant as the ocean on a clear day, so translucent you can see to the sea floor. But in Vicky's there is also an anxiety Jean-Paul can't help noticing.

'What's up, sweetie?'

Vicky squirms a little on her chair. She is paler than usual, seems chilled, sitting there in nothing but her shabby dressing-gown. The boiler, unreliable as ever, must have gone out again. And the autumn storm blowing through the night comes whistling in at gale strength in icy draughts through the uninsulated windows.

'Something Angela Holmes said today . . . I can't get over it . . .'

'Oh? And what did Angela say?' Jean-Paul sounds a trifle impatient. He is longing to go up to bed, sleep, forget; has had enough of complications and problems for one day. Yet realizes it is important to listen. Behind what Vicky wants to say he senses not only anxiety but also strength. A force.

'We were having tea in their sitting-room, in front of that new colour TV of theirs, you know, Dad, ever so posh, they must be millionaires, or very nearly!'

'That's as may be,' Jean-Paul says sceptically, 'Ralph Holmes has several irons in the fire, and some of them are not a little bent.'

'Angela's awfully nice to me, even though I'm younger than she is. She went on and on about a lot of things I couldn't quite understand: Vietnam, capitalism and communism, and starving kids in Africa, all that. She said she hates her father and would do anything to oppose him, because he "exploits" those Ethiopian workers of his. I'm not quite sure what she was on about . . .'

'Very interesting, I'm sure,' yawns her father. 'But what was it she said that upset you?'

Vicky's eyes fill with tears:

'All I said, was that our mums, both being Swedish and even distantly related, second cousins or something, ought to get together some time. Because Mum's so lonely . . . Didn't they once meet at a bazaar at the Swedish church in London? Anyway, do you know what Angela answered?'

'No, haven't the faintest idea. But most of us avoid our relations like the plague. I do, anyway . . .'

'Dad, you aren't listening! Angela said . . .'

'What did she say?'

'She said her mum, Karin, that is, had a crazy sister called Malin, who was a painter but went round the bend.'

Vicky chews nervously at a strand of her hair.

'Well, *ma petite*, what's that strange aunt of theirs got to do with Mum?'

124

'Oh, Dad, that's just it . . . "I don't think it would be a very good idea," Angela said. "My mum has had enough of people like Aunty Malin. She doesn't want to have anything more to do with them." Meaning . . . meaning that Mum's like . . . like . . .'

Jean-Paul tenses up. A cold rage wells up inside him, at people's stupidity in general, and at the Holmes family in particular. To see his nearest and dearest hurt by a bunch of narrow-minded money-bags, at the mercy of their dried-out little minds, cuts him to the quick. That Karin Holmes and Jenny happen to be related through their mothers and both have the misfortune to be clergymen's daughters does not make him feel any the kindlier towards her, least of all as there is obviously a sick strain running through both families. Too much inbreeding, he thinks, over there in Sweden. Thousands and thousands of years of it. Jenny, when in a good mood, likes to joke about certain similarities between Karin Holmes's mother, Hedvig, and Charlotte, adding hastily, 'Though Mother, of course, is by far the deeper and more intelligent personality.'

'Vicky, darling, don't take it to heart.' He taps his pipe hard against the sink. 'I'm not too keen on that Holmes woman. She is too domineering by half, hasn't an ounce of sensibility in her whole body. Mum's not missing out on anything by not associating with her. You know as well as I do she would only try to put Mum down, be arrogant and critical. As for her "crazy" sister, she probably envied her talent. What is she, after all, but a dumb blonde married to a pompous ass! Karin Holmes isn't worth your Mum's little toe!' he declares emphatically, to relieve himself of his own and his daughter's indignation.

'But, Dad, I can't stand it when people we know talk that way about Mum, as if they knew . . .'

'Knew what?'

'That Mum's sick in some way . . .'

Vicky stares down hard at the spotted plastic tablecloth.

Clumsily she tries to dry her eyes, but the tears won't be held back, trickle silently down her childish round cheeks.

'One can't always protect one's loved ones, Vicky,' he says, his voice suddenly tender and serious. 'Some people are like wild animals. Their only instinct is to tear apart anyone they think is weak or frightened . . .'

'But Dad, maybe she is right? Even if she is nasty. Perhaps Mum really is ill, I mean, in her mind or something. What's the matter with her? Whatever it is, it seems to be infecting us all, me and Michael and the little ones. We feel it too, though I don't think you notice because you are so busy all the time. If only she could get back to her poetry, do you think she would get well again?'

Jean-Paul's nerves are all on edge. He walks up and down the cold kitchen, exactly as his father, *Le Monde's* chief editor, used to do in moments of national crisis.

'If you only knew, Vicky,' he says stressing his words, 'how I've tried to get Mum to start writing again, or do something creative, anything! You are quite right of course. If only she could, it would be a blessing for all of us.'

'But why can't she, Dad? You told me she had a collection of poems published once – *The Heart's Mirror*, or something like that – just after Michael was born.'

Jean-Paul sits down.

'That's true,' he says, 'And everyone was so happy for her sake. Only your grandmother, Charlotte, I mean, was a bit sceptical, as usual: said something Cassandra-like about not counting chickens before they are hatched. I don't think I have ever seen Mum as happy as she was that day when she got the printer's proofs. She was a poet! Had visions, no limit to her inspiration. She was going to be a new Edith Södergran . . .'

'Who's that?' Vicky wonders.

'A great Finnish poetess who died of TB, isolation and poverty. Mum used to read her poems aloud to me. *The Land that Never Was*, I think one of her collections was called. Well, then it came out, Mum's book I mean, and we threw a party for all our Stockholm friends to celebrate her début; she looked so lovely and happy. Next morning the blow fell. A review in one paper said her collection was no good at all, not aesthetic enough, over-strung, I don't know what else! Mum almost went out of her mind. Smashed the sitting-room window and cut her hand badly. Then she tore up the next thing she had been working on. Went down to the cellar and threw it into the boiler. I tried to stop her, but it was impossible. She wept for hours. Kept trying to hurt her-self . . . Oh well, you must have heard about all it till you are sick of it . . . '

Yes, Vicky has. 'When I was little I thought a review was some kind of an injection she had had that had made her ill. Didn't she get any good reviews, then?'

'Certainly. Several, in the provincial papers, some very posi-tive indeed: said she was very promising, called her "highly origi-nal", "an intuitive" and so forth. But they didn't count. Only that diabolical scribble in Stockholms Tidningen. How explain that? It was beyond me. It was as if she had lost a child. Then she got pregnant again. And I had to take that job in London.'

'Reviews!' exclaims Vicky bitterly, suddenly agitated. 'What's the point of them? Why can't people make up their own minds? It's not as if poets were schoolchildren who've got to be given reports!'

Jean-Paul laughs. Vicky is bright.

'Couldn't agree more! But people want to be told what to think, I suppose. And take reviews at face value.'

But Vicky says she still doesn't understand how one bad review could have paralysed her mother's poetry for life. Like an amputation. 'I'd have been furious, too, but it wouldn't have stopped *me* from carrying on!'

The storm is beginning to blow itself out. Dark November rain falls steadily, beating monotonously against the old stone house. Jean-Paul, who never gets a proper night's sleep or a chance to relax, is consumed with fatigue. His life too, could be snapped off like a branch by the autumn gale.

Vicky is dismayed. Despite a boyish fringe that (truth to tell) is becoming a bit ridiculous, her father's face resembles a death mask, with eyes sunken into two dark blue hollows.

'You are made of different stuff from your mother,' he says quietly. 'She always sides with the aggressor. Thinks anyone who hurts her must be right. Defends herself by destroying herself. I have tried everything. Support, ideas, love, encouragement, that room in the attic with her typewriter and record-player to write in. Yet wild horses won't drag her up there. "There is only room for one genius in a family," she says. Sometimes it seems to me as if she has thrown away her creativity, given it to that Leo fellow. There is nothing much more I can do. *C'est un sauve-qui-peut.*'

Vicky's lower lip trembles.

'But, Dad! Can't you send her to a shrink? I mean, one of those doctors who help people like her?'

'I would if I could, but we can't afford it. And anyway, there aren't any around here. Not good ones. They're all up in London – feathering their own nests in Harley Street. Believe it or not they charge seven pounds an hour and I just don't earn that kind of money. We can't even afford a new boiler! That's the bitter truth. Come on now, let's go to bed. Turn the lights out, Vicky, love! We'll have a nice lie-in tomorrow, take a day off . . .'

'But can't you ask Mormor for some money then?'

A pleading girl's voice in the dark.

ACT II

The Pimple

Jenny

So we got off in the end. Despite the trains being on strike and Jean-Paul having to drive us all the way to Dover. It was a cold, grey rainy day. I was close to tears! I felt so let down, disappointed that Jean-Paul wasn't coming with us. I'd so looked forward to a few days in Paris with him – he'd have taken care of Mother, too, something I'm not really up to, not just now. Not after her outburst the other day when she called my home an 'atrocious mess' and criticized me for not being strict enough with my children and not giving them 'moral guidelines', etc. etc. Hardly surprising I feel humiliated and out of sorts. But I mustn't be unfair, mustn't forget the miracle on the ferry, Mother's transformation!

It was blowing hard where we stood on deck, the wind and the sun thrusting themselves on us by turns, and that's when it happened. Suddenly she turned ever so sweet and loving! Made light of all rifts, all complaints and criticisms, controversies and problems with the children that in Lindfield had almost crushed her; it was as if she had taken out a big red india rubber and eradicated them. Like an old fur-clad fairy godmother she stood there on deck with her head scarf round her greying black hair, all aglow. By a wave of her wand transformed this vale of woe into the happy dream it ought to be. How strange she is, my old mother. All she needs is a little sea air under her wings to soar up 'like a bird to heaven's heights'! Earthbound she certainly isn't! Carried away by her extravagant state of mind I stared down at green waves foaming by like Vichy water from one of her little bottles. And for an hour or so, interrupted only by a cup of coffee in the lively cafeteria, we were granted what for us is a singular happiness: to be together, intimate, happy, almost frolicsome; more like a couple of adventurers, two sisters or schoolgirls out for a lark, than mother and daughter . . . But our madcap state of mind soon passed, wasn't to be relied on; shifted suddenly, as our family's moods always do, and drowned in the muddy waters of Calais harbour. It was then the negative, self-humiliating thoughts came back. Among the rubbish in the women's toilet I wasn't able to help looking at myself in the mirror and have seen how this pimple on my cheek had blossomed during the crossing into a furious, flaming, shameful red for all to see. I've never been good enough. I've never come up to scratch in Mother's eyes – no matter how long or hard I've tried. For her I would gladly hew rock, cross deserts, swim the deep and dangerous waters. All in vain. When I was little I would pick flowers for her, weed obsessively till my eyes swam and my fingers bled. *Obeyed*, developed a sixth sense for her least wish; listened tirelessly to her perpetual complaints about Father; forced myself to follow her down grim winding paths and understand all sorts of other things I was still too young for. As long as I could hold her hand, cling to some part of her body, to *her*, I didn't do too badly. That time, ages ago, when we went down to bathe in the great river and I panicked at the sight of a herd of cows that stood there mooing and glowering at us. In the mud of the river bank was a old, rotten tree trunk, half in, half out of the eddying waters. Huge logs went surging past on the river's gleaming surface, flowing quietly between distant blue hills. Clutching her nude, softly rounded hips, I pressed myself against her rump as it bobbed up and down there in front of me in the muddy water. Why this unexpected memory, here in this Parisian hotel room on the Champs-Elysées? Little suspecting my thoughts, Mother sits there in a plush red chair, scribbling away in one of those little diaries she has been keeping ever since 1937. Day after day of her life has been immured in those little books' dark secret depths.

They are the only friends she can rely on not to tell tales. Her ever-faithful companions. Her attempt to stand life by setting its vicissitudes at arm's length, by describing it, capturing its all too-easily forgotten moments of light relief and, by finding words for the nameless agony that suffuses our whole family, keep it at bay, tone down its delirium; exorcise it, *look at* it. Why, just now, did I recall that scene by the river? Can't say. My pleasure at being so close to Mother's round white buttocks was immense, ecstatic as in orgasm. All my fear of those cows' staring eyes, of the swiftly flowing river, its icy waters, the rotting tree trunk, lying there huge and stinking like an old man's corpse, had turned into a sense of boundless well-being. The sun – a maternal sun, immense, more vast, brighter, more yellow and life-giving than any marigold or sunflower – had come out, lighting up a landscape that only a moment before have been heavy with thunder-clouds. But my ecstasy only lasted a moment. The maternal body shook me off impatiently. And she said: 'Go back, Jenny! I'm going for a swim.' But I just stood there in the water, shivering and watching her swim out like one of those logs to the boom, where she stood up, her naked breasts gleaming like juicy pears and her long black tresses clinging to her pale face that she never exposed to the sun. Her eyes looked away to the mountains, not for one instant at me whom she had forgotten, spellbound. She was no longer my chthonic mother of a moment ago, whose rump I would have been so glad to toddle after. A body I wanted to dwell in, a womb I longed to hide in and, safe from all terror of mooing cows, harsh human words and harrowing family scenes, become invisible again. She was a water-nymph. For this little woman, who sits there scribbling in her diary, deaf to the Paris traffic roaring by and blissful to be in the city of her dreams at last, I could give up my sham of a life with Jean-Paul and the children . . . The Champs-Elysées traffic is shattering my nerves. It is as if we were actually out there on the boulevard, among the giant, bright-lit posters, those glittering neon signs . . . Though Mother doesn't know it, her little daughter is still standing there shivering on the muddy river bank, whose dark undercurrents still flow swift and wild between us! My childish cries drown in its gurglings, in the thunder of Paris traffic. You are dangerous, Mother, dear. To be locked up alone with you in this Parisian hotel room is both heaven and hell. Heaven because I have so wanted to be alone with you, confess to you my soul's despair, be comforted, loved, give you the few flowers that my hands can still pluck. This anxiety inside me is gnawing at my entrails, has drained all the goodness out of me. My garden is so small, has only a few flowers left. Soon, laid waste by my anxiety, only weeds will grow between its stones and in the end only sterile cement. So take my flowers, while I have any left! Like the characters in Sartre's *Huit Clos*, we're stuck here in an everlasting silence. Nauseated, claustrophobically hemmed in, we too could start bandying harsh words; accusing each other; quarrel, fight; turn back the clock and chase each other round and round in a labyrinth of memories – yours faint, dim, grey; mine painfully sharp! Until in the end, after going through the endless register of guilt and old sins, we would collapse, exhausted, each in her plush red armchair, and I, your embittered daughter, would at last, at long last, realize we have no clocks to put either forward or back, time having ceased to exist: only this doorless room, closed in on us for all eternity. My longing to have you all to myself will have realized itself, irrevocably. And then, Mother, I'll kill you, and then myself – pointlessly, because we'd already be dead . . . I feel sick. Want to throw up. The mere thought of my hurting Mother in any way or, still worse, ridding myself of her, makes me dizzy. Without her there would be nothing. Like when I was little, stood there screaming my head off, all alone in my cot. If you had gone somewhere, vanished, if you didn't come to me, my little universe too would vanish. No one came and picked me up out of that cot – until Jean-Paul did . . .

Charlotte's diary, 10 November

What a deplorable start to our excursion; it could hardly have been worse. It was raining cats and dogs. Little Jojo clung to Jenny for dear life and Jenny, she just stood there the child in her arms, white as a sheet, in a state of utter despair. If Rita hadn't come to our rescue and resolutely taken the screaming child out of Jenny's arms and almost pushed her into the car I do believe she would have skipped Paris altogether. And then, when we finally got as far as Haywards Heath station, the trains were on strike. So Jean-Paul had to run us all the way to Dover, at breakneck speed, so that he was stopped by a policeman for exceeding the speed limit, which I suppose means he will have to pay a fine. Poor Jean-Paul, he looked so tense! I can't fail to see how overstrained he is despite all his admirable self-control and ability to keep calm in all circumstances. Jenny certainly doesn't make life easy, crying her eyes out like a small child, all upset at having to leave Jojo, I suppose. Then she started looking at herself in that cracked pocket mirror of hers, over and over again. These last two days she has had some kind of tiny pimple on her cheek, a mere nothing, a trifle. But seems obsessed by it. I sat in the front seat beside Jean-Paul, none of us said a word. The rain lashed at the car windows as if in a rage, the wind whistled and whined from all directions at once. Thank goodness I had had the foresight to bring my galoshes and Ma's dear old umbrella! We only got to the ferry and the ticket office and passport controls in the nick of time. Jenny clung to Jean-Paul as if she was never going to see him again. It made me feel *most uncomfortable*, standing there under my umbrella waiting for them to be done with their kissing. (Having to watch two people kiss like that is most distasteful. It fills me with repugnance, shouldn't be allowed in public!) But other people's reactions are of no account to Jenny, naively absorbed as she always is in her own primitive emotions. In this respect, if in no other, she is Leo's sister!

Once on board the ferry, the weather changed. The rain ceased, the sun broke through, lighting up the frothing green waves; seagulls screeched overhead and came swooping down impudently close to us, where we stood on deck watching the white cliffs of Dover disappear. A lot of Spaniards were gabbling away happily. Though many of them were dressed in gaudy, threadbare clothes, their zest for life was so infectious we too started talking and laughing just like we used to in the old days. All the suffocating tensions of the last few weeks were blown away by the sea breezes. A little colour came into her cheeks, her eyes lit up and she seemed to forget all about her domestic worries and – above all – about that silly little spot on her cheek! I felt like one of those screeching gulls, like a prisoner let out from solitary confinement, and my bleak, critical attitude towards everyone and everything of these last couple of weeks evaporated. We chatted gaily about the children, their pros and cons, without a care in the world. I found myself admitting, willingly, that I had been 'difficult', too hard on them, and assured Jenny how deeply I love them all. In this new mood Vicky, who has been so dreadfully trying, seemed merely sweet and amusing; a trifle rebellious perhaps, but at her age that is only to be expected. Mikael, far from being the weak or unreliable little boy I have sometimes thought him, is a fine brave little lad, sure to grow up into a proper gentleman like his father. And the little girls, how sweet they are! Perfectly adorable! Going through the nursery the other day, tidying it up as best I could and all upset to see so many broken toys cast aside, I had sworn to myself I would never come back. Now all that was forgotten, a faint irrelevant memory, light-years away! Jenny's mother-in-law – her outbursts of jealousy, her sanctimonious moralizing and chilly attitude towards her grandchildren – is an insoluble problem. I have advised Jenny to be patient, show a degree of indulgence, try to be kind to 'the old witch'. After all, it is Jenny who has the upper hand, since it is *her* Jean-Paul loves and is loyal to. That this leaves his lonely old mother to rage next door, like an abandoned tigress behind iron bars, is a shame, of course. But only natural and a trial that Jenny, as the younger woman, must simply put up with.

Wrapped in our fur coats and with shawls round our heads we chatted and laughed, undaunted by the gusty sea breezes. Rising and falling on the brilliant sea, a sharp light swept the clouds away, dispersed the grey English fogs and its sharp rays as if breaking into our hearts' sinister closets, encouraging us to throw out like old moth-balls and dingy threadbare garments the memory of sorrowful occasions; all gloomy days, domestic crises and conflicts, when floods of tears turn into bloodstains that the heart can never forget and are beyond sending to the dry cleaners. For the first time in years we were smiling spontaneously at each other, mother and daughter. And Jenny, putting her arm around me, began to resemble the daughter I was to Ma in her last years. My feelings for my own unhappy daughter, perhaps misunderstood and despised, exploded! To be happy is really so simple! Comes as such a relief! Always it takes us unawares and, for the few precious moments it lasts, shows us the way we should always live! For me, Charlotte, such dazzling moments have been few and far between and I can only be grateful for ever having experienced them at all. Of course I have many heavy regrets, thoughts and feelings almost beyond bearing; am always all too aware of the wrongs that have been done. But there on the cross-channel ferry's deck, all *that* was suddenly of no importance. Our relationship, after starting off on the wrong foot, had suddenly taken a turn for the better; become warm, simple, impervious to chilly intrusions.

So . . . here I am at last, comfortably installed in a delightful hotel kindly booked for us by Peter and trying to steal a few furtive moments with my diary to capture, if only fleetingly and in outline, the outstanding events of yesterday and today before changing for dinner and venturing out to meet Peter and Anne-Marie, who have so generously invited us out this evening. How I'm looking forward to seeing them both again! Peter, in particular, holds a very special place in my heart. Ever since the day we first received him in our home, a young rootless refugee from Nazi Germany, he has touched my heartstrings. Henrik, I know, has never really understood him; but then, he really has very little insight into human nature. He has led such a *sheltered* life. Neither did our boys take to Peter, made no attempt alas to conceal their jealousy. As for Jenny . . . well, that was a sorry tale. Let's hope she will let bygones be bygones – certainly she hasn't said anything about being reluctant to meet him again. Quite the opposite, so it would seem. At heart she is probably quite fond of him, or so I believe. Oh, how I wish she were different! Restless and depressed again, she is just now surreptitiously examining herself in the mirror, imagines I don't notice; but all these everlasting self-perusals, her way of staring at that wretched little pimple in her mirror – well, I find it utterly frustrating and irritating! Yes, I have a good mind to *forbid* her to go on doing it! It's so unhealthy, so self-centred, so vain, and it is poisoning the little time we have together – what a *shame*, after we got off to such a fine start on the ferry yesterday. But she is grown up, I keep having to remind myself, a mother of four children, and I have no right to interfere or forbid her anything. Exactly when did our moment of happiness abandon us and Jenny again become joyless, introverted? Well, it makes no odds, *mustn't* do. I'm not going to let anything spoil my days in Paris that I have so looked forward to!

We were joined in our compartment on the train by a couple of chubby Dominican nuns, who spent the whole journey fiddling with their black rosaries and reading little prayer books. They gave us such a friendly smile, I should have liked so much to talk with them (a marvellous opportunity for gaining a little insight into Catholicism!). But my French, I'm afraid, is sadly lacking. Our arrival at Gare du Nord was utterly chaotic. The whole place teemed with gesticulating, chattering people, fish in their own aquarium. But it made Jenny and me feel rather lost and far from home. In the autumn wind sweeping along the boulevards we had to hold on to each other to avoid being whirled away like two dry leaves. We had to wait ages for a taxi. The Paris traffic hooted and roared and whistled all around us; cars drive so much faster, are so much more impatient here than anywhere else. It made me feel quite dizzy. By the time we had managed to get hold of a taxi darkness had fallen, but there were still any amount of shops open and Paris twinkled gaily with a thousand lights – everything is so southern and lively! It is like coming to a city that never sleeps, or even takes a catnap. In the air there is a smell of roast chestnuts that frozen old men stand selling hot at street corners. All the while I have been on tenterhooks, taking it all in, the gigantic, glamorous shop windows, the noisy crowds. You could easily put the whole of Stockholm within the enormous avenues around the Etoile, between the Avenue de Neuilly on the one side and the Champs-Elysées, leading to the Tuileries, on the other. Oh, these splendid, unending avenues, at once fearsome and fascinating! By the time the taxi drew up outside our hotel here on the Champs-Elysées I felt quite stunned. My simple soul feels quite bewildered by such a festive mood.

What bliss it was to step inside the warm, snug atmosphere of this hotel with its soft-carpeted corridors and install ourselves in our (to my mind) spacious, comfortable room. Unfortunately single beds don't exist, only one double one, which means Jenny and I will have to share it these next few nights. But what of it? Jenny, though, pulled a face as if she was in pain or it were a hundred-year-old turtle, not her mother, she had been sentenced to sleep with! I must admit it upset me a bit. But I had armed my soul with *aes triplex* and let it pass. Our luxurious bathroom has something they call a *bidet* (whatever that can be good for?). Our room is furnished in crimson and overlooks the Champs-Elysées. Of course, the traffic outside *is* terribly noisy but it doesn't bother me in the slightest. Here in Paris at last I'm not going to let a little noise upset me! Children crying, whining, nagging; Vicky's pop music blaring out, morning noon and night; those dreadful Beatles she loves so; Mikael's obsession with the television (it can't be *normal* for a healthy young boy to sit sucking his thumb in front of it for hours on end, I really must have a word with Jean-Paul about it!) – all that is far, far worse. Not for Jenny, it seems, however, who seems quite *shattered*, says she can't stand what she calls the 'hellish traffic' outside our window. Homesick already, missing Lindfield's sluggish silence, I suppose, its almost monastic stupor. Or, anyway, longing for her children and, I'm sure, for Jean-Paul's tender (erotic) embraces . . . Oh well, there at least she has been lucky, making a marriage that gives free outlet to her sensual nature, inherited from Henrik. Something I have certainly *not* been able to do in mine – though I have no longer any wish to dwell on *such* topics. Not that I too didn't taste Eve's apple, once . . . In my case, alas, an extra-marital, thus a forbidden fruit. Sometimes Jean-Paul reminds me of X and that brings on a twinge of pain inside me, doddering old woman that I am; yet at the same time intoxicates me, like sipping champagne . . . only for a moment, mind, and this strictly *entre nous*, my dear diary. Nowadays no one is discreet about such pleasures; on the contrary, they advertise all *that* to the point of hysteria, whilst romance – the sweet blue flower of true passion and *sublimated* love – all that is forgotten and done with.

Jenny has borrowed my wax ear plugs, the ones I bought at the chemist in Lindfield High Street to survive the uproar in her house, and now she is lying on the bed with her eyes closed (seeing nothing and hearing less). She is a dreamer, my daughter, like her father, with no thought for others. Reality is something they can't cope with. I remember when she was just a little girl how, long after the fire had gone out, she wouldn't go to bed, protested that she 'could see so much in the dying embers'!

Anyway, when at last we ventured out for a bite to eat I was ravenous, curious to see Paris by night. Reluctantly roused from day-dreaming on her bed, she traipsed after me along the busy pavements. After being pushed and shoved hither and thither – why are Parisians always in such a hurry? – we ended up inside a sort of glass veranda and ate an omelette. I drank mineral water (real Eau de Vichy!). But Jenny had wine – half a bottle, all to herself! All we got to nibble at was some dry bread that crumbled to pieces. A waiter who looked as if his tight trousers were on fire served us, but in a most unfriendly, *nonchalant* fashion, and finally flung us a bill that told us this meagre snack, spent (vainly) conversing with my sullen daughter, had cost me a small fortune!

After that there was nothing for it but to go back to our hotel room in a glum silence and turn in. I washed myself, plaited my hair, which has become so thin of late. But all Jenny could do was smear Ponds Cold Cream all over her face and peer at it in the mirror, until she looked like a ghost, a white apparition with huge watery eyes like Henrik's! I took my sleeping tablets and digitalis and crept into my side of the bed, where I curled myself up into a small inconspicuous ball and closed my eyes so as to shut out her bedside light, which she, inconsiderate as usual, didn't switch off for at least an hour while she read *The Divided Self* by what's-his-name.

When I'd finished saying my prayers I added one more, asking Him to salvage my short stay in Paris, and in His infinite mercy grant me at least a few days of unmarred happiness and peace of mind. Also that He soothe my daughter's agitated nerves and (but how absurd!) heal that pimple that is tormenting both her and me! 'Many a great load is upset by a tiny tussock . . .' was my last thought before falling asleep.

Jenny

This underfurnished hotel room of ours has a high ceiling and only one bed, which we'll have to share, an old-fashioned screen, a couple of bedside tables with doors intended for bygone chamber pots, white walls (without any pictures). In front of the windows hang heavy, red velvet curtains. There are two small red chairs, a defunct fireplace and, above it, a mirror . . .

I mustn't, but I can't stop myself. It draws me to it like a magnet, drags me out of bed where I have been slumbering with thoughts of mothers and cows and others – equally ridiculous in a grown woman, still quite young, in Paris. Has she noticed? I hope not! No, she is still deep in her scribbling or perhaps writing a letter home to Father. Can't tell. How gently mendacious, euphemistically diplomatic, her letters to him must be. She keeps to herself her innermost feelings, her everlasting regrets – has to. Father is so sensitive, his soul is as fragile as one of those little glass animals that Rosalind is forever adding to her treasured collection: the delicate green giraffe, the blue turtle-doves, a pink spider – an odd assortment that she takes as much pride in as Muriel takes in her one remaining piece of Lalique. Father lives such an enclosed life, with the central heating turned up to twenty-two degrees and all doors on the outside world double-locked. Except for a brief glimpse of it on the nine o'clock news he hasn't a clue about what is going on out there. And even that doesn't perturb him in the least. The horrors and atrocities being committed by mankind, humanity's immense suffering, are beyond him, have always been beyond him, outside his hunting ground. Such things don't happen in Sweden. Earthquakes, revolutions, mass starvation, children burnt to a cinder – sitting there in his black rocking-chair he views it all with the same nonplussed calm. But the minutest draught, the slightest of quiver in his own or Mother's nervous systems, the merest hint of a storm-cloud on our horizons – Fredrik's, Leo's or mine – is capable of throwing him into a state of tense introspection, dominated perhaps by a single obsessive thought – either painfully unambiguous or ever more distorted – that rampages about in the arid wastelands of his soul until it assumes monstrous proportions.

Father, I am like you. On my left cheek, just beside my nose, I have a small, inflamed pimple that is completely ruining my otherwise clear complexion. It may be small but it is poisonous. Its seething red surface defies all camouflage, all makeup. It's dominating and destroying my face, destroying me – what is left of my self-confidence, my time here in Paris with Mother, our few precious days together. In such nightmare moments the whole world shrinks to a meaningless little pimple; and my pimple becomes a universe . . . Demented, I stare at it in the mirror. Study it. Gingerly finger it. And the panic rises. My heart beats wildly, irregularly. My stomach is empty and hollow. It was already there on our way to Dover: a little menacing lump. Aghast in the back seat I couldn't help looking at it in my cracked mirror. And now it has burst into flower on my pale cheek like some strange, repulsive rose. Paris, compared with it, is a pin-head. My compulsion to keep looking at this one loathsome little pimple – which seems just to grow and grow – in all sorts of mirrors, from the cracked one in my handbag to the huge ones in this hotel, is an agony I can do nothing about . . . Like you, Father, I don't give a damn for the outside world; or for Mother, who, amazed, seems to have stopped scribbling and be gawking at me; or for Jean-Paul or the children . . . My misery, my disfigurement, my leprous state throbs in my mind, eating me alive. If only I could run away – anywhere from this city with its glittering neon lights, its traffic's unending roar, its overflow of life! Hide away in some dark little mirrorless room, take an overdose and drop into a deep sleep, just sleep, until this loathsome rose tires of me and for lack of attention and sustenance leaves me with pale clear cheeks again, with my numb face a mask that doesn't betray me, doesn't trumpet out my inner torment!

'Jenny!' Mother's voice is plaintive. '*Can't* you stop staring at yourself? It seems a little odd, you know . . . No *normal* person carries on like that. You never used to be vain. That was what was so nice about you – that you didn't care what you looked like!'

'I'm not vain, Mother. I have got a pimple, a horrible pimple. And it's getting worse and worse . . .'

'*Nonsense*, Jenny, it's nothing. Dab on a little powder and forget about it! Surely you aren't not going to let something so . . . insignificant wreck my few poor days here in Paris?'

Turning away from the mirror I look instead into the face of this other woman, my mother, which looks back at me, disappointed but defiant, refusing to see either my pimple or the half-crazed despairing self behind it. She's in Paris. She wants to have a good time. She's determined to ignore her hypersensitive husband, her two thugs of sons, her daughter's pimple.

'It's time we changed for dinner, Jenny,' she says. 'In an hour we are supposed to be meeting Peter and Anne-Marie at that restaurant. We must get a move on, they are always so punctual!'

'I don't want to go,' I whimper. 'I have a headache!'

'But Jenny, you *must*! It would seem so ungrateful, so unfriendly, not to go.'

Her tone is final. Brooks no contradiction. At such a moment a whole army couldn't budge her. Feebly I object:

'It will look even worse if I come and spend the whole dinner looking myself in the mirror . . .'

'Stop it, Jenny, that's enough of neurotic silliness. Just try and look bright and cheerful and no one will notice anything. Jenny, *please*!'

I have neither the courage nor the heart to destroy this little interlude in what my mother calls the 'grey round' of her everyday life. Mustn't let on, no matter how bad I'm feeling. A tone of heart-break has crept into her voice, a plea for a respite, however brief, from her problems and miseries, real or imagined. A Parisian interlude. I neither can nor will get through to her. Murky, swift river waters separate us. I am screaming inside like a frightened child, but she doesn't hear me. The rush and swirl of the river, the howling and roaring of the Paris traffic, the French police's impatient whistles, my mother's deafness to her daughter's state of mind, it's all between us. Fuming with black silent rage I go out to the bathroom, change hurriedly, smear a thick layer of matte beige foundation cream over my catastrophic pimple.

Charlotte's diary

So to the day's great experience. I still have a little time left before changing for dinner. It would seem God did not heed my prayers last night. But as so often before, I accept His silence and grope my way through the darkness without so much as a glimmer of light. Can it be God intends something by His silence? Like a veritable Jeanne d'Arc I have struggled against dreariness, melancholy and disappointment. But now my efforts are beginning to flag. Jenny and I have had to struggle through a grey day with freezing November winds. . . In the morning, we had a few hours out at Versailles – interesting enough in its own way, of course, but nothing much to waste words on. I shall chiefly remember the tall wrought-iron gates the revolutionary women once stormed in through, the great cobbled forecourt and the vast cheerless rooms that made me feel no bigger than an ant: the Hall of Mirrors (where the French and Germans have repeatedly forced peace treaties down each other's throats); the magnificent baroque ceilings, swarming with naked gods and goddesses; and the Trianon, which Jenny insisted going to see even though it meant traipsing through an unending park only populated with shivering nymphs and leering centaurs. The fountains weren't playing; only the wind whined plaintively as it tore leaves off the trees and the courage out of my decrepit old heart. More than once I had to stop and take my digitalis; but Jenny, she just plodded on ahead, lost in her own thoughts.

Her indifference, which I find as hurtful as her constant spying on me in Lindfield, is an enigma to me. To tell the truth, her ruthless egocentricity isn't all that different from Leo's, though I find Leo's more excusable – it is only by being ruthless towards himself and others he achieves such remarkable creative results. Whereas Jenny . . . nothing. 'My poetry's *dead*,' she said one day in Lindfield, when I had plucked up the courage to ask her about it. And added: 'A bird can't fly without wings. And I have lost mine. Isn't Leo – scudding about over the whole world like an eagle – enough for you, Mother?'

'You sound envious, Jenny,' I said. 'Surely it doesn't *pain* you to see Leo . . .'

She shrugged, but blenched painfully.

'My brother's successes thrill me to death,' she replied joylessly, holding up the knife she had been peeling apples with. 'It's just that they're about as little to do with my life as this apple peel . . .'

And demonstratively held up a windfall, bruised and spotted after lying on the soggy English lawn. Quickly she picked up the knife, stroked her fingertips over its sharp edge and let it glint in the autumn sunshine.

'Oddly enough, Mother, just now this knife interests me more than Leo . . .'

Her words upset me *deeply*. In her eyes was a dull gleam not unlike that nasty knife's. But I consoled myself with the thought that Leo, Jenny, and above all Henrik, have a penchant for melodrama and take a certain sadistic pleasure in frightening people! The uncanny thing about Jenny, though, is that one can *never be sure* – she hasn't the same survival instinct as Leo or even poor Henrik. Sometimes it seems to me that her life hangs by a thread and recently the horrible thought has occurred to me she could throw it away on the spur of a moment.

No, Charlotte, this simply won't do! Pauline Bonaparte's bathtub, which that obviously immoral woman had grabbed after poor Marie-Antoinette, amused me. The Trianon's interior was more intimate, had more feminine appeal, than the Versailles palace, so grandiose yet so impersonal. I can well understand the lovely young Marie-Antoinette taking time off now and then from life's realities at her *hameau* and playing the milkmaid with her ladies-in-waiting! I'm sure I'd have done the same! Though, of course, I would never have been so *extravagant*! Why didn't she come to her senses in time, *intervene* to prevent the catastrophe . . . ? But then her husband, the fat, kind-hearted but simple-minded Louis XVI, was so stubborn! (Do I fancy I discern certain parallels between him and my own Henrik?)

Jenny

The restaurant is high up with a panoramic view over Paris glittering up at us like a shower of diamonds through the November night's transparent darkness. Everything up here is exclusive, Vietnamese, hushed. Tasselled Chinese lanterns yield a subdued lighting and on each table little night-lights burn in red holders. Along the walls hang carved silvered reliefs of Vietnamese landscapes, soaring mountain peaks, tranquil rivers where willows hang their heads and weep, fishing boats drifting weightlessly in their shade. We make our way across a mossy carpet to the table that Peter has reserved for us. Gently, tenderly he takes Mother's arm; she is radiant, already in her seventh heaven. I follow on behind with Peter's wife Anne-Marie. The lift we have come up in was nothing but mirrors and my pale face with its pimple, defying all makeup, is already making me feel so tense I can hardly grasp Anne-Marie's polite attempts at small talk or bring myself to respond to Peter's overwhelming friendliness. His greeting kiss, grazing my forehead, only made me feel still more panicky. As long as he doesn't see how horrible I look! How can he bear to touch such a hideous face as mine? He said: 'You haven't changed a bit,

Jenny! Young and pretty as ever! Not a day older than – well, when was it we last met?'

Don't know, Peter. Long, long ago. And I'm sure you are lying just to be polite, my thoughts run on. Because I'm no longer the pretty seventeen-year-old you fell in love with, a refugee from threatened extermination in some Nazi death camp, in our Stockholm home where for one reason or another you stayed on, became a member of our family. Doted on by Mother, who super-imposed you as an adored supernumerary stepson on Father, but in Fredrik's and Leo's eyes a despised interloper and very nearly my seducer. I don't come back with some cheery, no less conventional compliment. Nor are you the same person, Peter. From a fragile dream-prince with a hooked nose and jet black locks too hand-some to be quite manly – not that you could help your Jewish nose – hunted down, emaciated, homeless, trembling pathetically like a whippet in a freezing wind, you have turned into an exuberant businessman, somewhat overweight but glowing with health, suc-cess and money. Only your glance is still sad and shy and its diag-nosis sure, as swift as an arrow. No words are needed to tell you how bad Jenny is feeling. You see her stigma, her pimple. And pity her. Already your sharp mind is asking: How come Jenny has turned out like this? Why is she so thin, so worn-looking after four childbirths and probably several miscarriages, too, but obviously even more suffering from the cursed family sickness . . . the anxiety you, too, suffered from once . . . even if you have managed to lock yours away in a burglar-proof safe, you, if anyone, know what it is to suffer, to be persecuted, humiliated, terrorized. I can see it writ-ten all over you, a grim knowledge that still stares out dumbly through your forty-year-old features. Those lines under your eyes, the premature wrinkles, the hard, slightly tense lines criss-crossing your forehead as if scored into it by the rake – remember? – that you were so reluctant to use on our gravel path out at Dalarö. Telltale signs, hardly discernible in your otherwise plump, self-satisfied face, oh yes, Peter, I can see them, you can't pull the wool over my eyes. Caustically they contradict your air of success and the genuine warmth of your feelings – even love – for Mother, whose son, gentler, more grateful than her own, you practically became during those war years, when Father's intervention via the Swedish church in Berlin had also rescued your own mother from the clutches of that German hell. When you moved back to Aunt Sarah, Mother wept inconsolably for hours on end. She thought she had lost you. And when you came back to us in the end I seem to recall it sparked off a small-scale world war between the two women.

Do you know who you are, Peter? Half-Jew, half-German? Half of you, on your mother's side, chained to a superior but hunted race, forever threatened by new pogroms and fresh outbursts of hate; the other half in true Prussian fashion always standing to attention, like your father, the colonel. Well, whatever you are, Peter, you are certainly not a Swede, no matter how brilliant your attempts at mimicking our slow, dull, sulky wits that forever fluctuate between a hectic love of life and isolated withdrawal and introversion. Your ideal, funnily enough – what you wanted to become – was a real English gentleman, à la Evelyn Waugh. So what has become of you? *Who* are you, Peter, I wonder, really? I'm so confused, you see; here, high up in the night sky in this Vietnamese restaurant, I'm feeling even more lost and confused; even less than usual do I know who *I* am . . .

We seat ourselves at the table, where the three of you promptly disappear behind your menus.

I have Jean-Paul and the four children. You have your Anne-Marie and two half-grown sons. Though in no way stupid or narrow-minded, Anne-Marie, I feel immediately, is a sunny, outgoing extrovert. Everything about her is positive, normal, capable. Nothing grim, nothing negative could ever attack her. In all her plump, blonde ordinariness, here is something out of the ordinary.

I'm drawn to her like someone dying of cold is drawn to the fire, like a mouse to a star, or a prisoner doing life to those outside the prison walls who can still laugh. She is like Vivaldi's Spring, your Anne-Marie; our Swedish spring, a bit intrusive, pushy, but vivacious and full of fun. With Jean-Paul, Peter, I'm threading a pearl necklace that can snap at any moment. Dancing an ever-swifter dance that spins vertiginously and transiently onwards towards an end that neither of us can predict, while you and your Anne-Marie string yours on a strong thread and move on towards new life, away from an evil past and its shadows . . .

'Why, Vicky must be quite the young lady now!' Anne-Marie is saying. 'A donkey, you say? What fun! And Michael, do you really mean to send him off to Winchester? That's where his father went, isn't it? But imagine how you will *miss* him! I couldn't think of sending Orlando or Amadeus off to one of those places! It would kill me. They are such lovely boys. We really must try and meet up some time, all of us, the children too. Who knows, perhaps my Orlando will take a fancy to your Victoria! But why is your little Rosalind so sensitive? Oh dear, your mother-in-law isn't kind to you or the children? I'm so sorry, what a shame! Never mind, it'll pass, and you have so much to be happy about, with a two-yea- old in the house, what joy! Tell me, how is your writing going these days? Peter has told me all about it. Me, I couldn't write a poem to save my life! And what about that husband of yours, your Frenchman, I'll bet he is a handsome devil. Let's drink to him, *Skail* for Jean-Paul! Such a shame he couldn't be here with us! Now, let's make up a programme for you and your mother for these next few days, eh, Peter?'

Her talk sparkles like the wine in our glasses, she is so vital, has such an appetite for life. My mumbled replies scarcely have time to reach her before new questions come up. After an endless wait the Vietnamese (or Siamese, as Mother insists on calling them) padding about in their own secretive world at last begin serving up an array of unidentifiable dishes in perfect silence. Along with a heap of boiled white rice. But no bread. Bread! That is all I'm longing for. Behind my eyes my head throbs at the temples. I'm sure the wine and the heat in here are making the pimple swell up like an artichoke. I must take a look at myself in my cracked mirror – they can think what they like, I don't give a damn, nothing can cause me more anguish than this pimple. I feel myself drift away from them, from their happy chattering faces; their pleasantries and table talk merge and fade into the background . . . Through a haze I see Mother, whose spirits are so high they are almost ecstatic, is telling the others about Leo's latest triumphs at Carnegie Hall, in London, Tokyo . . . And the others listen, spellbound. For them, too, Leo is a slice of God, causing their own existences to dwindle away altogether, seemingly content in their own littleness, their inferiority to Him. And here I leave Mother in safe hands, Peter's and Anne-Marie's, their hearts glowing with warmth . . .

All I want is a bit of bread. Just a morsel. Crumbs for a sparrow. But Vietnamese restaurants don't serve bread. So I lie down in one of the boats bobbing on the river in green willows' grateful shade. Close my eyes. And drift away . . .

. . . to Berlin, 1938. In a petrified silence my girlfriend Inga-Lill and I are sitting on our camp beds in Peter's mother's back room, the only one she still dares to use. Its shutters have been barred on all the windows facing the street and only a few slim shafts of light filter through into the dark bedroom, whose parquet flooring is still littered with broken glass since a few nights ago, when a gang of Nazi youths smashed all its windows. Aunt Sarah hasn't even been able to bring herself to sweep it up.

'If they discover Peter and I are still living here,' she confides in a low desperate whisper, 'they'll be back for us, I know it! Maybe even this very night, and send us off to one of those, those . . .'

She gives a loud sob, twines a small tear-stained handkerchief round her bony fingers, where her wedding ring hangs loose, ready to fall off.

'Concentration camps,' Inga-Lill chips in, sententious, solemn. Half-German, half-Swedish, she is as bright as a new pin, not easily fooled. Speaks the language so fluently that not the least nuance escapes her. We have been visiting her relatives on Lake Constance and are on our way home. Our Berlin stopover in this barricaded Jewish flat is due to Inga-lill's being in love with Peter. They have been pen-pals for years. Overcoming all obstacles, they have finally arranged to meet up here in Berlin. We are taking a risk, but the typically Arian, flaxen-haired Inga-Lill, stronger both mentally and physically than silly little over-protected Jenny, makes light of all difficulties. These summer weeks she has been striding about in a dirndl dress – that is, when she hasn't sported a pair of provokingly scanty Swedish shorts, undaunted by the menacing atmosphere of a city that, despite official denials, rumbles with the muffled sounds of war. If Inga-Lill's and my parents had had a clue to what for years now has been going on here and still is – this systematic extirpation of Jews, gypsies, communists and the 'handicapped'; this satanic hunting down of innocent people by torture, gas chambers; these sudden mysterious arrests of undesirables in the dead of night – how could they have made so gross a blunder? Sent us, their impressionable young daughters, out here to polish up our German? Tante Frieda, her uncle's wife, is a tall, stooping woman whose mind is wracked by grim intuition and dark foreboding. In her long, whispered conversations with her at Bregenz Inga-Lill has sniffed out the true state of affairs behind the magnificent, seemingly solid stage set, the exaggeratedly cheerful songs, the never-ending parades, the resounding shouts of 'Heil Hitler!' Has been allowed to peep into Tante Frieda's terrible knowledge and cruel foresight; while I, shy, sixteen-year-old Jenny, who possess none of Inga-Lill's fluency in

German, have been shut out, spared such dangerous secrets. Tante
Frieda's husband, a confirmed Nazi, would kill her if he knew what
she has been saying. But though Inga-Lill has been sworn to secre-
cy, promised never to betray these monstrous confidences, she has
been too scared to hold her tongue. And under our eiderdown,
late into the night, she has been passing them on to me: 'Promise
me, Jenny, promise you will never tell! Not a word, to anyone!' I
promise. I don't want to get Inga-Lill into trouble. Anyway, it is all
quite beyond me, at least to begin with – a nasty fairy-tale I refuse
to believe in but in whose inconceivably evil reality I'm being
gradually forced to believe. And I'm terrified! Home, all I want is
to go home, as quick as I can; to be read to aloud by Father while
the angelus rings on Saturday evenings; to water Mother's potted
plants, to eat their Sunday dinners. Now my only longing is to
hurry back to their anxious, narrow little world, whose sense of
impending catastrophe I know inside out and can cope with. For
the first time, in a sudden flash of teenage lucidity, I see them
clearly: lying on their soft pillows like Hans Andersen's princess,
sleepless all because of one hard little pea – the pea of an anxiety
that the very safety of their cosy Swedish existence always compels
them to blame on someone or something else. For naked anxiety
is intolerable, like groping about in a dark cave swarming with
black butterflies, whose whirling and fluttering wings will infallibly
swallow you up if you let them, unless you kill them, pin them
down and label them.

But Peter's mother is starving. Her black widow's dress –
Peter's father has just died – hangs on her like a sack. Her
unstockinged legs are as thin as reeds and her eyes red from crying
late at night. In this wretched back room she stands before us two
young Swedish girls, a very embodiment of suffering; the suffering
of the Jewish people, the whole world, of which we know nothing
and perhaps never will.

'Death camps *für Juden!*' she exclaims in a loud sob. And falls on her knees in front of an embarrassed Inga-Lill. 'For us *alles ist verboten*: park benches, seats on the trams and buses, food, life itself; all that's left us is the barest necessities – and death. They are throwing its gates wide open to us – old and young, healthy or sick, rich or poor, even children, the little children . . . Oh, girls, girls, I implore you, listen to me! Listen to what I'm saying! Take home the truth about Germany, tell them, tell them what's going on here! And please, please try to save my son, Peter . . . Do everything you can to save him. Don't bother about me, they can gas me to death, if that is what they want. As long as he is saved!'

Inga-Lill puts her arms around her, says what she can to comfort her. In this situation we are out of our depth, both she and I. Our helplessness in the face of world events, a gigantic drama of which we, here in this back room in Berlin one hot afternoon in July 1938, are witnessing one little scene, overwhelms us. Two little princesses, each on her own pea.

Standing by the locked door Peter is holding out in his outstretched hand a loaf of coarse bread. I can't take my eyes off him – his finely chiselled features, his vulnerable face. And suddenly I'm head over heals in love. A single hour in this wretched back room and I have burst out of my infantile pupa, transcended myself. Come what may I'm determined to rescue them, both mother and son. How? I don't know. But as I watch him break off pieces of the black bread and share them out, all my silly girlish egoism falls away and for a moment I'm free from my security, my anxiety about nothing, all the inhibitions of my upbringing.

'You must be hungry,' he says, simply. 'Here. I've managed to pick this up on the black market.'

Bewildered I find myself back in Paris, with Mother, Peter and Anne-Marie, still sitting here, the four of us, in a Vietnamese restaurant high above the city. For an endless moment my shrunken life has taken part in world events so appalling, so sadistic as to kill all optimism, whether philosophical or psychological, for ever.

For a little while I have forgotten my pimple, my pea of anxiety. Instead I'm desperate for bread. Ready to drop, I turn to Peter, interrupting his conversation with Mother:

'Peter, please! Do you think you could ask them for some bread? Please Peter, just a little piece . . .'

And Peter, obliging as ever, turns to one of the impassive Vietnamese waiters. Who just throws me a half-mocking glance out of the unfathomable slits of his eyes and shakes his head.

There isn't any. This time Peter hasn't even a rough black crust to offer me. I try to get a hold on myself. Smile. Look interested. But can't. In their closed circle they are no longer reckoning with me, Jenny, who has nothing to say for herself, out there on the periphery. Poor thing, she must be a bit gone in the head, hardly touching any of this delicious food. Just going on about bread . . .

'What a weird creature,' I can hear Anne-Marie saying later on tonight in bed beside her Peter in their hotel. 'Surely you noticed the way she kept staring herself in that mirror of hers? It's true she had a little pimple beside her nose, but . . . but we wouldn't even have noticed it if she hadn't kept furtively staring down into her handbag . . . But even so! If you ask me the poor thing is going round the bend. Somehow or other she wasn't *there*, we couldn't bring her into the conversation. *Poor* Aunt Charlotte, and she such a delightful person, so full of life, even at her age. How awful for her to have to drag round Paris with a daughter like that! Do you think she is unhappy with that Jean-Paul of hers, or could she be in an early menopause?'

'No, darling, I don't think she is unhappy with Jean-Paul. Without him and her kids she would crack up all together. She is always been a bit different, hypersensitive. The fact is the whole family isn't quite right in the head, except Aunt Charlotte, of course. Jenny and Charlotte just don't get on. She is so dreadfully mother fixated, has never been able to assert herself against Charlotte's iron will; or her brothers', come to that. You saw for yourself how she shrinks and dwindles away to nothing in her mother's company, like a moth on a curtain! I feel so sorry for her; she is too damn frail, too weak-willed to cope with life. Who should know better than me, who lived with them all those years!'

And I hear Peter, for what must be the hundredth time, telling his pretty, vivacious Ann-Marie just what that home had been like:

'Aunt Charlotte decided everything. Squashed the poor little thing completely until sometimes she seemed half-witted. At times they squashed me flat, too. Almost managed to crush me . . . If I hadn't been such a crafty devil and known how to wriggle my way out I could have ended up glued down like Jenny! Her brothers hated my guts, were bloody awful to me. In their eyes I was nothing but a Jewish lout, an intruder in their home. And though Jenny's father helped mother and me to get to Sweden I know he never really cared for me – nor I for him, come to that. But Aunt Charlotte really loved me and I loved her too. She is amazing, don't you think?'

Now they are making plans. Mother's voice; youthful, enthusiastic:

'Oh, I have just *got* to see the Louvre; see the Mona Lisa and the Venus that my Ma used to talk so much about! We even had a reproduction of the Venus, from my grandfather's time. For years it stood in his home, and then in the Trädgårdsgatan apartment in Uppsala.'

Uppsala, New Year's Eve, 1939

Alone with Peter. Stumbling along hand in hand through the snow-drifts by the banks of the Fyris stream's black rumbling waters. It is very late and icy cold. We press close to each other. No one can see us here. Unchaperoned by Mother's and Father's eyes, we are on our own, on leave of absence from our Stockholm home. Peter's aunt, who has set up a centre for Jewish refugee children here in Uppsala, has invited Peter to come and see her. But Peter isn't living with her; he is living in the attic of a professor's villa in the town's outskirts. The professor shelters refugees and is the man behind the Jewish children's home. My lodgings are with some of Mother's close friends, on Övre Slottsgatan. And that is where I ought to be right now, if – Peter brushes aside my apprehensions: 'You've got your own key, haven't you? Come on, then. You are not a child any longer. They won't eat you up if you get in a bit late. After all, it is New Year's Eve!'

So cowed and reticent in Berlin and in our Stockholm flat, he is suddenly so self-assured, so audacious that I, seventeen-year-old Jenny, can hardly recognize him. His hold on me has tightened, become hard. I'm trembling all over, suddenly aware of a strange heavy warmth in my lower parts as if my heart had sunk down there, become all damp and excited. Recklessly I fling all thoughts of God and parents on to a snow-drift. And turn my cold young face up to his for the kiss that I have secretly been dreaming of all these months Peter has been living with us. Yes, ever since the July afternoon in that back room in Berlin I have known something must happen between us. Exactly what, I don't know. Only that fate has threaded our two black threads on its sharp needle and knotted them tightly together, as Mother does hers.

I am not in the least bit afraid. Without any evil presentiments whatsoever, I follow him in through the back door to the professor's villa, hardly even noticing where I am. Unlocking another door, he pushes me on in front of him up a staircase.

'They've gone away,' he whispers. 'We are all alone, Jenny, all by ourselves!'

Suddenly panicky, I want to run away. But also to stay. Now we are standing very close to each other. Though the snow is still on our overcoats, our bodies are so hot, so steaming with excitement that we scarcely notice how cold it is inside the unheated house. Dimly I make out a hallway crammed with furniture and book-shelves, a little writing desk and a Victorian sofa group. Somewhere in this big house a clock chimes twelve, followed by twelve dark strokes from the distant cathedral. In this unfamiliar villa's silence its bell is tolling in a new year; one more, to unleash death and terror on a ravaged Europe . . . Passionately I cling to Peter's taut, thin body, pressing myself close. Already I belong to him. Assuredly Fate's seamstress has tied our two threads together with a double knot and then, with a sharp snap of her teeth, bitten it off, in my girlish fantasy uniting us – this Jewish refugee boy and me – for ever more! A *fait accompli* that neither God – if He exists – nor parents, brothers, Jewish children, Jewish aunts, end-of-term exams or a war that in this instant seems to have lost all reality can reverse. Eyes closed, blind with desire and adoration, I cling to him like an olive still unshaken from its tree's gnarled and silvery trunk.

He is leading me into a dark room. All I can make out is a few book shelves. Nothing more. Through a window a puffed-up moon stares in at us with a look of blank amazement. Suddenly, to my horror, Peter starts pulling my clothes off, flinging them frantically aside onto the floor and a rocking chair, where they land on a black cat. Startled out of her sleep, she emits a loud, indignant miaow; leaps from the rocking chair, streaks out of the room, leav-ing me, half out of my wits, naked and scared, alone with a mad-man. With one deft movement of his hand he undoes his flies and brings out *something*, a huge, elongated, swollen monster shaped like a bread roll, holds it menacingly in his hand . . . Never in my wildest dreams have I have imagined anything so grotesque or that Peter, delicate, refined Peter, should . . .

'No, Peter, no!' I scream.

Ignoring my anguished cry, hands still cupping the hideous rep-tile, he closes in on me. Shivering with cold and fear, I try to grab the rocking chair and cower behind the home-woven antimacassar hanging over its back, gleaming dully in the full moon's creamy light, a deep blood-red. Undaunted, smiling a superior Prussian smile and with a crude insensitivity I would never have believed of him, Peter rips it away from me. And tries to ram that thing at me, force it in between my thighs, which are so stiff they seem to have grown together.

'Go away, Peter!' I scream. 'Take that . . . that *thing* away!'

But Peter is no longer poor persecuted Peter. In the pool of lunar light shed by the chubby ??professorial?? face up in its black night sky, he forces me down on my knees. Sobbing hysterically, wholly in his and that horrible thing's power, I feel it being shoved into my screaming mouth, hear the man who a moment ago was Peter utter the words: '*Sauge doch, sauge doch!*' Nauseated in my whole being, I obey, sucking mechanically at his pale hard thing, filling my mouth like a snake in its pit. Suddenly a sticky, glutinous sweet-sour liquid squirts into my mouth, down my throat, chokes me. Or would have if, in my last convulsions, the thing hadn't suddenly shrivelled up and recoiled like a banana withdrawing into its skin. Overcome by nausea I stumble out of the room. Not knowing where the bathroom is, I throw up all over the hallway carpet, upsetting a pyramid of books as a new spasm shakes me – my whole being, not just my shuddering body. Where is Peter, anyway? He's nowhere to be seen. Somewhere far off there is the sound of a toilet being flushed. Utterly abandoned, alone, I crawl about the floor looking for my bra and panties, my skirt and jumper, find them in the rocking chair, underneath the black cat who, having resumed her rightful place, is purring loudly in the night, witnessing my agony through luminous, unfeeling ginger eyes.

Next morning Peter turns up in my mother's friend's apartment on Övre Slottsgatan. He has brought me a half-frozen bouquet of pink carnations and roses.

'For you,' he says, guiltily. 'For my little Jenny.'

'Where on earth did you get *them* from?' I ask. 'I mean, today, with all the shops closed . . . ?'

'From the churchyard,' he replies. 'They were lying by an open grave, so I took them. No one will notice, there were any number of others lying there . . . and they would only have withered in the cold.'

Standing behind me is the house's prim and proper daughter, Catherine, scrutinizing Peter from behind thick glasses. She is an intelligent girl but tends to be sarcastic, malicious even.

'You are a thief,' she says coldly. 'A ghoul, stealing from the dead!'

Peter goes all Jewish. Takes offence. Humiliated, without another word, he slinks off.

'How could you be so cruel?' Involuntarily I find I am defending Peter against this Swedish Valkyrie of a family girl. What does *she* know of anxiety, terror, persecution, suffering, death? For her they are just abstractions. 'He isn't a thief. He hasn't stolen anything!'

'Oh yes he has!' Catherine insists, her eyes behind their thick lenses cutting through my already frail and distraught state of mind. For some reason I can't understand it is imperative I fight off her insinuations, her intolerable self-importance.

'What . . . what has he stolen?' My voice trembles timorously, as if this slip of a Swedish family girl in front of me were my judge. Mine and Peter's.

'Your virginity,' she asserts with a chill smile.

'My . . . my what?' I stammer.

'Oh, cut the silly stuff,' she goes on brusquely. 'He has seduced you, that's what! Lain with you. *Had* you! It's written all over you!'

And when I still understand nothing, just stare dumbly at her, unable to react or even stir, as if I have ceased to exist, she throws me a searching glance. Takes off her glasses and peers at me, a kind of cruel, short-sighted stare.

'Don't you understand *anything* then? About sex? Are you just plain dumb? A silly innocent? How do you think they make kids, eh? With a magic wand?'

Giddy, unable to stand up, I sink down on to a chair. Can't get out a sound. My mouth has gone dry, my heart flutters like a dying moth. Between me and her a whole row of those white things are dangling like bread rolls or sausages. I shut my eyes.

'Don't you even know what a *penis* is?' Her amazed voice reaches me from some indefinable distance. And when I don't answer, she fetches an illustrated work on anatomy, opens it at a page showing 'the male organ' – that's what she calls it – in its normal position and then, with a strange smile, turns the page and shows me another: the same thing in a state of 'erection'. At this I scream loudly. For a split second I, who am so small I can hardly reach up to the washbasin, see Father standing naked in our bathroom. Suddenly, as he sees me standing there, his hands convulsively cover something between his legs. Flushing red, he roars: 'Out! Get out, girl, this instant!' Again I scream, this time right into Catherine's horrified eyes and the picture book, out of which that *thing* seems to be thrusting its way into my mouth, like a disgusting bloated nipple. My mind reels . . . Three weeks later I wake up at the city hospital. Beg the nurses not to let either Mother or Father visit me . . . I never want to see either of them again . . .

Charlotte's diary, late that evening

Before tumbling into bed I must tell you in confidence, my dear diary, that this evening spent in Peter's and his delightful wife Anne-Marie's company has given me back my courage and (despite the ridiculous – not to say embarrassing – fuss Jenny made about wanting some bread when there wasn't any, which ended with her collapsing!) my delight at being in this marvellous city. We were so perfectly in harmony, our conversation was so spontaneous, so full of fun, it was *revitalizing*! The dishes and the wines were superb and the view from the skyscraper enchanting! It was as if I were right up there among the stars. Peter's overwhelming kindness, so genuine, coupled with Anne-Marie's interest in everything and her sunny disposition, really helped me so much that at times I almost forgot Jenny was there at all! Her silence, her refusal to eat or even let herself be drawn into the conversation – in other words (to put it mildly) her *neurotic* staring into that mirror of hers – *could* so easily have ruined the evening; but Peter's and Anne-Marie's *joie de vivre*, their perfect contentment with each other and all the interesting things they had to talk about were so infectious that the three of us, in spite of Jenny's ever-more piteous performance, soon settled into a kind of spiritual *mènage à trois* and by silent agreement we quite simply *excluded* her. Ruthless? Perhaps. But sometimes one just *has* to be ruthless if individuals like Henrik and Jenny aren't to drag you down into their black pot-holes. But then what does she do but suddenly, pale as a sheet, get up from table and ask Peter to drive her back to the hotel! Says she is feeling sick and just *has* to go straight to bed! Naturally Peter, being the gentleman he is, drove us straight back. Embracing me he mumbled something in my ear I didn't quite catch, but it sounded like 'Poor Aunt Charlotte!' Fortunately they have promised to look after me tomorrow afternoon.

Jenny is asleep. She really looks terrible, poor child! Too thin and haggard for her thirty-eight years. I find it frightening, being alone with her. (Can't help wondering what is in those tablets she keeps taking. Valium? And she is drinking too much, hardly eats a thing.) And there I was, ready to unburden my heart to her, to tell her what professor S. told me before I left . . . When I think of how my ma used to confide in me! But how can I possibly confide such a thing to *my* daughter? What support or comfort can I expect from someone in her condition? I wish she didn't keep that book with its gruesome title *The Divided Self* lying on her bedside table. She hasn't got the energy to read it anyway. Just goes on staring at the same page all the time. How I wish Jean-Paul were here!

Charlotte's diary, 12 November

We made an early start, took the Metro to the Louvre. A most intense morning. I saw both the *Mona Lisa* and the *Venus de Milo* that my ma used to talk about so much. We used to have a reproduction, the one that first hung in his home and then in ours at Uppsala, from Grandfather's time. Jenny is a little better. Her French, of course – thanks to Jean-Paul – is quite remarkable. Otherwise I don't think I could have managed with my rusty French, alone in this city with its fiery chatter, whose excited rhythms I find both wearisome and enchanting. Jenny has a way of stopping whenever she sees one of those miserable beggars (and the Metro is swarming with them!); it is more than she can do not to put a few francs (not so few, either!) into their filthy, out-stretched hands. As she also does if she sees one of those thin, long-haired youths standing there in their gaudy clothes, playing a flute or a violin. Instead of just hurrying past like everyone else she always stops, praises their playing and tells me what piece it is – a flute sonata by Loeillet or one of Bach's violin partitae. And then she drops a franc or two into their violin case or greasy upturned hat. Jenny has always had a soft spot for 'these the least of our brethren'; it is as if she only has to set eyes on one of those poor wretches to wake up out of her trance, her *fog*. In *that* way she is more genuinely Christian than Henrik or me . . . Almost puts me to shame.

But where was I? Oh, if only I were younger, what a lot there is I would like to experience! The truth is, I have missed out on far too much, living as I have done boxed up with Henrik in his narrow existence. How different my life would have been if I had been born later, been one of these modern young women of the sixties, who put their careers first – self-assured, emancipated, politically and socially aware! The eternal submission to male authority that I have suffered so cruelly from – despite being Henrik's superior when it comes to intellect and force of character – is now *putz weg*, gone away for ever – perhaps even too much so? First and foremost, the woman of today seems free to 'find herself', develop her own personality. The mere sight of all these young women in full flight of self-development fills me with envy. I bleed inwardly when I realize how completely my own life, dictated by the older generation's prejudices and restricted views of life, has been spent in a male-dominated society that we women have tamely *accepted*. If only I could voice these thoughts to Jenny, make her aware of her chances, infuse into her some of the enthusiasm and energy I still have inside me! But in the Metro she just sits there opposite me, inaccessible, lost in her own dreams. The truth is she is a product of Henrik's old-fashioned romantic ideals of the self-effacing woman. Admittedly there are lightning flashes. Then she becomes either aggressive or insinuating. Surprisingly intelligent and imaginative. Shows a mental acumen and, despite her dreamy detachment, a certain ability to pilot us through Paris. Then she is *my* daughter, at such moments I recognize myself in her! Unfortunately they are few and far between. Believe it or not, she just drooped along behind me through the Louvre, showed not the least interest from one end of it to the other, despite all she has learnt about art from Jean-Paul. As for the paintings, she didn't even seem to *see* , far less experience them; just stared *into* them, particularly the chiaroscuros behind glass, staring compulsively at her own reflection and that diabolical red pimple of hers – verily a case of 'through a glass darkly'! My soul revolts against such apathy – in front of centuries of masterpieces! It is as if this little spot on her face were persecuting me, awakening in me an inward fury, though I am trying hard to control it – a furious impulse to grab hold of my daughter, shake her, slap her cheek *hard*, so that pimple bursts and all the puss and blood comes oozing out! I would like to give her a real shock, cure her with a sudden violent blow, the way one cures the hiccups . . .

Charlotte, Charlotte, may God forgive you your thoughts!

But at least I have seen Ma's *Venus. Mona Lisa* smiled at me a bit sarcastically, I thought, surrounded as she was by flocks of noisy American tourists. Sarcastic, yes, yet as if she secretly understood me: 'You see, Charlotte, life is only a farce, soon over. For you, anyway. But not for me. I am eternal.'

Jenny

Mother is very tiring. Paris, its constant noise, is wearing me down. Soon there'll be nothing left of me. My heart is so trapped by anxiety that I am drugging myself with Valium, smoking one cigarette after another, drinking too much wine to numb my panic, numb myself. Until I'm only half-conscious, indifferent, idiotic. All I long for is a quiet, dark room, a bed of my own to rest in! Our hotel room vibrates with street sounds from cars, from noisy, lively Parisians. And we have to share the same bed! Mother, touchingly enough, curls up on her side, not to bother me. Yet all the time I am hyperaware of her, that she is there, only pretending to be asleep; of her sighs, suppressed but deep, speaking louder than words.

She's as tense as I am.

Why?

We hardly have a word to say to each other, only to plan our days or exchange conventional remarks about the weather. Otherwise this silence, which leaves so much unspoken, unsolved, conceals an oppressive hatred; even more, suppressed love. Why can't I overpower my mother, force her under me – like a lover his mistress – and squeeze all her secrets out of her, everything I want to know about her, about Father, about myself? Before it's too late . . .

I am gradually falling apart, I am in such a state. As long as I could keep it invisible, inside me, I could cope with people, no matter how hard it was, no matter how it demanded all my concentration and female charms to fool them. But now, when my decline has manifested itself in the form of a pimple on my face, all my defences are down. And I am driven to mirrors, to get close to them, into them. Forced to look into my face, distorted by this pimple, all too well aware of the looks people are giving me and how weird they think my behaviour, even a bit mad! They think I'm vain, narcissistic. And I am, seized by a sick narcissism and a wild desire to flee from Paris and back to Jean-Paul. Home, to be soothed by his love, which never condemns, always understands; back to my little Jojo, to hide myself in her; to Rosalind, Michael and Vicky – *they* don't care how I look, I'm just their mum, they'll forgive me . . .

But today something happened that relieved the pressure. Anne-Marie is so elegant, so untarnished, so healthy. But there is a deeper side to her too. She seems to understand a little of the torment I'm going through. When we were having lunch yesterday as Peter's guests at the Swedish Club overlooking the Place de la Concorde, she whispered: 'Put that mirror down, Jenny! You are so lovely, you don't need to worry about that silly little spot on your cheek. I have got some medicated makeup with me. Let's go out to the ladies' room and I'll help you put some on!'

We excused ourselves. Mother was anyway in her seventh heaven again with her adored Peter, who was heaping their two plates high with a copious smörgåsbord. Deftly, almost professionally, Anne-Marie took over; I closed my eyes, relaxed.

'Don't look in the mirror, not until I'm done with you,' she said.

For the first time since we have been in Paris I calmed down, became almost drowsy as her warm hands stroked my face, massaged my throbbing temples, lightly, ever so lightly, touched my evil, detestable pimple.

'I've been watching you for the last couple of days,' I heard her say, as if from a distance. 'You are over-strained, poor Jenny. Your energetic mother is too much for you, isn't she? I mean, you are hardly up to coping with yourself, are you? This little pimple is nothing really, but something's worrying you, gnawing away inside you, isn't that so? I'm a trained nurse, you know, though I'm not working right now, and I specialize in psychosomatic symptoms. I have learnt to love eyes like yours, shy, suspicious, sad eyes. How do you think Peter looked, when he first came to us? Bewildered, scared to death! And now, Jenny, dear – take a look at yourself!'

Looking up into the mirror there in the ladies' toilet I didn't recognize myself, or anyway not the terrified, ugly Jenny. I looked as smooth-skinned, calm and fragrant as this merciful Samaritan of a hostess who had so unexpectedly lifted me up out of my misery. Pretty, new, radiant, overcome by gratitude and relief, I flung my arms around Anne-Marie's neck and embraced her. Hugged her as someone one loves; and a sensation of deep happiness, the same sensual thrill went through me as in the river when I had clutched Mother's haunches. I experienced again those childish moments of bliss before she had swum out and left me alone. It was so intense that without stopping to think what I was doing I found myself kissing Anne-Marie passionately, not on her lips, of course, but on her cheeks, forehead, hands.

'There, there, Jenny,' she said, a little taken aback, pushing me away gently but firmly. 'Calm down! And for heaven's sake don't cry, or you'll spoil my little job as a beautician. Come on, let's go back to the others. Now you won't have to keep looking down into that mirror of yours any more, will you – promise?'

Perhaps this was just a ridiculous little semi-lesbian interlude and I am making too much of it . . . But at that moment I worshipped Anne-Marie, would gladly have given her all my jewellery, spent all the francs I had put aside for Jean-Paul and the children on flowers for her. Cool and unruffled she resumed her place between Peter and Mother. Possibly didn't even understand what

166

she'd done for me. But she had broken through my anxiety, my isolation. For a moment given me a little loving, sisterly sympathy, a mother's tender affection . . .

Charlotte's diary

After a divine lunch at the Swedish Club, Peter drove us all round Paris in the glorious autumn sunshine. I am filled with such a myriad fragmentary impressions, dear diary, that I am unable to give you a coherent or concrete report. Sleepy and not a little light-headed from the wine we had consumed at luncheon, I was feeling at peace with the world and transported by the beauty of Paris: the Seine, the Eiffel Tower and so on. I sat in the back with Anne-Marie, who pointed things out to me, explained what everything was, etc., but, as I have said, I wasn't all that clear in the head. What did astonish me beyond words, though, was the sudden change that had come over Jenny. Sitting in front next to Peter, she was chattering her head off, laughing! – full of life, quite the coquette, every bit as sweet and charming as she used to be in the old days, so long ago. It almost looked as if she was trying to turn Peter's head (no risk of that though, he has a truly wonderful wife and Jenny has her Jean-Paul!).

Jenny

They have dropped us off by the doors of Notre Dame. Mother and I enter the sanctuary alone. At the entrance two nuns stand with collection boxes '*pour les pauvres*'; I give them what I have. Wordlessly we wander through the endless gloom of the cathedral, flocks of tourists trailing past us, to and fro; passing by small altars dedicated to various saints, passing confessionals, heading up the main aisle, towards the burning candles. High above our heads is the rose window. Rays of November sunlight burst through in an intense play of light tinted by a myriad hues. Here and there people kneel deep in prayer; everywhere reigns a reverential silence. Suddenly somebody begins playing on the organ, the great Cavaillé-Coll organ that Jean-Paul so admires. It must be Widor he is practising. We sit down on two chairs in front of a statue of the Madonna and Child, surrounded by white lilies. Gone is Mother's exuberance of only a moment ago. Unmoving, with eyes closed, she seems to have withdrawn into herself, lost in her own thoughts of which I know nothing – perhaps she is praying. At that moment the light from one of the rose window's panes glides over her face, illumining and transfiguring it as if it were the face of someone who has already died. Yet at the same time that she is slipping away from me over the horizon to a sphere that I'll never reach, she feels strangely close; an intimate, wordless, sacramental feeling I've never felt before. It is as if for a few minutes we have been transported to another, unearthly sphere, without disputes or anxiety, a place wholly in harmony with itself; as if in the gentle but piercing light, mirrored in the rose window's eye, we are being transfigured and somewhere far above ourselves are being changed, becoming one. Deep down I know this experience can only be an illusion brought on by my overstrung nerves, fed on candle-light, the organ music, all this cathedral's immense but muted history. At the same time a piteous little prayer rises in me, Jenny, to this mirror – no, this window, this eye – and to a great strong heart, if there is one; a plea that at last it will help me, Jenny, in my need; and Jean-Paul and the children, who I fully realize are also suffering under my terrible burden . . .

Without my having noticed it, Mother has left her place. Confused, my eyes seek her until suddenly I see her stumpy, fur-clad figure over there among the candles. She must have bought some for a few francs. Now, under my gaze, she's fixing it on a holder, lighting it from another's stump. Then, her hands clasped, she stands before it a long time, gazing into its flame, burning there tall and brilliant amid all the others, some of them flickering anxiously in the cross-draught from the doors, others, already half-burnt down, melted away to dripping candle grease. It strikes me that my dark little mother hardly stands out at all among these Catholic South European women. It is here in this candlelit mystical world that she belongs, not in our chilly, extroverted Protestant churches.

Coming back to me, she hands me a candle.

'Light it for me, Jenny', she whispers, 'when I'm gone – I have just lit one for my ma.'

Her eyes close and she is withdrawing from me again. It is in my heart to refuse, despair, defy her, but the words can't come out. For the first, perhaps only time, I realize she may not have long to live.

Holding the tall, slim candle in both hands I turn her statement over in my mind. Find it true but incomprehensible, impossible. Dismiss it, forget it.

Mothers don't die before their children.

Charlotte's diary

Went to the opera last night, Beethoven's *Fidelio*. Peter had got us tickets. Wonderfully beautiful, splendid. What a pity Jenny wasn't up to it. Said she was too tired, just wanted to sleep. I say a pity, because I know how music relaxes her and what a great pleasure it affords her. Afterwards, instead of dining out, I went back with them to their hotel room, where I had a chance to lie down and rest for a while. Anne-Marie was making sandwiches and tea, just like we do at home. Such a woman, it seems to me, has a knack of creating a cosy atmosphere wherever she goes. A little reshuffling of the furniture, some photographs of a delightful son, flowers, a bowl of apples and grapes like a still life, soft, subdued lighting, and the impersonal hotel atmosphere yields to another, home-like and intimate. Women like her may not call themselves artists, yet it seems to me that they have exactly the same inner resources, the same artistic sensibility, as so-called real ones. How lucky Peter was to have met her after his first, catastrophic marriage to that Renate woman; the beautiful young Jewess who was so haunted by her experiences in the concentration camp Folke Bernadotte that our Swedish Cross had rescued her from that in the end she took her own life . . .

Our easy-going conversation became more and more confidential because Jenny wasn't there to disturb it. We spoke our minds about all sorts of things, joking and generally having a good time as friends do. Our evening might well have turned out quite differently if Anne-Marie hadn't suddenly said: 'I know this may upset you, Aunt Charlotte, dear, so please forgive me. But there is something I really must say before we go our separate ways. This is the last evening we'll spend together, so it's my last chance . . . We've been discussing this matter, Peter and I; and, well, he thinks you will appreciate us speaking our minds, even though your health obviously isn't too good and we can see how bravely you are bearing up, despite your tricky heart and blood pressure. But the fact is, we feel Jenny's in grave danger!'

Here Anne-Marie paused. In the wan pink light I saw their eyes watching me intently. And she went on:

'Mentally she is *very* frail, obviously suffering from an acute neurosis that, if it isn't treated, may well turn into a psychosis. I would almost go so far as to say that she is already hovering on the brink of schizophrenia. The fact is,' she added hurriedly, '*she has just got to have some help* – and the sooner the better! It seems as if she is in a state of deep regression' (that was her word: 'regression'). 'No longer really living in the present but mixing everything up with old traumas from her earliest years.'

Anne-Marie's tone of voice was calm, professional and final but not insensitive. She waited to hear what I would say, ready to share my distress. Realizing such a dire warning might come as quite a shock to me, she had even had the foresight to have a glass of water and some tablets to hand. An unnecessary precaution because, although I didn't understand the professional terms that she used and that she patiently tried to explain to me, what she said, though daring, actually came as a relief, gave me a chance to unburden myself to them, something I had not had the least intention of doing – 'silence is my heritage', as the poet puts it. But now, in these two young people's company, I finally found myself speaking freely without the least feelings of guilt. I told them all about my stay in Jenny's and Jean-Paul's home in Lindfield, everything! It all came pouring out: Jenny's confused, unstable state of mind, how it affects them all. I described Jean-Paul, his near-saintly efforts; the children, the poor rootless children, and the problems they are having with the mother-in-law; how Muriel had made herself scarce throughout my stay – the whole sorry story. It was like going to confession, a luxury I no longer permit myself. By the end I was weeping tears of exhaustion and relief. I even told them about my visit to Professor S. and the 'verdict' she, at my own insistence, gave me: that after two heart attacks I am living on borrowed time and a third may prove fatal. Out it all came. They didn't say a word. Anne-Marie gave me a paper handkerchief and Peter put his arm around me, as if he had been my own son. When I had calmed down a little and Anne-Marie had brewed another pot of tea (they have one of those electric tea-makers in their room) my first question, naturally enough, was: what ought to be done for Jenny?

As for my own condition, there is nothing that *can* be done; and anyway I am quite an old woman and not afraid of dying. The terrible pains in my chest *do* frighten me, of course . . . but all I can do is trust in God and the doctors. But about Jenny? Well, according to Anne-Marie she needs psychoanalysis or, at the very least, some other lengthy and probably no less expensive therapy, coupled with a considerable period of convalescence. She may even need to go into hospital. She also said that Jenny looks physically weak, eats too little and ought to give up smoking and taking all those tablets!

Anne-Marie, who has worked at Långbro among other mental hospitals, says Jenny is not the only victim of such sufferings, far from it; people nowadays are saturated with anxiety and take any amount of tranquillizers. It seems British housewives, according to a recent survey, are worst of all. They feel aggressive, left out, 'different' and therefore ostracized by normal people. In our highly rationalized society, she said, any number of people can no longer cope, are always off work sick, sometimes even prefer to accept early retirement. They feel so bad and are so lacking in self-confidence that they get addicted to tranquillizers, antidepressants or to alcohol and are all in desperate need of help. They feel crushed, oppressed by all the rest of us – as she put it – 'efficient people' and often get it into their heads that we would like to put them away.

Another thing she said was that people like Jenny simply don't want to live in the ordinary world. However awful their anxiety is, it can give them experiences, excitement and strange, fantastic associations of ideas . . . Well, I can't remember all she said, but the gist of it was that everyone of us has a raving lunatic inside him or her, whom we are terrified of. And the mentally sick person gives vent to this madness of ours on our behalf. As she warmed to her subject it crossed my mind that Anne-Marie is possibly just a shade *too* interested in such morbid matters . . . Nevertheless, in Jenny's case I agreed: a psychiatrist ought to be consulted and as soon as possible!

While Anne-Marie and I were discussing these matters Peter, who seemed more and more agitated, was stalking up and down the room, chain-smoking. He seemed nervy, all on edge, irritable somehow. Suddenly, with a vehemence altogether uncharacteristic of him, he pointed at a vase full of freesia and said: 'Jenny is like those flowers. Delicate, ethereal; unlike anyone else. In my own way I think I can say I know her quite well, and it's obvious she needs psychological help. Anne-Marie is absolutely right. Jenny is heading for a breakdown. She's withering away in that dull English village with its pond, whose 'silly little ducks and two evil-looking swans', as she put it, 'just float round and round looking for a way out!' Jenny can be satirical, even sarcastic at times; and we laughed at what she said. But afterwards I felt the sadness in her words. After all, Charlotte, she is a Stockholm girl, Swedish through and through, and I don't think Jean-Paul quite realizes it! Her roots have been pulled up and she's wilting away for lack of light and water . . . If we don't look out it'll kill her. It was the same with Renate; I saw her . . . fade . . . gradually lose her hold on herself. And I would have suffered the same fate too but for Anne-Marie. If we hadn't met . . .'

Here his voice broke, his words became disconnected. I could sense the pain of his lament. All his bonhomie had blown away like thistle down. But then his voice levelled out, became confidential. And he said: 'Aunt Charlotte, dear, there is something I have never told you. Never told anyone. My old mother's clairvoyant: that time Jenny came to us in Berlin, that summer day with her friend Inga-Lill, she recognized her instantly! She had dreamt of her, she said, our guardian angel, come to rescue us from the Nazis! Which is precisely what she did, *nicht wahr*? After all, it was Jenny who told Uncle Henrik about us and got him busy working on his contacts, even went to see the bishop, to persuade him to get the Swedish Church to smuggle us out of Berlin. Well, you remember how it was . . . And one more thing: though my mother is virtually blind these days she still does the tarot cards. All that time ago, back in Berlin, she saw Jenny's fate in them. And said:

'This girl has a very special destiny.' I remember her words, sitting there chain-smoking in our back room. 'Very bad, very good. Like Sleeping Beauty, she'll prick herself on a deadly needle, exactly as the evil fairy prophesied, but won't die. Just fall into a long and deep sleep before waking up to a better life.'

He repeated what his mother had said, word for word, in German. How strange it was, after all these years, to hear him speak his mother-tongue again! Anyway, we went on talking until well after midnight, and when Peter finally drove me home through streets that for once were quite silent, he said something else that has also affected me deeply:

'I lived with you a long time, didn't I, several years, in fact. But one thing I could never understand was why Fredrik and Leo treated Jenny so arrogantly, so humiliatingly. Like they treated me, too, though of course that was different, understandable; me being an outsider, an intruder in their home and Jewish to boot! But to treat their own *sister* like that . . . Though I have the greatest respect for Uncle Henrik, I'm convinced he was wrong to do what he did. That abortion business must have harmed her no end! It wasn't as if she didn't want her child by that fellow – what was his name? The one who was obsessed with Valéry. I know because she told me. Surely there was something you could have done, Aunt Charlotte – intervened and put a stop to it?'

His question, with its accusatory undertone, took me aback.

'No,' I answered indignantly, 'there was *not*. I tried, but Henrik as you know has a will of iron and dominated the whole situation. You know what the men in my family are like, hard as granite! Come to that, Peter,' I interposed, 'you are not completely innocent either, are you? Not that I know any of the details,' I added hastily.

Pulling up outside my hotel, Peter averted his face:

'You're quite right, Aunt Charlotte,' he said. 'I behaved badly. But I was young and foolish. Too young to realize how fragile she was . . . Besides, aren't we all damaged in one way or another, except perhaps people like Anne-Marie?'

I had half a mind to contradict his 'all'. But was too tired and let it pass. Our farewell, though hurried, was heartfelt. Candour, which at times can be so devastating, hasn't frayed our deep fondness for each other.

Jenny was asleep. On my pillowcase lay a goodnight note, of the kind she used to write as a child:

Jean-Paul rang. He was wonderful! Jojo's cold is better. Forgive me for fretting and being so silly. Sleep well. A big hug from your Jenny!

Touching.

Charlotte's diary, 20 November

I am sitting on deck aboard the Swedish Lloyd boat on my way home to Sweden. I have been reading, resting, watching the sea rise and fall. What is in store for me, I wonder, at home with Henrik? My life in Stockholm has quite fallen by the wayside these past weeks, but by and by I suppose I will get back into it!

Yesterday after lunch Jenny and Jean-Paul drove me to Tilbury. It was overcast, wet and cold, and it felt hard to leave them, particularly Jenny, who was beside herself with what Jean-Paul calls 'separation anxiety'. A long while I stood watching the shores of England recede. Sad!

Time has slipped away. A glance at my diary tells me I haven't written a word since 14 November! Our homeward journey was tiring. A gale in the Channel and other delays meant we didn't get back to Haywards Heath, where Jean-Paul was waiting for us, until it was dark. Came home to a cold, chaotic house. Rita had gone up to London, Muriel was in bed with a bad cold, Victoria standoffish, and Mikael, as usual, glued to his television. There had been plasterers at work in the sitting-room (planks laid out all over the carpet, amid pots of glue and old newspapers); everywhere utter disorder and almost nothing to eat, only some sardines on toast, with a pot of tea kindly made for us by Jean-Paul. Oh, how I wish Jenny could make that house of hers just a little more comfortable, more homely! When I think of what a woman like Anne-Marie could do with it – the comparison has a bitter sting! Yet I was deeply grateful for having had the chance to be in Paris and to have delivered Jenny back to her Jean-Paul; sparks of passion flew about them, even though they have been married so long.

At last, the next day, I had an opportunity to speak with Jean-Paul. He had taken the day off. Jenny had taken the older children to see *The Sound of Music*. And Rita (who seems to me to be at least five months pregnant, her protruding stomach can hardly be due to English cooking!) took care of the little ones, so we had a couple of hours to sit down in peace and quiet in front of the sitting-room fire.

I described, as precisely as I could, our days in Paris. Not so much the outward events; I gave him a detailed account, rather, of how Jenny had been: her obsession with that little pimple on her cheek, her obsessive staring into mirrors, her sudden switches from elation to anxious depression, her strange, distant manner towards the rest of us in the Siamese restaurant, for example; and finally her aggressive outbursts, all the inordinately mean and impertinent things she had come out with on our last evening – yes, my dear Jean-Paul, it was *dreadful*! Monstrous!

Jean-Paul listened to every word, sipped his tea, didn't react much; just asked me to tell him exactly what had happened. Actually I had meant to spare him the details of our last Paris evening and go straight to Anne-Marie's and Peter's (particularly Anne-Marie's) advice that we take Jenny to a psychiatrist. But since he insisted I told him, as briefly as possible, how Jenny, dur-ing our last evening in Paris, had got it into her head that she absolutely must see some Cocteau film that was showing. And upon my saying I wasn't up to it and was quite simply *exhausted* (which was true, I had overstrained myself, was afraid my heart would start playing up) she flew into a rage, accused me – *me*! – of being false, devious, double-dealing. 'It wasn't too much for you to stay up half the night with that Peter and his Anne-Marie, was it? But now, when *I* ask you to come to the cinema with me, then you are 'exhausted'!

Then she screamed at me that I had *never* loved her, not like I loved Fredrik and Leo, that now she *knew* it. All her life she had been nothing to me, nothing but a nasty little rash, a *pimple*; oh yes, she saw it all now, it was crystal clear!!! 'Never, never' (if I remember her words correctly) 'had anyone been so afraid of her own family as she was of me, of Henrik, of Leo, of Fredrik'; all she wanted to do was to 'run away, vanish, never again have to share her bed with me, it was *unbearable!*'

Grabbing her coat, she had rushed out into the rain, Jean-Paul, leaving me alone in our hotel room. I felt dreadfully upset, became more and more frightened, more terrified for every hour that passed – and not just because of her cruel, unjust words, which are simply untrue! In the end I had had to take far more tablets than was good for me. I went out again and again and stood in the corridor to see if she was coming. *Dreaded* to think what could have befallen her. There wasn't a soul about, no one to confide in or turn to for help. Peter and Anne-Marie had left Paris and in my despair I very nearly rang you, Jean-Paul, but at that very moment she burst into the room.

It was well past midnight. Oh, Jean-Paul, she looked awful! Soaked to the skin, dripping wet, bedraggled, her lank hair clinging to her face, she was as white as a ghost – apart from that pimple, which was blazing! She must have been scratching at it; it was huge, scarlet, like one of those birthmarks, you know. And she *stank* of alcohol and nicotine. She fell to her knees, right there on the carpet, in front of me, sobbing. 'Oh, Mother, forgive me, forgive Jenny for being so nasty, so bad. She will never say such horrible things again!'

Like a little child she let me undress her, tuck her up in bed, all the while rambling on quite incomprehensibly about some flowers that had been stolen from a graveyard; how some apple slices that her grandmother had stuffed down her throat had choked her when she was Snow White; how she had 'gone from one bar to another with men hanging after her, but nothing had happened', no one but Jean-Paul was to touch her, though he wouldn't want to any more, not with the worms crawling out of this hole in her face, 'the worms that were eating her up as if she were already dead . . .'

That was how she had gone on, a lot of nonsense from beginning to end. Until suddenly she threw up all over the carpet (I'll never forget the stench!). I had to open both windows, wash her off and clean up the mess on the carpet as best I could. After a few sips of mineral water she calmed down a little but complained of a terrible headache. I gave her a couple of aspirins and half a sleeping tablet, smoothed some disinfectant cream on that vicious little spot and covered it with sticking plaster to stop her scratching at it. At which she got all excited again, began kissing and hugging me, mumbling on about 'this being the way it used to be when she was little and she had been ill and I had sat by her bedside; *now* I cared for her, and must never leave her again . . .' In the end – it must have been close on 3 a.m. – she fell asleep with her hand clasping mine. Naturally I didn't have a wink of sleep!

Then I told Jean-Paul, as best I could and even if I was afraid it would shock him, what Anne-Marie had said about the need to get Jenny to a specialist.

When I had finished, he looked both stricken and pale, very pale in fact, with his growth of black beard (he had obviously not bothered to shave that morning). There is no doubt in my mind that for a long time now he has been every bit as *scared* as I have that Jenny is heading for total mental collapse; but so far hasn't wanted to admit it, either to me or anyone else. It is my belief he is been fooling himself that his strength of character, understanding and *amour* will carry them both through a while longer, and that his refusal to see how *sick* she is, 'with her artist's tentacles always out, vulnerable, but *très intelligente*, definitely not mad or out of her wits', has simply been putting off the moment of truth and delayed anything being *done* about it! And this humane and considerate attitude of his, alas, has merely aggravated Jenny's deplorable condition.

For once he had nothing to say, no 'existentialist' theories, no psychological tirades, no more talk of an 'artistic' block; he could no longer take refuge in his embarrassingly hearty '*tout va bien*'s. Without a word he stood looking out of the french windows into their green but water-logged garden, its green lawns and trees wracked by autumn's gale-force winds. He seemed older, heavier somehow, than before we went to Paris, as if his worries over Jenny and the children had changed him physically, made his tread heavier, made him put on several kilos and engraved even deeper shadows under his eyes. His Parisian vivacity, his *esprit* had deserted him.

Finally he said: 'You are quite right, Aunt Charlotte. And so is Anne-Marie. Her verdict hasn't come a moment too soon. Something must be done, and soon. Otherwise Jenny's horrible life or death anxiety will be the end of her – and of me – and cause irreparable harm to the children. She can't go on like this. Nor can we. She can't go on living in what she called – only the other day – her 'hellish void'. I have a feeling that she, very early in her childhood, was as it were castrated, mutilated in some way – or rather, mutilated herself – so that some crucial bit of herself got lost.'

His voice faltered, dumb with a despair almost at breaking point. Even in this intimate moment he seemed to be making an almost inhuman effort to control himself. Something the men in my life, Henrik, Fredrik and Leonard, *never* do. Always they fly off the handle, rant and rave and then, tough and masculine though they may seem to outsiders, break down in front of me – and *expect me to feel sorry for them!* And I, being a woman, have had to put up with it. But Jenny's Jean-Paul is different. He is quite phenomenal. And in that moment I, too, realized how boundlessly this foreigner loves our Jenny and how much he has suffered on her account. More, even, than we have . . . (who, if the truth be told, weren't all that unhappy to see her safely married off, off our hands, so to speak). Just what he meant by 'castrated' was beyond me, nor did I trouble him for an explanation.

'I think you ought to know, Jean-Paul,' I said in a – for me – unusually humble tone of voice, as if trying to excuse myself, 'that Jenny was a most unusual child.'

Without in any way ever directly reproaching me for or accusing me of the way we, Henrik and I, had brought her up, he has a way of making me feel guilty about her and ransack my, our, conscience. Is it my – our – fault if she is a failure in life? Can't it be some inherited handicap?

'Compared to the boys,' I went on, 'she seemed characterless, withdrawn. But we really did *everything in our power* for her, *you must believe me*, my dear Jean-Paul! It is so painful to see her in such a state, she who was so beautiful, so talented . . . I remember how happy she was when her collection of poetry was accepted. And her bottomless despair after that stupid review. Whenever I think of Jenny, Hans Anderson's story *The Ugly Duckling* comes to my mind. She who was within an inch of becoming a swan . . .'

Ignoring my literary allusion, he sighed deeply, picked up some of the hard little pellets left on the carpet by Mikael's rabbit and threw them on the fire, in which was hardly more warmth than in the setting sun. And said: 'I'm so very grateful, Aunt Charlotte, that you've come to realize that something must be done. But a so-called psychoanalysis, which is what *cette Anne-Marie-là* recommends – and which I, too, of course, have long had in mind – would take a lot of time and above all money. My income simply isn't equal to it, no matter how hard I work! Vicky and Mikael ought to be off to boarding school, but that's impossible. The house needs modernizing and all kinds of repairs doing to it, we need to put in double glazing, get a new boiler and so on. I can't see how . . .'

'. . . How it could be done, Jean-Paul, my dear, is that it? Well, I have been giving some thought to the financial aspect too, and I have come to the conclusion that Jenny will simply have to take her share of my capital, in other words take out her inheritance in advance. There can't be any question of taking it off Henrik's pension. In fact, I would prefer Henrik to know nothing at all of our transaction. He is so dreadfully old-fashioned, as you know, and would never understand this analysis business. He has a petty bourgeois fear of spending money, watches every penny! But I have a little capital, left to me by my grandfather. As soon as I get back I shall arrange for my bank to transfer what you need. And I beg you, get hold of a clever psychiatrist as soon as you can and send me an estimate of how much it will cost.'

With a look of sad triumph in his eyes, he looked at me. I realized he had long been wanting to appeal to me for the help that was now, without any pressure on his part, being offered them.

'Je vous en remercie de tout mon coeur, ma chère Tante Charlotte. Vous êtes trop généreuse! But – can you really afford it?'

He bent down and kissed me with a warmth that touched my heart, yes, he would consult a certain Dr Shaw, whom he had been at school with, on Harley Street, the very next day . . .

It is about ten o'clock. I ought to tuck myself up in my bunk. But the ship's gentle rocking motion has induced in me a state of tranquillity that I have no wish to disturb. I remember Ma telling me how, even as an infant, I suffered from a strange restlessness and could never drop off to sleep like other babies do. In the end they had had to call on a 'wise woman', an old Dalecarlian peasant who had used her ingenious tricks to make me drop off. When I finally fell asleep in her arms or in my cradle it must have felt like it feels now, rocked in this ship by the sea. An unending calm, an ever-lasting repose. Well-dressed, well-fed Swedes, who have spent the day buying drinks, cigarettes, perfumes, silver, jewellery, etc., keep passing in front of me on their way to or from dinner, which I intend to miss. Lights from passing ships twinkle through the night, between a sea and a sky that at this late hour have merged into a single black whole.

My little diary has been put away, I'm too tired to write. Thoughts of my grandchildren come to me in vivid flashes, as if they were all seated around me here as they were those last few evenings, when Jean-Paul and Jenny went out and left them in my care. After they had had their baths, washed their hair and their little hands and nails had received a much-needed manicure, they clustered round me in front of the fire; clung to me in the stained old chintz sofa, whose yellow roses are turning grey, and asked me to tell them a story. How could I refuse? To the little ones I read *The Tomtebo Children*, with gentle little Jojo sitting sweetly in my lap and Rosalind, pink-cheeked and adorable, snuggled up beside me. She is something out of a fairy tale herself, little Rosalind, a `princess without a kingdom'. Then, after they had gone to bed, Vicky and Mikael (his rabbit is *still* allowed indoors!) demanded slightly more advanced entertainment, so I gave them a few glean-ings from my own childhood at Hedemora, which they found so fascinating they even forgot all about the television programme they had been planning to see, and even Vicky for once sat still without wriggling about or chewing the ends of her hair.

It was then I experienced a feeling of belonging to these chil-dren; a vital, inspiring feeling of belonging, burning like a diminu-tive fire between us. All the problems, age barriers and the so-called generation gap were wiped out, burnt away, and we became like one happy person. How I wish I were a young mother, could start all over again! Take on these darling children, each so talented in his or her own way, thirsting for love and so devoted, yet so gravely at risk as a result of Jenny's mental illness and Jean-Paul's busy, over-strained life and his mother's chilly moralizing – which I find utterly incomprehensible.

But of course it is quite impossible; my own advanced years and poor health forbid it. Yes, Henrik, my dear, we are in truth reaching for the final rungs of life's ladder before we fall off. It isn't easy for us to stand by and see our children and grandchildren's troubles towering up, after so many of our own, and having looked forward to a peaceful, relatively unproblematic old age, to at long last being able to live, as you are so fond of saying, 'like the birds in the sky and the lilies of the field'.

All we can do, my dear old Henrik, whom I'll be reunited with tomorrow, is to commend Jenny and her flock of little ones into God's hands and hope that He in His infinite wisdom and mercy has a hidden meaning with her life . . .

Wonder, finally, where and when I'll make my next journey – in spite of everything I'm hoping there will be one. Yes, I'm looking forward to it already!

ACT III

The Knife

Violet

Ugh, it's cold in Mrs Muriel's house, damp and nasty. Can't take my coat off, nor my woollies or wellies. Not until I've been out in the coal cellar, shovelled her coal into the bucket and lit a fire in her sitting-room, even before I draw those faded velvet curtains, not until then do I even start thawing out. And now I'll put the kettle on and make myself a cuppa before going upstairs with the old lady's breakfast.

This drag up from my own dainty little house with its violet-coloured door, all the way to Mrs Didier's at the snobby end of the high street, gets more and more tiring for each year that passes. Particularly on a morning like this, with the wind beating into me and ripping at me like it had a mind to tease me for being so little. Not that I mind being small, for some medical reason or other stopped growing at the age of ten. Not at all, I loves little things: small children, small animals, myself too . . .

On this particular morning she's still all tucked up under her eiderdown quilt, the one with pink roses on it. Her face looks ever so small and sort of yellowish like a Chinawoman's against the old lace pillow. Slamming the tray down on her bedside table, I shouts: 'Morning, sleepy head!' Fact of the matter is, she's getting to be a bit hard of hearing. I pulls back the curtains, takes the cosy off the teapot and noisily pours the old crone a nice cup of tea.

Yawning like an old cat, she stretches her limbs out lazily, and anyone can see she would rather not get up at all. Who does, come to that? There's them what can go back to sleep, and there's them what can't. Them what has beds with frills on their sheets . . . Not

186

me, not little Violet, standing scarcely four foot above the ground, she's always had to get up before dawn, ever since she was a kid! Eight of us there was, all crammed up together in a draughty little house in north London. There wasn't no opportunities for idling about there, I can tell you! House? More of a shack, really, 'cause I don't mind calling a spade a spade, even though it was my childhood home. Our mum would drag us out of bed into the cold grey smog, off to school, or to work if there was any to be had. My mum did too for the likes of Mrs Didier. Ladies of the kind what's above doing anything for themselves.

'Just a little bit longer, Violet,' she whines. 'I was up half the night playing bridge.'

She gives me such an obsequious look, humble-like, makes you wonder who's the boss around here.

Upper-class ladies, I ask you; with stacks of money, nannies, cleaners, cooks in the basement! Thought I'd end up a crack above my mum . . . That's a laugh! Charles hadn't got it in him, weak he was. Died in a sanatorium, leaving me to fend for myself and the boys. What was there for it but to grit my teeth and follow in my mum's footsteps. So there I was, on my knees, scrubbing and polishing, carrying heavy buckets of coal to them posh ladies' fireplaces, waxing their antique furniture, shining their silver, washing their blood-stained knickers and the unsavoury insides of the gents' underpants.

Charlie had his sick lungs; what a cop-out that was! Didn't do a stroke of work, just lay about reading his Marxist books, about how things *ought* to be! Me, more often than not I was in a mad fury, doing all the dirty work; but somehow it seemed the madder I got about them so-called social injustices the faster I worked, and those nice ladies was *ever* so pleased with their dear little Violet, thought the world of her they did! Oh yes, it had its perks, sometimes they'd slip me a little something, sweets for the boys, or a little extra. They'd be standing about, chattering, as I did the polishing or ironing . . . And all of a sudden they'd get confidential and start complaining about their husbands, or their kids, or their cushy lives, quilted like eiderdowns I always say, like I was their *equal* or something, socially like, not just their charlady, an unnaturally little one at that, who goes about with her heart in her mouth trying to make ends meet; pay the rent, feed her kids, put clothes on their backs and her own.

'Oh, and by the way, Violet, did you happen to see my son's car today?' she says.

'No, I didn't,' I answers, all pert. 'All I saw was the postman and the milk bottles, and I took them in, but left the postman outside. And if you ask me, your son's gone gallivanting off to the moon,' I tells her, jokingly. 'The way he rushes about, he's probably gone for good. So it's as well you gets up now, Mrs Didier, and turns over a new leaf, so to speak, and makes friends with that poor Mrs Jenny next door, now her mum's gone back to Switzerland and the two of you left all to yourselves.'

She starts up in bed, with her hair all on end, gropes for her falsies that are floating in a glass of water on her dressing table, and stutters out: 'You can't mean that, Violet, dear, can you?'

Goading her, grinning to myself like the Cheshire cat, I tiptoes back downstairs. It'll do her good to sit on the edge of her bed up there, unravelling them knots in the ball of yarn I'd flung her way, in my little gesture of playful ill will!

Perhaps it was on account of my littleness and my chirpy moods, 'cause I weren't really happy, just clowning about to stop them noticing how far down that black barrel I was, with no hope of getting the lid back off, or ever getting out again and seeing the light of day. Maybe I should've remarried, but I was too tired and worn out to get myself all dolled up for some affluent gentleman, and anyway who'd want a widow with two sons? And the sons didn't want no stepfather neither; not unless I'd managed to get myself something out of the ordinary, and men like that don't grow on gooseberry bushes. Anyhow, I listened to those missuses, every word they said, as they drowned me with their secrets, all that twaddle about their feelings, sometimes they'd start falling all over me, bawling their eyes out, just like they was little girls! I kept a kind of notebook in me head, where I made notes of the things they'd come out with, and I learnt a wealth of things my mum never spoke about; about the kind of feelings women can get in their private parts, and about male impotence, and 'nerves' and the like, which those rich people can afford to have, 'cause they've got the time and the energy for it and can afford some fancy physician for. I'm not saying we don't have things like that too, but we have to sit on it, swallow it – with alcohol, more often than not. It made me feel a bit queasy having those nice perfumed ladies half on top of me.

In my opinion, they was humbling themselves to the wrong person, 'cause I didn't care for their crying and their souls no more than what I did for their dirty laundry, and in me heart of hearts I wasn't the nice, understanding 'little Violet' they thought I was. They didn't know it, but me heart was as cold as Mrs Didier's house and so full of fury it was fit to burst! Charlie understood that, he knew I was mad, he liked me that way, I'll say that for him! He had his head screwed on all right, though he was taller than me, could have become a teacher, if he'd studied – but my mum, she said: 'Little Violet's a work of the devil, she is, with that foul temper of hers; I never saw such spite, for all her littleness!' And then she'd add: 'I'm warning you, if you've a mind to start moving them class barriers in this old country of ours, or if you and your sick husband Charlie wants to have a revolution, please yourselves – but don't expect them genteel folks to let you do it without putting a lot of difficulties in the way, 'cause they wants things to stay *just the way they are*, and'll make life hell for you! You mark my words. Your wicked temper and Charlie's red inclinations'll be the undoing of you. You'll end up in prison, the both of you, and get yourself deported to one of them colonies. No, I say, put up with it!'

That's what she said, as she scrubbed at the floors until her knees swelled and her back packed up and the rheumatoid arthritis forced her into a wheelchair, which was the worst thing that could've happened to her, 'cause if there was one thing she hated it was idleness! And now she couldn't even move her fingers to crochet. It was wicked, it was! God, how I hate to remember the sight of her poor, crippled body, contorted with the rheumatism, sitting in that wheelchair over by the fireplace; her sad eyes following us everywhere we went, like they were glued on us, stuck on her eight kids, when we come to visit her, our comings and goings, 'cause none of us could stand to stay, not with our dad there. He'd been laid off work, and would drink himself into a rage the likes of which I've never seen! Maybe it'd been there all the time, his rage, but he hadn't dared show it before, not until our mum started rotting away, disintegrating, giving in, despite her strength.

To tell the truth, I'm quite fond of old Mrs Didier. She's got her peculiarities, she's spoilt, thinking she's still a catch, at seventy (or seventy-five!). But she is reliable, not one of them gloomy old owls. She tells me all about that sinful city, Paris, and all those countries she travelled to with that famous husband of hers. It's as exciting as one of those series in *Woman's Own*.

She is raging mad, too, not like me and Charlie was but about her daughter-in-law, Mrs Jenny – can't stand her, she can't. Poor Mrs Jenny, creeps about like a sick lamb, she does. Oooh, I'd like to put a bit of marrow in that one, comfort her like, but the missus won't have any of that, even though she *is* a lady, knowing her place and not to confide in me, not without cause, that is; 'cause there are days she can't keep it to herself any more and lets me in on her suspicions. Sometimes she thinks Mrs Jenny's mad, sometimes that she is possessed by an evil spirit, like in the Bible.

There's always something amiss with her and her brats, and she's *ever so sorry* for that son of hers! No way can I let on that I'm drawn to Mrs Jenny, and that I feel sorry for her and her little darlings!

The old crone don't pay too well, either, not more than half-time. Time's sort of stopped for her. But she does give me things, precious things, like a silver bowl, several pairs of white lace gloves, a beautiful silk shawl, lots of things, and I can dress myself up in them and make my house look fancy, which makes me feel a bit like I'm a lady myself!

By one o clock I'm done with Mrs Didier. I fold my apron, pick up my shopping bag and shout 'Bye-bye, see you Monday!' to her where she is sitting over by the puny old fireplace, eating her cold lunch.

But as I shut her front door behind me, I get the feeling I ought to pop into young Mrs Didier's house, see to her and her little girls. I've always had sort of a little voice what whispers in me ear and it'd be foolish to disobey it. 'It's as if you had a guardian angel right there behind you, Violet,' my mum used to say, 'no matter that you've stopped growing, you've an angel of God behind you, no bigger than yourself, and that's why I never needs to worry about you!'

There is something not quite right about Mrs Jenny's house today, something grey and shut off. The windows in the front of the house looks at me from under heavy eyelids, and the front door, which is a dark red colour, isn't standing ajar like it usually does but is shut and staring at me in a most unfriendly way, as I stand there shivering in the mean wind. Like the shut entrance to a church when you wants to go in and pray for a while. Or the veterinary surgeon's office at weekends, when you comes running with a sick pup or a kitten in your arms. Shut. And I know how that feels, 'cause I've had a fair amount of them little beasts in my house since me sons grew up and left me.

The doorbell's out of order again and, failing to make myself heard, I give up knocking and walks right into their orange-coloured hallway, which is plastered with mould spots, filled with cracks and needs a good lick of paint and repairs done to it. Climbing over some muddy children's wellies and coats in a heap on the floor, I knock hard on the door that leads to their so-called day room. By and by little Rosalind opens up.

She's dressed herself up as a nurse and is wearing one of them white aprons with a red cross on the breast pocket and has an air of importance about her, like she's extremely busy, so I hurriedly says I won't stop, but she says it don't matter and could I please stay 'cause she's all on her own. All of a sudden she throws her arms about me neck, the little love, and she is trembling all over, seems to me she is upset about something. So I says: 'Where's your mum, dear?' but instead of replying, she flutters off like a butterfly in nurse uniform.

Well, I've seen some sights in my day but what meets my eye when I steps into the day-room takes some beating; there ain't no words to describe it. All I can say is it's like one of them modern paintings, everything topsy-turvy, and nothing looking like it does in reality, with people with green faces flying about and offering each other black flowers, and the sky's a blood red. Outside the window the donkey's dining off the newly planted bulbs, with the assistance of the dog, Tittine, who's having the time of her life scratching them up out of the earth. In the middle of the floor, sat half naked in her play-pen, is little Jojo, her eyes red from crying. Seeing me, she stretches out her dear pork-sausage arms and shouts: 'Mamma, Mamma!'

Next to the play-pen stands a birdcage, empty, the watering door wide open, its inhabitants, two budgies, having escaped and found themselves a perch up on the curtain rail, where they sits, chirping their blue heads off, free at last but not knowing what to do with their freedom. Seeing them sitting there like two blue spots makes me insides turn . . .

On the foreign white table-top two guinea-pigs are dancing a jig, dashing to and fro, squeaking anxious-like in their bewilderment, like they're trapped in a labyrinth. Flat on their backs, two teddy bears lies in the play-pen, their little tummies all bandaged up, the rest of them stuck with Rosalind's drawing-pin injections, staring up at the ceiling. From the whereabouts of the kitchen a steady stream of water is spurting out all over the floor.

'Heavens above!' I exclaims. 'What a circus!'

'Oh no, Violet, it isn't a *circus* ; it's Noah's Ark,' the little one corrects me. 'I'm playing Noah's Ark and I'm trying to save the animals from the flood *and* be a nurse at the same time. The teddy bears are being very good, but Jojo's *naughty* and won't let me give her any of my injections, even though they are not proper ones and won't hurt her! The water's from the washing machine and I don't know how to stop it . . .'

Double quick I takes me coat off and follows Rosalind into the kitchen. It's flooded out, water mingling with spilt cat's milk. The place is a mess, littered with unwashed dishes and half-drunk cups of tea, a frying pan, the black remains of eggs and bacon stuck to its insides, dirty jeans, wet socks piled up on the washing-up unit, and there is a nasty smell coming from the unemptied rubbish bin. Not holding out much hope, I turn to the family's he-cat, Pinky, who's round as can be, is just now lording it on top of the fridge, his eyes riveted on them two budgerigars what's got out. But his yellowy green eyes, what seems to express either something or nothing according to which way you sees them – they gives me a look of 'I'll thank you for not disturbing me, 'cause I'm *thinking*!'

It was all a bit much, even for little Violet. I found myself beginning to perspire. Something must've happened, there must be some explanation for all this, I think . . . Where's Mrs Jenny? Surely she can't have walked out on her little girls, not just like that?

As if Rosalind had read my mind, she says: 'You see, Rita went away last night. She left a letter, wait, I'll go and get it . . .'

She shows me a slip of paper, and with some difficulty I read:

To Mr and Mrs Didier

I can't stay here any longer.
I'm pregnant, and it's impossible, you see. I can't do all this heavy work any more. And I don't like being here anyway. Mrs Jenny's far too lenient, everyone does just what they want, and so there is a terrible chaos here. In my home everything was always very orderly, and I'm used to that. That's why I got knocked up here, and I can't go back to my parents, who would punish me most dreadfully. I'm at an unknown address, so that you won't find me or try and take me back, which I wouldn't anyway. I want to be left alone.

Rita

PS I have not taken Mrs Didier's gold heart, so don't set the police on me! I know I have committed other sins, but I'm not a thief.

'Bitch!' I say beneath my breath. But what can you expect from foreigners! Gone off with that road worker I suppose, the one who hangs about stripped to his waist by a hole in the ground, eyeing up all the women.

'She only told *me*,' Rosalind's saying with pride in her voice. 'She even showed me her tummy, with the baby in it! It was *this* big!' Demonstrating, she pulls up her frock and sticks out her tum. 'Mummy read me the letter. She was ever so upset at Rita saying she didn't like her . . .'

Picking little Jojo up out of the pen, I holds her close, saying 'hush' and giving her a biscuit to chew and some milk. I play with her toes, 'This little piggy goes to market, this little piggy stays at home . . .' And then I ask Rosalind: 'But where *is* your mum, dear? Is she down at the shops? Or is she up on her bed asleep?'

Rosalind looks me straight in the eye, her self-important attitude and her excitement all gone, and takes my hand.

'Put Jojo in the pen and I'll show you where she is.' Her voice is solemn.

Several steps up the crooked staircase, almost half way up, we find young Mrs Jenny Didier, sitting stiffly, not moving a limb, leant up against the wall.

'Mrs Didier,' I says to her, but she doesn't seem to hear me. 'Mrs Jenny, Jenny, dear, it's Violet!'

She doesn't stir. Could she be asleep? Since I can hardly see her face for all that hair hanging down in front of it I brushes it aside; the ends are split and need cutting. Her eyes are shut, her forehead cold and damp. She is grey in the face, kind of bloodless, and her cracked lips are moving, like they are trying to say something, but I can't make out a word. She won't answer me, isn't properly awake. She is miles away, somewhere where her little ones can't reach her, far from her untidy home, the guinea-pigs, them budgerigars, the unwashed dishes. I take her hands in mine. They are cold, with an unnatural bluish tinge to them. Clenched in the palm of her right hand, is a small gold heart with a pink rose on it. Her pulse is faint but fast.

'Rosalind, love, go and get me some water, there's a dear,' I say. She is back in a trice with a glass, but when I carefully try to get Mrs Didier to drink she won't swallow; and the water trickles down out of the cracked corners of her mouth.

'What's happened? What is it, love?' I asks her anxiously, not really expecting an answer. 'Oh, do try and drink, just a drop, please,' I implore her. But to no avail; she is like one of them wax dolls at Madame Tussauds.

'How long's your mum been sitting like this?'

Rosalind shakes her head. 'I don't know.' She sounds troubled. Screws up her eyebrows in consternation.

'Ages. No. Just before you came, I think. She came down the stairs to me and Jojo, and then she sat down, and sort of fell asleep. I didn't want to disturb her, because she's been crying all night about the gold heart . . .'

'What gold heart, love?'

'Not that one, that's *my* christening heart, I gave her that one. I mean her own gold heart. The one she gave to Vicky. But Vicky lost it – and we were out looking for it last night with torches and everything, but we couldn't find it! And then Rita left and this morning Mummy read the letter and Daddy didn't really want to leave her, but had to anyway, and he told us to look after her, but Vicky and Michael had to go to school, and that's why me and Jojo and the animals are all on our own . . .'

Throwing herself into my arms, she bursts into tears.

'Oh please don't go, Violet, please don't go!' she sobs, heart-rendingly. 'We need you much more than Granny does! I tried to stick a pin in Mum, but she still didn't wake up . . . She won't say anything and she won't eat or drink anything, not since, not since Mormor left . . .'

'When was that, lovie?'

'Well, it wasn't yesterday, no, I think it was the day before. I'm not sure. A long time ago, anyway. Mummy isn't dead, is she, Violet?'

'No, love, she isn't dead. She's just not very well. But why didn't you go into your Gran's and tell her your mum was sick?'

'I didn't dare,' she sobs, poor mite. ''Cause Granny doesn't like us . . .'

At that moment I hear footsteps downstairs in the lobby and the next, Michael, red-cheeked, hair all on end and soaked to the skin, walks in, throws his school satchel on the floor, bounds up the stairs and leans over his mum, calling to her: 'Jenny!' Not 'Mum' but Jenny. Slaps her face gently, then strokes her cheeks in a kind of resigned sort of way.

'I'd better call Dr Matthews,' he says worldly wise. 'If you and Rosie get her into bed . . .'

At long last – evening! Now I can settle myself down on their sofa and get some rest. It's a bit dirty but comfortable enough. I'll make myself a cup of tea. Phew, what a tiring afternoon!

It's a bit eerie, 'cause even though the house is filled with sleeping kids and all species of animals I feel a bit lonely, sort of anxious despite my tiredness. My little dog, Tiny, is asleep in the kitchen, snoring her head off. It was obliging of Michael to run down to my house and fetch her, but she couldn't have stayed there all on her own all night, not without her mum.

I hear the hoot of an owl, out there in the woods, in the thick fog. When I went out to put out the milk bottles I could scarcely see my own hands, it was that thick. Damp too, dripping with it! And someone was burning up old leaves, I could smell it in the air.

I never feel like this in my own home – kind of desolate, anxious. The feeling's boring a hole right into my insides. Maybe it's because the ceilings here are so high up, dwarfing me somehow. And the furniture's kind of odd, even though it is classy. There is a grand piano what Mrs Jenny sometimes used to play so nicely on. And a great big picture in a gold-leaf frame showing Our Lady , her son Jesus and a very old Joseph, though he's hardly visible. Mary isn't looking at her child but into the distance, into another world; a bombed-out, devastated garden, a wilderness, an overgrown place that no ordinary healthy person in their right mind could see. Maybe that's what's making me feel so on edge.

For a split second, just as I was laying her down in the unmade-up double bed, she looked up at me pleadingly, thirsty, like she wanted to drink me up. Her hand, the one clutching on to the gold heart, reached out for mine, she whispered: 'Violet, Violet . . .' On her face was a faint smile, as if she recognized me – like a kind of sparrow in the fog – she tried to hold on to me and mumbled something, but then just falls back on her pillow, opens the gate to that garden and vanishes . . . The look in her eyes! I recognized it, it was one of those hasty but penetrating looks that goes right into you, seeing everything; but at that moment Dr Matthews walked in and I couldn't recall where I'd seen it before. Now, with everything so quiet around me, I remember: it was the look in my mother's eyes, following us from her place in the wheelchair. The same pleading look, asking the impossible of us, before it went out for good, faded away into the blackest of grief, making us loath to stay by her side, making us want to run away as fast as our legs'd carry us. The way anyone would run away from suffering, dying. Though since then life's taught me different: it's the madness, the difficulties and us being doomed to death that is life, or anyway a part of it we've no right to cut off or run away from. No, we has to stay right where we are, biding and keeping watch; like we do with the little ones when they're sick, or with animals in pain . . .

I wonder what Dr Matthews meant by what he said when he came downstairs after seeing Mrs Jenny? It was me he had spoken to, not old Mrs Didier, who'd finally found her way into this house, only to be horrified by the disorder – not to mention Noah's Ark.

'Well, Mrs Walker, she is not too bright, I'm afraid. Try to get her to drink something. Most important. Seems she is in a state of exhaustion and semi-starvation. I've given her a shot of something to help her sleep, but I think it's probable we'll have to take her into hospital tomorrow . . . I very much suspect a case of nervous aphasia. And the kidneys are playing her up. Could you possibly stay the night here, Mrs Walker? Is there any possibility of getting hold of Mr Didier? And of course Mrs Didier will be of great help in this unfortunate situation, won't you?'

This with a quick, knowing glance at Mrs Muriel, who'd gone white as a sheet underneath all that rouge and powder of hers.

'Aphasia? What's aphasia?' she asked aghast.

'Greek for not being able to talk,' the doctor replied, all terse, picking up his bag and hurrying out to his red Mini. Mrs Muriel looked like a haddock with a hook in its mouth. Not disregarding the gravity of the situation, I had to laugh, she looked that funny! 'Not able to *talk*!' she echoed, gaping; an affliction as far as I know she is never suffered from. 'Oh, poor dear!' she said; seemed genuinely moved for once, even a bit doddery. But soon enough she gathers her wits about her, becomes every bit as heroic as no doubt she was during them air raids. Her son Jean-Paul, bless him, was naturally shook up good and proper when she rings him in France and tells him the news. He's promised to come home as quick as he can. Then she actually offered to cook supper for Vicky and Michael and play solitaire with them afterwards, if I'd see to Mrs Jenny and her two little ones.

It's taken some doing, getting this house in order. The older children gave me a hand with carrying out the guinea-pigs, but no amount of wheedling has been able to get them budgies off their perches up on the curtain rail, so they're still there . . . The little ones, Rosalind, in particular, wouldn't hardly let go of me when I'd tucked them up in their beds, all over me they were, hugging and kissing, making me feel quite giddy with happiness in the middle of all this misery. But that's life for you! I had a little girl too, once, Mary her name was, but she . . . How I wish Michael could only catch them bleeding budgies and put them back in their cages! 'I want to go to fairyland with you,' Rosalind said as we was hugging one another. 'D'you know, Mummy wants to go to a country that isn't *there* . . .' There's something not quite right with that little Jojo – but I can't put me finger on what it is. She's like a little plant Mrs Jenny's watered with her tears so long her roots are near enough waterlogged from all that anxious crying . . .

The last time I popped into Mrs Jenny she was lying very still, fast asleep, looking for all the world like a young girl, with her long fair hair spread out on the pillow. She is like a flower, delicate, too fragile to stand the knocks of life. Even so, it strikes me as a bit peculiar, it does, that she, who has everything life has to offer – a husband like Mr Didier, four darling children, a big house and plenty of money, so I presume, *and* love – just about everything old muggins don't have and never will – should go off her rocker, leaving her loved ones behind, off to some wasteland, or to that there garden – how should I know where. I'm so sleepy, think I'll lie down on the sofa, sleep rough, just this once . . .

. . . The baby's due any time now. My little body's so heavy with the child I'm expecting. Simply breathing's an agony, and my legs have swelled up really bad; I'm sitting here weary as my own mum, knitting this cardigan for the baby, but every now and then I gets this feeling inside of me, sort of a nagging anxious feeling, dragging me down. Outside our house, sitting in the sunshine playing his mouth organ, is my Charlie. The effort's making him cough, but that don't worry me, because the doctor's said his lungs are on the mend now. He's happy, and the tune he's playing is about his love for me and our first child, a tender, loving little tune, secret-like. Lost in a feeling he couldn't ever let out in words, he plays like there was no poverty or tuberculosis, no death – nothing but our love, our fumbling hot embraces, and our daily bread, scant but sufficing, and the life that's awaiting us thanks to this child that'll soon be born. But the worry is like a rope around my heart and the baby's not moving or nothing inside my bloated little body. Is it sleeping, maybe, having a rest before the grand effort it's about to make, before the great event of being born? My mum's swapped her wheelchair for the grave, and my dad's suffered two strokes, both at the same time, and is in the hospital now, looking like a sick ox with its mouth shut and body not moving an inch, lying there alongside the other remnants of human life. The only way he has of communicating his suffering to us is through grunts we can't make nothing of. But my child, our child, is going to even out all this death and dying and mourning, lift me and Charlie high above our miserable station in life, stuck away nowhere. This child will give us the courage to work for ourselves and others that lives the same lives as us, help us to rise against oppression, against all them what exploits us, as Charlie puts it, help us kick down them barriers that's holding us back; this child will set us free. In a different world, unlike the one we grew up in, knowing nothing but necessity. No, my child, our child, who is shortly to be born out of my stunted body what's anyhow female and ripe enough for its task, will give my Charlie the guts to tell the world all that stuff he's read about in those books of his. Then we'll be resurrected from our hard mattresses and the damp kitchens, the scouring-pails and other people's rubbish, and then, then we'll – what? What do we do then? What does he mean, my Charlie, my love, my revolutionary dreamer, sitting out there on the porch playing the Internationale in the sunshine, amid the daffodils and narcissi what's bursting into bloom? Do we, me and my child, really understand him? No we don't. Don't care to. Closed in on each other like we are, sitting on two ends of a rainbow, noticing nothing but our own warmth, cooped up together; because soon, very soon it's going to burst apart, our oneness . . . Suddenly realizing that I don't want to give birth, don't want to rupture, don't want the blood and the pain that takes away this treasure I have inside me, the only treasure I ever had in my hard-working life, Charlie's mouth-organ playing bothers me no end. It's grinding on my nerves, his false notes, his whining greeny-yellow tune like a nasty mixture of dandelions and spew. I can't stand it. Clumsily I stands up, the white ball of yarn rolls off my lap like a kitten, falls to the kitchen floor. And before I has a chance to stop his playing in flies this great big bird, right through our kitchen door, and heads straight for my tummy, my heart. Horror-struck, I shout: 'Charlie, get it away, *get it away!*' But Charlie's too little and lightly built to stand up against that big blue and black bird. It flaps its great wings around us, round and round, distracted, as if we was chasing it, like it was all trapped in and attempting to escape, beating its body and its wings against the window pane. Desperately I tries to catch hold of its wings; my fretting's turned into this bird, my reluctance to give birth turns into a rage against Charlie, the bird, myself, the self that only moments ago was all knotted up with the unborn baby. Making a last grab for the bird I fall, not gently, like that ball of yarn fell off from my lap, but heavily, like one of them old-fashioned flat irons, steaming hot, falling out of a hand that's burnt itself on me. With the water and the blood gushing out of me, I lie in a pool of my own red blood, a pain worse than Charlie's mouth-organ playing's tearing my insides apart. Moaning like my dad did with his strokes, like a sow led to slaughter scenting her own blood, I give birth to a dead child. A girl, a little Mary . . . 'Mary, Mary, quite contrary, how did your garden grow?' It didn't. I wouldn't let go of you, for hours I sits on my bed, holding you close to me, with that nursery rhyme going round and round in my head. In the end they tear you away from me, leaving me cold and trembling to wander along that same lonely path as this here foreign woman lying upstairs is wandering along now. Heading towards that same dreadful garden where, I believe, my Mary is . . .

I'm wakened by a sound like my red-hot iron falling to the kitchen floor. Dawn's broken. The light's streaming in. The sun's dazzling my eyes. Starting up, I hurries out to the kitchen.

There, on the floor, lying in a pool of blood, I sees Mrs Jenny, dressed only in her nightie. More and more blood is coming from her slashed wrists, already the tresses of her fair hair are tinted a pale red. Under the kitchen table I see the glinting blade of her carving knife.

Michael's coming down the stairs, two at the time. Shutting the kitchen door firmly behind my back, I shout out to him: 'Michael, call the ambulance! Your mum's had an accident!'

The Cell

Their faces hover over me, their contours are hazy, I can't hear what they are saying: I don't know them, they don't know me or my crime, that isn't how one speaks to a murderess . . .

This cell they have put me into seems to have floated up from the ground to the top floor, yes, even higher, the sky is so close I could almost touch it, if only . . . But these shadows, my gaolers, have tied me down to my bed. Soon my judges will be here . . . But here in this cell I'm not scared; there is endless light in here now, with the sky breaking through and the clouds touching my skin. Why is my hand too weak to touch them? My grandmother is smiling at me out of this great light, waving to me, smiling death's smile: don't be frightened, Jenny, don't struggle! My grandmother, who never cared for little girls, cares about me now I've committed a murder . . . Oh, Mormor, the deepest of all secrets lies in your smile, you could explain it all to me, but I'm too tired to listen . . .

And I see little cousin Jan too, also in that light, standing beside my bed, holding a model aeroplane. You are dead, too, Jan, aren't you, didn't you die ever so long ago? Yet you haven't grown at all, you are no taller than my Michael . . . You want me to come and fly your plane with you, Jan-Michael, is that it? But I'm too tired, haven't the strength . . . Now we are off, the earth is far below us, I can hear its church bells roaring, filling all space and my cell with their noise. It is Whitsun morning, I know; and I'm back in Sweden, that's why it is so light, no mists or fog between me and the sun . . . I'm running through long uncut grass, through long, long grasses, all upside down, waving in some summery meadow, filled with midsummer flowers . . . Michaelmas daisies, poppies, buttercups, cornflower . . . Father is coming closer through the poppies' red glow – Father, how I have longed for you! 'Tell me, Father, we've so much we must talk about. Time . . .' 'It's we who decide over time, Jenny, dearest; in my gold watch it's always creeping backwards. See, I'm holding it in my hand with your heart . . .' And there, lying in Father's hand, my heart is panting like some small red animal I daren't touch. 'Come along, let's visit my childhood home at Mörbylånga,' he says; but we have no sooner stepped over its threshold and caught a glimpse of my other grandmother's black dress and Father's little two-year-old sister sitting there on the floor under a tree that has grown up through the house than I'm in a desert, screaming for something to drink. Sand, only sand stretching away under a monstrous spider-like sun, like this one here on the wall of my cell! I must shut my eyes tight not to see that spider and all those loathsome little animals crawling around it: red-eyed mice, cruel armies of ants, eternally on the march, a yard-long worm that keeps falling apart only to mend itself again, tiny lizards darting to and fro, a tortoise slowly making its way up the pale-green wall. But the spider is worst, most wicked of all! It is on fire, burning! Oh, I'm suffocating, my throat is full of sand. Water, water . . . Someone I can't see properly gives me something to drink, it can only be Jean-Paul; his face is swinging towards me, coming and going. The water trickles down from the corners of my mouth, but it seems they have bound up my wrists in thick heavy bandages. Suddenly any number of people are standing all round me: it must be my judges who have come in . . . One of them is dressed in white; bends down over me.

'Mrs Didier,' he asks quietly but his words roll like thunder among mountains. 'Do you know where you are?'

'In prison,' I whisper.

'Why do you think that?' his voice insists, and the cross-stitch face is as huge and close as Mother's best table-cloth. Why is he hiding behind it?

'Because . . . because . . . I have killed my mother-in-law,' I answer wearily.

'Who are you?' Another question from far away.

' *Nobody*,' my lips mumble as if sprinkled with salt and sand and pepper. 'It's my punishment.'

'*She won't last*, her temperature is still rising . . . some infection must have set in, kidneys packing up,' mumble voices from space, as in an oratorio. Kidneys. Two little objects, I'm religiously cupping them in my hands as I go down to the sea that I hear roaring behind the sand dunes here in Denmark. There is a storm, the sea is a lion; but I will lay my little kidneys in its jaws to soak while I lie down on the beach and let the roaring, cold, shimmering green-blue breakers roll over me. Jean-Paul is on top of me in the sand. I would like to throw my arms around him, if I weren't tied down, swaddled, pegged down by all these needles and tubes they have stuck into me. He will have to take me as I am, love me without my loving him back.

'It wasn't my mother you tried to kill, darling,' his voice says. 'It was yourself . . .'

Words he has no sooner uttered than they become lies among all the other bubbles in the leonine frothing ocean all round us. I can neither understand nor reply to what he is saying because my tongueless mouth is a vulva, my lips labia . . . From out in the corridor comes a laugh. It is Leo, his footsteps. Why doesn't he come in, I want to see him a last time, before . . . But he is chatting up some policewoman, their sallies of laughter reach me in deafening gusts as the sea does. Father is sitting on the edge of my bed, stroking me with frail, trembling fingers; it hurts a bit, but the pain is lovely, makes all the other noises go away. 'You only did what was right, my girl,' he is saying in his pulpit voice. 'Here's five kronor for killing Krabatska. People who poison our lives must always be killed off. Jesus said so.' I long for him to cleanse me with the snow all around, it's snowing, we are in a desert of white snow in the Söderhamn forests. 'Please, Father, cleanse me of my sins, I can't go on much longer . . .' The cell door is flung wide open. An icy draft blows in.

'Hello there, sis! How're you doing? Oh, for chrissakes, what's it to you that you've killed off that old witch! Dead or alive she was rotten to the bone anyway. Look, let's fly off together to Tokyo and leave all this wretched business behind us . . .'

'But I have no clothes,' I whimper. 'Well then, make yourself invisible, like when we used to play hide-and-seek and you fell asleep inside that old chest up there in the attic, remember? Come on, hurry up, because I'm conducting Lohengrin tonight.'

Lohengrin? Who's green grin or smirk is he hiding behind? Don't know. Couldn't care less. I have no more need for alibis. I'll hide behind my children. They will protect me from all our neighbours in Lindfield, who have burst into my stone house at dawn, armed with mops and buckets, shouting as they wave their yellow dusters: 'What this place needs is a thorough spring-cleaning! Your garden's an eyesore, a pimple, your crime an act of madness! Why haven't you brought down all those spiderswebs from the ceiling? Well, now we're going to make a clean sweep of you and your snotty-nosed urchins . . . !' Most of all I'm afraid of Ulla Trots and the rattlesnake raising its ugly head out of her bucket. How has she got in? She who used to be so horrid to me and Marie in primary school; sneering at me with her protruding nail-like teeth, the skin taut over her high cheekbones and her quivering blotchy neck sinews: 'Here's what you get for leaving us nothing to talk about, so we can't talk badly of Jenny any more.' But in the nick of time I evade the broom she is about to bring down on my head, grab hold of the children and with them find myself walking along a sunbeam in the company of three nuns on their way to Notre Dame, to Mother . . . Sunk in praying for souls in purgatory they have no words. I'm running through the streets of Paris, alone, through a sombre, pink sunrise. Where are the children, where is the candle Mother gave me, that wan, two-franc candle she asked me to light for her when she . . . Is Mother dead too? I must ask Marie, standing here by my bedside. How lovely she is, how infinitely tender and full of compassion and sorrow her eyes are, like these two golden-brown roses she's laying on me. But she doesn't reply either, just turns her head towards her Ragnar standing there stiffly, black funeral tie against his white collar. Then bends down and kisses me. Oh, why am I tied down like this, I who want so to kiss you, my own little sister; but all you do is lay a bunch of keys on top of the roses. 'To Memory's Closet and the gate to our garden!' And are gone. To an accompaniment of suppressed organ music Fredrik comes hobbling in on his crutches, followed by his red-haired Diana. She is shamelessly swilling vodka out of a bottle and immediately they start up a loud quarrel, trying to drag me out of bed. Their flushed, furious faces, their hatred, fill me with pain: 'Come on now, Jenny, you stupid little thing, decide! Tell us who is right? Who is wrong?' 'Oh, Jean-Paul, Jean-Paul, you who once saved my life, please, please take them away!' But Diana hits out at Fredrik, knocking him over, and then kicks and stamps on him . . . Poor Fredrik, poor Diana, why are you so cruel, so dreadfully cruel to one another? You make me weep and weep . . . Wasn't that my Vicky who just now rode through this prison cell on her donkey and out of the window? Michael, Oh, Michael, darling, how sweet of you to come all this long way with that huge television set – though Mummy, my darling, won't ever be watching television any more, never again . . . Where's Rosalind, where's Jojo, my youngest? Why is she sitting all alone on the floor of this world's temple, crying, while Rosalind toys with the beads of a black rosary. Stop it, I say, you are not to play marbles with religion, it's dangerous . . . Throw them away, do you hear me, at once!

Why is it so hot in here, so cold? It's summer, isn't it? So why am I shivering? Maja is sitting with her bandaged thumb on my bedside. What a long way she must have come. She is explaining why I . . . her bandaged, bleeding thumb . . . I don't quite understand . . . Has she found my gold heart out there in the garden? Oh, what a relief, no need to wash myself any more, now that my heart has been found. All sins forgiven . . . Water, blood, gold, stone, light, sins, found, hearts forgiven, candles lit. No more washing, ever. Face-flannel gone, wash-basin cracked, eyes screwed down, voices behind locked doors, further and further and further away . . .

Jean-Paul

I have been sitting by her bed all this evening and half the night. She was in a terrible state, rambling deliriously, seemed to be going from one place to another, tormented by thirst, by people she imagined were in her room. I am so exhausted, so confused, I understand nothing any longer. She is in some timeless, feverish world of her own imagination. And all this a whole week since it happened! At first things didn't seem too dangerous, but then she suddenly got worse as complications set in – this kidney infection, the high temperature. And she began going on about having killed my mother. Thought the doctors were her judges, the nurses policewomen, her room a prison cell . . . and now Dr Vlemingck here in the London clinic is leaving me with hardly any hope at all. 'I'm sorry to have to tell you, Mr Didier, but your wife's state is extremely critical. She is sinking, she is weaker than she ought to be. We are doing all we can, but . . . perhaps, Mr Didier, it will be best if you stay the night . . . '

I'll never forgive myself for being away, even though I couldn't help it. Michael and Rosalind say that she didn't eat or drink anything after Charlotte left. But Vicky thinks it was the little gold heart getting lost and Rita suddenly leaving us – that impertinent letter – that brought on the crisis. I'm trying to catch up with all this . . . Of course she was still full of morphine when she . . . slashed her wrists, didn't know what she was doing . . . Dr

Matthews didn't know Jenny is allergic to the stuff. Always has been. Thank God Violet has stood by us, is looking after the kids and doing the cooking. All she has said is how she found Jenny on the stairs 'in a faint'. Matthews thinks it must have been some kind of a shock that brought on the aphasia – very rare state indeed, he says. Luckily none of us have told my mother exactly what happened and the little girls didn't understand anyway. All my mother knows is that Jenny is in hospital in London. Not to be able to confide in one's own mother in such circumstances is tough, but she would only get all upset, start moralizing and criticizing, and that would be more than I could stand. Best to keep her in the dark.

Jenny, Oh, Jenny, my love, why did you have to do it? Why did you have to cut yourself? How can you have felt so alone, so self-destructive, so far from the children and me?

Again and again my thoughts come up hard against this incomprehensible fact, against Vlemingck's near-final words. Against stones. Darkness. Death. Jenny's death. That the woman I love so is going to die . . .

If only I could pray. Here, now, in this winter night, in the dim corridors of this hospital, in this cubicle they have let me have to tonight, I would pray, if only I knew who to pray to, or how . . . God? He is somewhere far away in my childhood. Beyond reach. Without Jenny my life is over. No love. No happiness. No future. A black starless existence. The children? They're standing here bewildered, waiting, can't grasp what has happened to their mum. Only Vicky knows she is dying. She came during visiting hour, took a look at her, tried to control herself, but burst into tears and cried and cried, till I sent her home. Only adults are privileged to know about death. It's icy cold. Soon Christmas. Sleet is falling over London's one million houses and streets. But Jenny thinks it is Whitsun, 'time of ecstasy'. There are moments when I feel she is walking in her Swedish summer meadows. And if it has got to happen I hope it will be in one of them, among her 'own flowers'. God, if you want me to slash my own wrists, destroy myself, *anything at all* to save her life, let me know what it is. At once!

For the sand is running out in her hour-glass. So at last in my desolation of heart I cry out to Him. Impulsively in my distress to Someone who long ago perhaps watched over me in a cold English nursery.

The night nurse touches my shoulder.
'Mr Didier, Mr Didier, wake up.'
'Is she . . . ?'
The nurse gives me a cup of tea. 'Drink it before it gets cold.'
'Is my wife . . . ?'
'No.'
She looks so young, cold, too. Wearing a grey cardigan over her uniform. Grey London dawn behind two uncurtained windows. 'Your wife's awake. She's very weak but fairly clear in the head. Wants a word with you.'

She is expecting me. Her eyes seem to fill her emaciated face. I have to sit very close, very close indeed. Her voice is weak but she knows where she is, what she has done. Suddenly remembers everything. It was only in her delirium that she thought she had killed my mother. 'She is still alive, isn't she?' I nod, can't help a tear or two trickling down on to her hand. But she begs me not to grieve, not be unhappy. She is still quite lucid, almost feelinglessly so, seems in a hurry. It will be best for her, for us, she says. Anyway she can't go on living wracked by anxiety, a burden to herself and others . . .

Leaves everything she possesses to me, only doesn't want to be buried here in England but up in Dalarna 'under the big silver birch'. Then she whispers something I don't understand about lighting a candle for her rather than for her mother. Closes her eyes, seems to be resting so that she can go on. Wants Violet to take over the children, console them – 'particularly Jojo, she never wanted to be born, no more than I. Happier before . . .'

For a few moments she looks at me in a way she never has before. It's unbearable. Then she dozes off again, becomes quite still as if she were at home listening to music – only so white and worn. On her way away from me, from the children. Where to?

I rest my forehead on the blankets. Can't weep, feel only utterly powerless. A long while I sit like this, with only one thought: that our long struggle has been in vain. Dawn turns into early morning, Jenny is still breathing, is still alive. And I'm still not all alone in a world that without her will always be one long, grey winter morning.

'Mr Didier,' says one of the nurses who keep slipping in and out of the room, taking her blood pressure, feeling her pulse, adjusting her drip, observing her. 'She asked to take communion today. We have an Anglican clergyman who comes to us on Sunday mornings. Did you know?'

No. Nor that it's Sunday morning.

With the consultant

'Not so fast, my friend!' Dr Vlemingck interrupts my excited monologue. 'You always tend to get stuck in psychology.'

He takes his time. I sit here observing him silently, without another word. A robust middle-aged man possessed of a special sensitivity, at once quick off the mark and lingering, soft and sharp, all that at once, or nearly, only a step apart. Just now, here in his surgery, I feel as if I were a patient myself, as weak as water, depressed even though I ought really to be relieved. No. Today I see everything draped in black. What Charlotte calls my usual 'mindless optimism' lies in ruins. It is like during the war, when one stepped ashore after surviving those torpedo attacks. All of a sudden one felt so terrified one could hardly stand up on the dockside.

'Against all the odds we've managed to bring her back over the threshold, out of the crisis.' Vlemingck goes on, as if from far away.

Could it be that I simply don't believe Jenny will ever change? Be the same lovely, cheerful, vivacious person she used to be only a few years ago? Do I really wish it had been the end?

The world outside these Victorian brick walls has begun to wither away, my work has become unreal, irrelevant. I have only been home twice. Hardly recognized the place as my own, everything so scrubbed, polished, shining, tidy. Governed by odd little Violet – whom the children adore – and by her overfed Tiny (whom Michael, not without reason, has rechristened Smelly), the house received me like a guest, a stranger, a tramp at the end of his tether. In these rooms without atmosphere it was as if Jenny had never existed, as if their impersonally gleaming mirrors had never set eyes on her, as if her hands had never so much as touched the record-player, now dusted off and put away; as if she had never lived, slept or loved in the immaculately made-up double bed that seemed under lock and key. As if her troubled soul, her anxiety attacks, but also her at times no less exaggerated *joie de vivre* and her passionate love for us all had been rubbed away with Ajax, soap and furniture polish. Only Tiny's fartings pierced the odour of Dettol. And of me. And much though I relished Violet's Yorkshire pudding, the neatly laid table and the children's unnaturally saintly manners, I felt a pang at my heart. Sipping my mother's sherry, the thought tormented me that perhaps it would have been better if Jenny *had* died. Everything *seemed* so much better, more peaceful, without her.

Isn't anyone indispensable?

There was a sadness in the eyes of Vicky, Michael and Rosalind – a great empty question mark. So many questions passed unspoken between us! In their hugs when I left again, in their hasty English kisses, their whispers so that Granny shouldn't hear 'give Mum a hug from me', 'Tell Mum we are always thinking about her', 'Ask her to get well soon', 'When can we come and visit her?' – in all this was an immense barely suppressed love. Only a contented Jojo clung to Violet, who dotes on her chubby little protégée. Rosalind gave me a drawing to give to Jenny: it shows a mother, as thin as a matchstick, in a frighteningly high bed and a girl who, likewise matchstick-thin, is running towards it with a bouquet of roses in her sticks of arms. In the blue sky above them a golden yellow heart.

'I can so well understand that you are trying to find some sense in all this chaos,' Vlemingck goes on calmly. 'Some leitmotif in her ego-dystonic fantasies. To be quite honest, I pay very little attention to what delirious patients babble on about. Rather, in that case, it would be that Rorschach test that you say was taken in Sweden in the fifties and which even then revealed strong suicidal tendencies, which could tell us more . . . You say she is obsessed with mirrors. Well, your celebrated compatriot Lacan, my colleague in the psychoanalysis business, has written a big book about all that – unfortunately it is quite beyond me, probably because of the lousy translation. Though he must have got his basic notions from dear Dr Winnicott. All we see in a mirror is ourself, isn't that so? Or do we? But I'm just a doctor, a medico. And just now we won't get anywhere peering into your wife's doubtless very traumatic past. What we have got to do here in this clinic is pilot our patient back into life again.'

'No one can be forced to live who doesn't want to,' I observe gloomily. 'How do you think she'll react when she really comes to and realizes she has got to try?'

My words seem to reach him only as an echo of the words from so many other worried next of kin. His whole dreary office is staring at me with the bored look one gives someone who is senile and never stops repeating the same silly question.

'Nowadays we have excellent drugs for psychological problems. For a while we'll just keep her more or less asleep. It's unavoidable, if we are to get her on her feet again. And please don't ask me for prognoses,' Vlemingck adds hastily. 'Her psychotic and suicidal tendencies will probably remain, you must always bear that in mind, no matter how well, physically, she may be. But we are always here to turn to!'

'But in that case,' I interrupt, 'wouldn't psychoanalysis be best? As I have told you, her mother's already sent me some money for . . .'

'Use them to pay our fees here at the clinic,' he says abruptly, a shade irritated. 'I'm afraid it's going to cost you quite a bit. It's still too early to tell. And her problems probably lie very deep. Speaking of her mother, I have a feeling she is a key figure in this drama. The crisis seems to have been unleashed when she left.'

'Yes, but it was *my* mother she thought she had killed?'

'Can we be so sure? The mother figure. The fairy godmother, the evil witch. In her state of mind there may have been a sort of double exposure.'

I'm too tired and confused to understand.

'Well, in that case, why did she try to take her *own* life?'

'The infant, Mr Didier, has no life of its own. It's all one with the mother. Originally it's not aware of any difference between itself and its mother. And in a deeply regressed person everything melts together again. Though, as I say, just now I'm not all that interested in psychology. I suppose someone's looking after your children?'

'Couldn't be better cared for. A . . . a friend of the family – and my mother.'

'Who I hope is in the best of health? And will now at last have a chance to get to know her own grandchildren?'

Dr Vlemingck – for the first time – smiles broadly. Then at once turns serious again.

'But, not a word to the old lady that she's been murdered!'

Suddenly I feel monstrously sorry for my mother, that lonely, excluded, self-excluding woman. It feels as if Jenny had really assaulted her.

'Leave your wife in our care a few days,' Dr Vlemingck says, getting up out of his well-lubricated swivel chair. 'Take a room in a nice quiet hotel and get some sleep.' And adds humorously, amiably, 'And remember: love can go too far. Look after yourself, Mr Didier, or it will be you who'll be our next patient!'

These Strange Days . . .

There is nothing terrifying about being close to death. It is a new kind of rapture, an intimation of eternity. Though the street noises float up from far below, they don't disturb me. Gusts of muffled music reach me faintly, broken, as if played on our old virginals some evening long ago when the embers in the fireplace gave a last spurt of flame before going out and the only light came from the candles in the two brass candlesticks as they gasped for breath and dripped ephemerally away into the darkness. Or can it be the sea, which at times drowns out all other sounds? The tide coming in on the shore? It would be so easy to let the waves snatch my body and for a moment experience again an immensity of sea and sky, as in that early summer morning in Devon, and then, unresisting, sink . . .

Suddenly I feel scared at my weakness. From immeasurable distances children's voices cut through to me. A hand, a man's hand, encloses mine and his tears are falling on it and his forehead pressing against it. Inside me a struggle begins, a return to my loved ones. Death's smile fades. I tear myself lose from it. Begin a strange grey journey through shadows. Little by little I struggle out of their immensity and see again his tormented face, a face pierced through with a love I have perhaps never before really grasped. I too would like to shed tears, but the long way back is so difficult, life down there so unliveable, and yet I both must and will go back to it . . .

Strange days, floating past. A river flowing between soft banks. For long moments I am lost in dreams more real than the reality around me; than my room in this hospital with its everlasting pale-green walls; than the nurses, especially the plump coffee-coloured one who is looking after me as if I were her child, making me drink, getting me to swallow just a few morsels of food; she washes me, plaits my hair, helps me up out of bed over to the chair and back again, all the while smiling her gleaming white Jamaican smile. I neither may nor need to do anything for myself. Their pills and injections have plunged me into a voluptuous twilight trance. At long last, after a life filled with fear, I'm allowed to rest from it. I'm so tired, so weak. Sometimes I wake up and call out for Jean-Paul and the children. Then it is as if I were searching for something I have lost, just what I don't know . . . But it is never long before they help me to doze off again, relieve me of it.

Where is he? Where is he? Exhausted though I am, I long to make love to him. Often in my dreams we are making love and the orgasm comes – it is ages since I have felt it that way . . . Our love-life has been a flight from terror for so long, without any real enjoyment, a moment of security and darkness, a pause taken together with him, like my 'dark weather' moments with Father when I was little; or else a game of make-believe, an effort, for Jean-Paul's sake, that I was no longer really up to making – all wrong, how wrong . . .

It is so empty here now that he has gone. It must be several days since he was here. The doctor says he is celebrating Christmas at home with the children. Poor, dear Jean-Paul, my poor children! Why have I wrecked everything for them? It will take aeons of time to make up for it, expiate it . . . Christmas? Surely just now it was Whitsun? How quickly time has gone by, it's these pills. I can't keep track of anything. Outside my window the air is heavy with wet English snow. One day they sang Christmas carols and left my door ajar. A few inquisitive faces peeped in at me and were quickly shooed away, but I caught a glimpse of paper chains and tinsel. On my bedside table there are some Christmas cards, along with a Swedish candle and a pink hyacinth, whose scent is so strong I have asked them to take it away, but they haven't . . . And from Mother and Father a letter that I have neither the courage nor the strength to read. Not yet. They must be terribly angry with me for what I have done. But I often look at Rosalind's drawings and read Vicky's and Michael's little letters.

These strange days . . . A new fumbling life, lying here listening to everything that has lain buried deep down in me for several years like someone buried alive in their cellar after an air raid or earthquake. Few survive, mostly the rescue teams find just corpses, though sometimes they get to them in time, reach down helping hands and drag them, apathetic, suffering from shock, back to life . . . But what kind of a life? To search among the ruins, among the rubbish and rubble that was once their possessions in feeble hope of finding a saucepan, a screwdriver, a blanket, a poem? From the depths, several poems. For me, life's barest essentials.

Why am I, today, so painfully, so fiercely aware of Father and Mother, of their unidentifiable suffering that stamped its hallmark on everything? Why, ever since I was little, without understanding it, have I tried to carry part of their burden, always been their anxious, meekly admiring shadow? A child weighed down by their cross? Why must they for ever carry one? An insight that throws a sharp merciless light on my whole life, cracked and distorted like a broken mirror. Can it ever change? Do we ever see the truth about those we are most inwardly and tormentedly tied to? About oneself?

Just now I don't think so.

The doctor smiles at my little cracked mirror lying on my bedside table. The one I had with me in Paris.

'Ask your husband to buy you a new one, Mrs Didier,' he says encouragingly.

'I don't want one,' I answer.

A long while he looks at me, thoughtfully. No comment.

Jean-Paul

In my dream I have lost Jenny, she has vanished. We are out looking for her, the children and I. Deep in the woods we come across traces of her, a bracelet, a slipper, a scarf. And finally track her down to this moss-clad house where she is in hiding among these dwarfs but can scarcely recognize us. Nor we her. Once so thin, she is now plump and rounded, almost fat, and wearing a white maternity dress; dark, uncombed tresses hang down around her pale face; she stares so strangely at us out of empty eyes. The children, terrified at the sight of this absent, indifferent mother who isn't theirs, scatter, run away. Leave me alone with the dwarfs. Strange little all-knowing beings, they are trying to explain that for some unknown reason she has taken refuge with them. They ask nothing of her, these ugly little red-nosed beings, yet complain that she won't keep house, won't use the huge broom to sweep up with or cook them any food like the real Snow White did. Good-natured, they don't want to turn her out to become a prey to wild beasts in the wood. Even so she is a parasite, a problem-woman, has no place in their fairy-tale. And despite their wisdom they are worried, don't know what to do. They tell me she is obsessed with mirrors and though they have hidden them all away she always manages to find new ones. When they go to hammer out silver in the woods and leave her on her own, an evil fairy comes and visits her, and though they have forbidden her to have anything to do with this fiendish woman, she sells little mirrors to her. It is this last mirror that has killed her by showing her something she couldn't stand; just what, the dwarves don't know; they are completely at a loss. Without any transition, she is lying in a coffin that the dwarfs have made for her; she is not like my Jenny, this dark-haired, swollen, terrifying female. Yet though I know, in some obscure way, what the fairy tale expects of the prince – a kiss of life – I am overwhelmed by fierce lust and in front of the dwarfs, shocked yet delighted, I pull off my trousers and rape this dead woman, pumping up and down inside her till I have a tremendous ejaculation. Then I notice that her soft, wet genitals are twisting and turning underneath me and she yawns, a wide-open, scarlet gape, and her empty eyes open. So – she isn't dead, has only pretended to be, deceived both me and the little men! Suddenly she smiles at me, a sarcastic, humiliating smile, and gives a disgusting, voluptuous groan. And in the same instant I know this *is* Jenny, the other side of my lovely, refined Jenny. I have under me a wild, sensuous, greedy, destructive woman. In a fit of rage I strangle her. But no sooner have my hands let go their grip on her throat than the real Jenny is lying there, as in her hospital bed. A woman consumed by torments and pain yet transfigured by a quiet purity. Then, suddenly, all that is left of her is a crushed rose whose white petals the dwarfs' coarse withered hands are grabbing at as they are blown away by the wind. Their hymn-like lament rips my dream to pieces and I wake up . . .

Sweating all over, bewildered, I try to understand my own dream. What can it mean? I have never lived in a fairy-tale. Have I read *Snow White* too often to Rosalind? It shakes me to the core that I'm capable of rape and murder, even if only in a dream. My feelings for Jenny are infested with guilt, split, defiled. Surely this horrible dream is only a reaction to the shock she has given us all? I try to calm down, tell myself I'm overwrought, that I have been living too long in the stuffy hospital atmosphere, approached too close to the edge of that nothingness we are all terrified of . . . But I don't succeed. Have I ever loved Jenny? And what do we mean by loving someone? That I'm in some way fastened in the mesh of her tangled being, have drowned in a desire that has robbed everything else in life of meaning – and that this has been my irrevocable *choice* – is obvious. And such a choice can only be the starting point of one's entire existence. Such limitless giving – even if only to survive – must surely create a hidden resentment towards the person who is so utterly charming and befuddled. Otherwise one would be letting oneself be ruled and made a fool of *ad infinitum* – what a temptation to the other party! Especially, perhaps, for a woman like Jenny, who knows no limits.

Limitlessness belongs to art, not to life. And she has given up her art. None of her family accept any limits,which is why they are always putting a stop *to each othe*r, which is perhaps just as well. Such individuals don't draw the line at murder, they kill either themselves or others, anything as long as they get their own way. Not to get one's own way, for such a person, is death . . .

Everything is going round and round in my head. What did Jenny really mean by her suicide attempt? Was it just an expression of her extreme despair, her fury, her resentment at her mother going back to Stockholm; or was it a primitive desire to give another turn to the screw under which we are all pinned down? No sense in asking her; she would just stare back uncomprehendingly out of those china-blue eyes of hers and say I must be overwrought even to ask so stupid a question. Is everything just a tragedy then or, rather, a grotesque horrible comedy that she is subconciously exposing us all to, *daring* to expose to us, because she knows we all love her? At some level unknown to herself is she confusing us with her parents and brothers in her childhood? Don't know. Impossible to say. Perhaps we've all got uncomprehending, all-knowing devils inside us? Dwarfs?

Maybe everything will get better now, at least for a while. Why, incidentally, did she react so violently to Vlemingck's parting words? After all, they were only a joke. Does some part of Jenny hate me? Would she really like to shake me off, shake us all off, but daren't? That wouldn't really be so strange, boring as I have become as a result (at least so I tell myself) of carrying such burdens. I who was once such an apostle of freedom! I don't even amuse myself any longer with my everlasting talk, my analyses of everything under the sun. But though I really try to understand her – and I mean understand at a deeper level – perhaps she doesn't *want* to be understood, even though she is always begging to be? To really understand someone is to gain a kind of power over them so that they become to some extent in one's thrall and have to cast their behaviour in the mould of the other person. Understanding! In which case could her incomprehensible act have been a kind of attempted escape to free herself by hiding in the chaos of everything that is incomprehensible, even if it should cost her life? Don't know. It's possible. Fragile as she is, Jenny is peculiarly strong. Has had to be, in order to survive what she experiences as the everlasting power struggle of family life. She must have learnt every trick of the spiritual trade at an early age, even the most lethal. No, I mustn't underestimate 'my' Jenny, who acknowledges no limits. Never has. Never will . . . That is where the immense difference between her and the rest of us lies. In her own odd way she is as great a virtuoso as her genius of a brother. And the sad thing is that no one appreciates her deathly arts, while the whole world admires his, as he stands up there on the concert podium, overcoming death with his magic wand. Oh, Jenny, if only you could begin writing your poetry again! Don't you realize that your conductor's baton is lying gathering dust up there in your writing room? Why is it too heavy for you? If you could, you would gallop away again on your imagination's white steed, instead of yourself being ridden by the evil black mare. And in a flash everything would be quite different, I'm sure of it! Imagination is always true to itself, and imaginative people have no choice. Either they must commit themselves to it, use it – or drown. No one plays with fire and doesn't get burnt.

Christmas day has been no fun here at home. Michael and Rosalind took endless trouble to deck out the Christmas tree with tinsel, colourful shiny balls and the little straw stars and blue and yellow paper flags that Charlotte had sent them in her Christmas parcel; but despite that, and all the little presents that they had saved up their pocket money to give each other and me, it was as if the law of everything's impossibility – Jenny's favourite expression – had got in the way. What a wretched little row of Christmas cards, this year, hanging on red string across the day-room! I couldn't help thinking of all the ones we used to get, even only a couple of years ago, when Jenny – except for a few 'down' periods – was still herself, baking, cooking food and arranging parties for our friends and the children's. Where have all those supposed friends gone? A few, a very few distinctly eccentric faithfuls apart, most have abandoned us, especially this last year. They are as scared of Jenny's 'mental illness' as of cancer.

I had only stepped in through the door after getting some sleep at that hotel when along came Violet with Jojo in the pram and Smelly dragging behind on a leash, saying she was ever so sorry but she couldn't possibly stay with us for Christmas. Has her own family, of course. Though she would be only too happy to take little Jojo with her; her own sons have small children and perhaps I – and my mother – would find it easier without the baby? Hoped Mrs Jenny was feeling better and would soon be home again. At this point she broke off and looked up at me with that unfathomable, quizzical stare of hers that always makes me suspect some guru's or prophet's soul has taken up its abode inside our petite charlady.

Of course she didn't let us down, gave us a hand as long as she could, though she is no chicken and not quite up to the heavy work as she used to be. She looked rather wrinkled and weary, like a half-withered violet in an egg cup with too little water. Kissing her cheek gratefully under the mistletoe I stuffed a crumpled fiver into her pocket, feeling utterly ashamed of myself. And in that instance realized she had been one of the dwarfs in my dream! Jojo, too, all white and angelic looking, got a kiss and a hug and made no objections about being carted off away to some unknown rave-up. It felt a bit sad, seeing our youngest go off and leave us on

Christmas Day, but in my dulled state of mind a certain indifference came to my aid.

In the house the mood was tense, overstrained. Michael looked depressed as he went off to church to sing carols in the choir and Rosalind seemed shy, not altogether well perhaps. Suddenly I heard wild sobbing coming from upstairs, from Vicky's room. I ran up and found her lying on her bed, furious. Rosalind was standing in the doorway, with three fingers stuffed in her mouth. I ask Vicky what has happened. Well, there had been one hell of a row that morning between her and her granny, who had asked her to stop playing that infernal 'What Are We Living For? record, which understandably gets on her nerves, to wash her hair and put on a dress 'of decent length' for our Christmas dinner. All of which Vicky had refused point-blank to do. Whereupon the old girl had lost her temper and called her 'a badly brought-up slut'.

Feeling helpless I tried to console Vicky, passed my hand over her undeniably filthy tresses, begged her to calm down and not pay so much attention to her granny's sharp tongue. After all, she is growing old, maybe a trifle senile, and it had all been as difficult for her as it has for us all.

'Vicky darling, you must try to remember that Granny belongs to another generation that regards pop music and miniskirts as horrible, indecent.'

'I *wish Mum really had killed Granny!*' she groaned out amidst her sobs. 'She makes me feel so unhappy, doesn't understand either Mum or me. It's all *Granny's* fault that Mummy . . .' My mother, losing her grip on her jealousy – which isn't too firm at the best of times – and her frustration at being so isolated, had apparently also blurted out 'like mother, like daughter'. And slammed the door behind her so hard that another bit of plaster had fallen from the lobby wall.

It was quite a while before I managed to rescue my eldest daughter out of this whirlwind of hateful, conflicting feelings.

Evidently she is the only one of the children who knows that Jenny had deliriously believed she had murdered my mother. Poor girl, she had sat out there in the corridor during the crisis, all alone and in despair; and in between times slipped into Jenny's room, listened to her ravings and seen her slowly gliding away from us. The shock had been too much. Poor girl, for weeks and weeks she had been bottling all that up inside her. And now it had exploded.

'I want to go to Mormor and Morfar,' she snivelled. 'They like me and understand me. Granny only likes Michael because he's a boy. Well, I can't help it, can I, if I'm not a boy? She is teaching him to play bridge and slips him pocket money. But she *hates* me! Violet's lovely, but she's busy all the time with the little girls and that horrible Smelly and keeps on getting at me for not behaving like 'a young lady'. I'm like Mum, all wrong, wrong, wrong.'

Gradually I managed to put a stop to her despair with an impulsive promise of a trip to Sweden at Easter. Her 'But, Daddy, do you think Mum'll *ever* be well?' cut me to the quick. It felt so impossible, so false trying to sound optimistic when I myself am so uncertain, so full of questions! And with my own courage suddenly having abandoned me.

Just as we were about to sit down at the table, decorated by the kids with English crackers and Swedish-style dwarf tulips, to have our Christmas dinner, there was a sudden loud crash outside the house. My mother, who had spent the whole morning in her damp kitchen roasting the turkey and all its trimmings, had tripped over her threshold and fallen flat on her face on the stone patio; wrenched her arm and given herself such a shock that it needed both me and Michael together to help her into the sitting-room, to lay her on the sofa and give her a sip of cognac. Meanwhile Vicky and Rosalind were picking up the mossy but otherwise unhurt turkey and sweeping up the fragments of the huge antique flora-dora it a moment before had been enthroned on.

226

Thanks to the exquisite turkey, the flaming Christmas pudding, Violet's mince pies, French wine for my mother and me, and Coca-Cola for the children, the mood lifted. My mother passed round the pagoda bonbonnière with its almonds, crystallized orange and lemon slices and marrons glacés, forgot all about her accident and began telling the kids about pre-war Christmases in Paris. Both she and Vicky seemed to have forgotten about their morning quarrel, at least for the moment. At last I could relax, smoke a Christmas cigar in memory of my grandfather, who could only afford such a luxury on this one day of the year, and enjoy the atmosphere – with all its inevitable limitations, but heroic even so – of our motherless home; warm myself at the crackling flames of our Scandinavian-style fireplace, see the children's faces shining between the candlesticks, hear them cracking nuts, admire my mother's never-failing Parisian aptitudes as a hostess and, gratefully if half-asleep, meet the thin blue twilight of Christmas evening, creeping in behind the Matisse-like reds of Jenny's velvet curtains. I quite simply couldn't give another thought to her, lying there doped up to the gills in that revolting pale-green room in the London clinic. Nor to my dream.

And so, little by little, even to us desperate little celebrators of Christmas, doing our best despite our heaviness of heart to tag along in its hypnotic dance, there came a sense of belonging, of cosiness, of trite domestic good cheer, though only a fraction, a ghost of Christmases past when Jenny has been with us, so lovely, so glowing, so happy as she fed us all with her good food, overwhelmed us with her presents, her jokes, her music. I remembered how, just as her father had done, after playing the piano and singing Swedish, English and French folk songs with the children, she used to sit down in the corner beside the Christmas tree and read us the gospel story, both in Swedish and in English, so that my mother shouldn't feel out of it. And how she and I, alone at last after all the others had gone to sleep, used to listen to King's

College choir and then, in the faint glow from the dying fire and guttering candles, make love on this old sofa. The same old sofa that I was sitting on right now, still comfortable though it has lost half its springs, reflecting on my own memories, some black, some gilt edged.

Suddenly my daydreams are interrupted by Michael, standing there unusually pale at the open french windows that are letting in a dank, cold draught to disturb our overheated attempts to celebrate Christmas.

'Daddy, Daddy, Lady's escaped!' he almost shouts. 'She's run away!'

I jump up and follow him. Quite right, his beloved white rabbit's cage is empty. She must have got out somehow. Hurriedly we put on our anoraks and wellington's and leave my mother and the girls in front of the television and Her Majesty the Queen speaking in a chilly, upper-class accent to the British nation from Windsor Castle.

It's damp out, almost wet. The brownish-green landscape, its hedges and fields, is asleep; not the least blade of grass stirs, comatose in this midwinter stillness. Not a bird flies past, not a bat, not a glimpse of anyone stirring; even the grey squirrel with its fluffy tail seems to have withdrawn to its nest to crack nuts in peace and quiet. Torch in hand, Michael rushes desperately on ahead of me in the hazel copse. Sometimes I almost lose sight of his little boyish figure. The blue dusk is turning into night.

After an hour or so, we find her lying in a heap of leaves in the wood behind our garden. By then darkness has fallen all around us. There she lies in the torchlight's beam, exhausted, panting, shivering. Gently Michael picks her up and wraps her in his jacket.

'She must be ever so ill, Dad,' he says. 'D'you think she's got flu?'

We lay her in a shoe box full of cotton wool. Try to get a drop of my mother's cognac into her mouth. But this little rabbit's life is on its way out into the unknown. Michael doesn't leave her for a second, his dirty, schoolboy hands stroking her white coat, talking to her all the time, saying hopeless little loving words that he has torn from the book of his childish yet endless grief. In a lonely circle, as quiet and unstirring as the English countryside now at Christmas, he sits bowed over the shoe box, inside which Lady is irrevocably growing whiter and stiffer in her rabbit death. Though it is late, I stay with him, seeing in my little boy and his dying rabbit a memory of myself and my Jenny; how two weeks ago I, no less silently, no less distraught, watched at her bedside, seeing her life-flame go out . . .

Who, for Michael, is 'Lady'? A little white rabbit, stand-in for a mother whose illness has gradually taken her away from him? A mother to whom he has been perhaps closest of them all? A mother whom he has seen lying unconscious on a blood-drenched kitchen floor, a sight he will probably never be able to leave behind.

When Lady has ended her brief but – thanks to Michael's tender cares – happy rabbit life, he sobs for a long time in my arms. And it is as if his distress of soul lifts me up out of the split, depressed state of mind into which my dream had plunged me.

The children, at last, are all asleep (Rosalind in our double bed on her mother's side with her doll Petronella – so filthy but, alas , unwashable – in her arms). I go out into the garden to refresh my spirits if I can before turning in as well. In the night's gentle darkness with its dripping sounds I remember the evening two and a half months ago, when Jenny's mother had just come. It is as if my swarthy little mother-in-law had wrenched open a curtain and set the play going. Act by act, scene by scene, Jenny's illness had passed into its last act: her attempted suicide. Or is it really the last act in our drama? Suddenly I have an intuition that more scenes, as yet scarcely rehearsed, are lurking in a script of which I know nothing and that perhaps some other drama, outcome likewise unknown, remains . . .

But I'm no longer the same Jean-Paul as I was a month and a half ago. No longer so naive, tense, so omnipotently determined to be forever making reparation and setting everything to rights. There is been a change in me this autumn. Dr Vlemingck's words about love sometimes going too far didn't exactly come as news. And I have no intention of letting myself be exterminated or letting my own life be wrecked by Jenny's illness. I'm no masochist and certainly no saint. But one thing I see clearly: the evil, the destructiveness in her, in myself, is in us all, is in the world . . .

Yet somehow I still believe in love. Jenny's and mine. And intend to fight for it, for our children. Even if love can't always win out, at least it can keep evil, sickness, at bay – if it keeps its wits about it.

The Invisible Sun

It has come back, I can hear it. The music that has been forcing its way into my room these last few days, through the guarded doorway and over to my bed where I'm lying half-comatose from their pills. Pills that I have so come to detest but am being forced to swallow every day.

There it is again, faint but beckoning, summoning me from my dull lethargy, my indifference. From my pale-yellow childhood home, its white doors and window frames, from my secret garden, its notes reach me, pure and innocent. And a ray of light flashes through my muddled mind, a lucid note, trying to rouse me out of my sick, numb state, all these tranquillizers.

Trembling, I try to get out of bed, put on my dressing gown and slippers. Though I am so dizzy I can hardly stand, gradually, step by step, I arrive at the door, open it and go out into the corridor.

No one notices me. At the end of the passage, through a large window, I can see roof-tops against a chill grey sky. The music is coming from somewhere up there. Some stairs lead up. I have to drag myself to where someone's playing.

So long since I've heard music.

Up there, in a big cold room, sits a long-haired hippie trying to play Mendelssohn's *Fingal's Cave* on a piano like the one we had at the vicarage, though painfully out of tune. I sink down into a sofa facing a dilapidated billiard table, listen.

I'm running through the rooms of an apartment that is vaguely familiar. It is silent, empty. No furniture, nothing. I can hear that note, now sad, now playful, now pathetic, now questioning. What

231

does it want of me? 'Jenny, where are you? Who are you? What have you done with your life? I'm always here, you know, inside you, loud or strong, though you've let me wither away, terrified me with your anger, silenced me with your anxiety, stifled me with the hatred that never ceases to throb inside you as you run and run through these empty rooms . . .'

Then, abruptly, I come upon them: Fredrik, Leo, Mother and Father. They are standing in a room with bay windows, empty, too, except for a few suitcases. One of them is open. It is full of my old dolls, broken, eyeless, legless and armless like Thalidomide patients; of old Victorian bookmarks whose angels' faces stare up out of smudgy, well-thumbed children's books. It is strange. Bewildering. It is ages since I saw all these faces, these bodies, since I was in the same room, with them at the same time.

Instead, fury is rising inside me. Weak as I am, I hold up my bandaged wrists for them to see and scream at them that it is *they* who are guilty of this deed of blood, that it is all their fault, they who are to blame! You, Fredrik, who never cared about me. Only once did you ever comfort me, when Mother and Father were quarrelling; and for that I will forgive you your hard, frozen heart. I see you are in pain, lonely, suffering. But I too have suffered, Fredrik! Each of us is hanging upside down on his own cross, the one I saw in my delirium on the old brown cupboard in my sickroom . . . And you, Leo, once I loved you. Then you deserted me, trampled me underfoot as you have so many others. I will never be rid of you, even if for you my life is nothing, my destiny grey, petrified, and I just a silly female on the verge of the menopause, a poet who has buried her talent . . . When I broke with you, married a foreigner, you threw me away; I was no longer one of your fantasy women. As for Jean-Paul, Leo, you despise him, don't you? He doesn't belong in our insane family!

Cruel, unjust words that I had never before dared come bursting out of me. There is no checking them. In my drug-induced dream a hatred I have never felt before makes me insult Mother and Father. Mother for never wanting me, never loving me, not as she loves Fredrik and Leo; downgrading me, making me dependent, sick. I see she is weeping and her tears appall me. But I have no desire to throw my arms round her, to beg her to forgive me; I am being ravaged by a wrath as terrible as a forest fire . . . Only Father I spare, my hatred stops short at him. Exhausted, with the blood pouring from my wrists, I throw myself into his arms.

'Oh, Father, why did you do that terrible thing? How could you have taken away my child, forced me into that abortion? Where is my child that you forbade to live? It was murder, Father, shame-faced murder! On the very day it should have been born I met Jean-Paul; it is as if that child has grown up invisibly among my others.'

'Forgive me, Jenny, you don't know how often I have regretted it! The child we took away is in heaven. Come to me, with all your burdens.'

'No, Father, I can't. I no longer find rest in your aged arms that try to lull me into a false sleep. You loved me too much, Father, with a love that should by rights have been Mother's, not mine!'

'But, Jenny, she didn't want it. She was the one who threw us together. I loved you innocently, Jenny, as a father loves his only daughter. Have mercy on us, Jenny! Can't you see what a bad way Fredrik is in, on his crutches? How can you say such awful things about Leo? He has changed. Nowadays he is so sensitive, so good to us. Don't let envy's worm eat out your heart . . .'

'Father, Father, how can I ever atone my guilt to Jean-Paul, to the children?'

'By asking God's mercy and forgiveness, my little Jenny!'

'But, Father, I no longer believe in God. Only in Jean-Paul and the children.'

Our exchanges are hurried because Mother is waiting for him, all her potted plants and suitcases, all her sealed jam jars filled with stewed apple and cranberry sauce, ready to leave.

'Jenny,' he says. 'Don't distress yourself so. Or wrack your brains over religious matters – at times even I have found them troublesome . . .' I clasp his black clerical overcoat, try to prevent him from going.

'Oh, Father, I'm so *frightened*.'

My words echo through the desolate rooms and my only exit from the dream is by way of an icy ladder, propped against one of the uncurtained windows. I am forced to climb down it, to the street, to the earth.

Suddenly I feel cold, steely fingers gripping me, hurting me like surgical instruments.

'And what, Mrs Didier, do you think you are up to? Patients aren't allowed up here! We've been looking high and low for you! Such disobedience sabotages the whole hospital, upsets our routines.'

I slip on the icy ladder, fall into the street; wake with a jerk. I am mistily aware of the bony ward sister, of her stony little eyes, so utterly insensitive to patients' sufferings. She towers over me like a tree charred by lightning, her ill humour blackly silhouetted against the dove-blue dusk of a January sky. Disturbed, still only half awake but resentful of her cruel twig-like hand, I bite into its thin flesh. She howls, flings me back on to the sofa. A whole army of nurses come rushing in and – I don't know what happens next.

'In this hospital we are not in the habit of biting people,' Dr Vlemingck says sternly. Disapproving, condemning my behaviour, he looks down at me as if I were a nasty insect who has somehow climbed into one of his beds, certainly not a patient he has just snatched from death's jaws.

'She *disturbed* me.' I defend myself hotly. 'When I was listening to *Fingal's Cave* and the last notes were just dying away . . .'

'So, Mrs Didier, you thought you were home again, did you?' His punitory mask falls from his face and to his own relief he again becomes the fundamentally good-natured, jovial father figure. 'Well, of course, that's quite another matter.' He sinks down on to my bedside chair. 'So you are fond of music are you, Mrs Didier?'

'Very. I can listen to it for hours. Sometimes only music brings me peace . . .'

I would like to talk to him. So many questions, so much lies in ruins. 'It must have had something to do with my gold heart . . .'

'Gold heart?'

'Yes, the one they gave me when I was christened. As a child I used to suck it, so it has a dent in it. One day I remember . . .'

'Yes, Mrs Didier?'

' . . . Losing it in the garden and feeling utterly distraught! I'd been standing washing myself, crying, splashing my hands about in the wash basin and spilling water all over the nursery floor, when suddenly Maja – she was our nanny – came in. She had felt so sorry for me that she had gone out into the cold to look for it and found it on the gravel. I remember feeling utterly ecstatic, standing there all wet and with nothing on I hugged her . . .'

Doctor Vlemingck listens.

'Yes?'

'Well, the next day, when Maja was sitting by the sewing machine – one of those old foot-pedal things, you know – the needle went right through her thumb. She bled so dreadfully they had to take her to hospital and sew her up.'

He is still listening.

'A day or two before all . . . this happened, I gave the heart on an impulse to Vicky – our eldest daughter, that is.'

'Oh, and why?'

'Because I was sorry for her, wanted to make up for being such a bad mother . . . Not that she really wanted it. In fact she promptly lost it . . . outside in the gravel. We were out there for hours searching for it. Michael, that's our son, was holding his torch in his little fist while he turned over pebble after pebble – didn't give up until it was quite dark. He is such a good boy, Michael!'

Between Dr Vlemingck and myself follows a silence.

'And then?'

'I . . . I don't remember much, only standing in the shower for a long time, until I was shivering with cold. The dawn outside the bathroom window was pale yellow. My mother had just gone back to Sweden. Jean-Paul was away on business. My gold heart had disappeared. The house was so quiet, numb in some strange way . . . That's when I saw Maja's bleeding thumb in the water running from the tap. I was getting more and more confused. Felt sick. All I knew was it was time for me, too, to feel pain, see blood.'

Exhausted, I appeal to him, want him to explain the inner contexts, find some hidden meaning in my halting words.

'Do you still hate your mother-in-law?' he asks suddenly, as if he hasn't heard a word of what I have been saying. 'You remember you thought it was her you had . . .'

'Of course I remember,' I say, a bit upset. 'But all that was delirious. No, of course I don't hate her. I only wish we could move away from her!'

Another long silence.

'Are you deeply fond of your own mother, Mrs Didier? Wasn't it simply that you couldn't bear her leaving? Starved. Stopped drinking. And ended up dehydrated and began hallucinating?'

'Of course I love my mother . . . but . . .'

Dr Vlemingck pats my hand amiably.

'No doubt your golden heart was a talisman from your childhood, up there in the north, isn't that so? But then you wanted to be a mother yourself and so gave it to your daughter; at the same time the little girl inside you couldn't stand being separated from her own mother and childhood. She isn't strong enough to cope with adult life in a foreign country, not really mature enough to manage several children of her own or run a home. So she collapses. Is this the first time she has wanted to hurt herself? The ultimate, most dangerous act being seen as a release, as a way out of a life that she is not up to?'

Questions that in the stuffy hospital atmosphere hover between us. In my mind's eye I see an unending row of half-open doors, all leading to a more feasible world, an unfamiliar light . . . vague memories . . . of a little girl straying, alone, deep into a dark spruce forest, never wanting to go back to the others' cruelty, their indifference, hoping in its depths to find a fairyland . . .

'My dear Mrs Didier, I fancy you are a bit tired.' Dr Vlemingck stands up. 'You have given me one version of your accident, and I find it interesting. Personally I believe there were many reasons for what happened. But just now I don't want to go into them. The main thing is that you get well again, can go home to your husband and children. We'll see to that! It almost seems as if your illicit outing, listening to that music, has been a turning point . . . But please, Mrs Didier, don't start biting Sister Ethel again. Between you and me, I'm sure she doesn't taste all that good. We'll soon be cutting down on your pills, so you won't feel so fuzzy and can come out into the ward, get to know the other patients.'

He goes over to the door. Pauses at it. Turns and smiles.

'And when you feel up to it, do try and write down your experiences here. Your husband tells me you are a poet, once even had a collection of poems published. Why hide your light under a bushel? I read quite a lot of poetry myself in the evenings. It's relaxing after all the sadness in these wards. Reminds me that there is such a thing as beauty, rhythm, another dimension to life.'

Suddenly his look is quite serious.

'When I look at you, Mrs Didier, I'm reminded of a quotation from my seventeenth-century colleague, Sir Thomas Browne. He writes: 'Our life is a pure flame, and we live by an invisible sun within us.' Words worth pondering on, Mrs Didier. I do, often.'

Jenny's hospital journal, January

Dr Vlemingck's right. There have been several reasons for my life going to pieces. One of them is my inability to focus. I have always been running away from my poetry. For fear of new failures; for lack of inspiration, of finding I'm empty. Perhaps he doesn't understand what an effort it would be to start writing again, how much anxiety it would entail. Like Beate-Sofie, the actress that I'm always dreaming about, I have forgotten my lines. Wearing a white dress, I – Beate-Sofie, that is – am about to go on stage any moment now, but find I have forgotten my lines, while the others know theirs! Panic. Before the curtain goes up I flee. Or else stand there gaping in front of a packed house, can't get a word out. But an actress who runs away leaves others in the lurch. A poet who gives up on her poetry leaves only herself. Myself.

January

In the day-room, for the first time. Just a short while. All I could manage. Hopeless atmosphere, half-doped. The television is on. No one bothers to look at it. Everyone is lost in him or herself; we are all itching and scratching at our own lives, which have gone so wrong. We just stare hour after hour into a green cesspool. It's like a grotesque party with no drinks, no chat, no movement. Either we castaways just aren't able to relate to each other or our feeble attempts to communicate lead nowhere. But though we seem half-asleep, stunned, at a loss for something to do, in reality we have so much to do that we have no time to bother about anyone else. We are forever putting our own houses in order, from dank cellars up to dusty little attics, climbing worn, creaking staircases, straying in and out of rooms where so much has happened that we can't recall. Past mirrors we no longer dare look into, past empty fireplaces, bare windows that overlook streets all leading to 'then', to 'now', to 'what's to come' . . . How should I know?

The air is hard to breathe in here, despite the television's never-ending babble, despite some nurse's hearty suggestion that we play some games, despite the coffee trolley forever bringing us biscuits. An air heavy with collective suffering, it stifles any flicker of life. So I'm not the only one. Jenny is just one among thousands – many hundreds of thousands – soon millions – of the incomprehensibly sick souls. . .

January

One by one they are detaching themselves from the anonymous group and I am beginning to get to know them. Frail, tentative approaches. We are all afraid of Sister Ethel, of the hospital, of all this surveillance. These eyes! We aren't allowed to visit one another in our rooms, only to meet out in the corridors, the day-room, or else sneak off for a smoke in the loos. Susanne and I are spinning a frail web of common friendship. Like two sisters of misfortune. Having no future beyond the hospital's confines, we both know our friendship will end. She is chronically unhappy, depressed. No amount of pills or conversational therapy bites on her misery. Still too weak to stand, I sit down on the bathroom stool. Susanne is sitting on the edge of the bath looking as if she could fill it with her tears and still find no relief. We smoke and talk spasmodically about this monotonous hospital life that we have doomed ourselves to; our fear of their treatments, their cures, their medicines, their imposed routines. About our even greater fear of having to live outside these walls again, as we long to, in our own homes . . . Strangely, I'm not ashamed to tell her about my anxiety, my dissociations, my mental absences, my abhorrence of going through the same misery again. She understands. I don't need to explain. She knows. She too has tried to open doors into Never-Never Land. Young though she is, she has an intuitive insight into our two sick souls. Theories, psychiatric terms she is suspicious of, dismisses. Nothing shocks her. The horrible thing is that she is given up, has lost hope. Takes it for granted that her life must be a vicious circle, from brighter periods to black ones. Strange to say, her suffering, her apathy stirs in me an appetite for living, a determination to change, radically . . .

Her guilt is greater than mine. She says she has been unfaithful to her husband, slept with another man, got pregnant and given birth to a boy suffering from Down's syndrome. All this happened a couple of years ago. Her husband has forgiven her, even helps her with the little boy, whom she loves deeply despite his being mentally retarded. But she can't forgive herself, escape her depressions. Though she is still quite young, the electro-shocks treatments are destroying her, affecting her memory, and the anti-depressants are making her fat and ugly, chronically dry in the throat. She thinks I ought to be blissfully happy to have four healthy kids, a husband who loves and satisfies me; she has only experienced sexual pleasure once, that time when she conceived her son . . . this sets her off again, round and round, tears, self-reproaches. Nervously she lights another 'ciggie'. Perhaps it would have been better, I think to myself, if her husband *had* punished her? But say nothing. Dwindle to a mere listener, whose misfortunes are nothing compared with hers . . .

January

Today Sister Ethel attacked my copy of *Thérèse Raquin*, the one Jean-Paul borrowed for me. 'I don't think that book's good for you, Mrs Didier,' she says. 'Nasty TV serial it is, absolutely nothing you, Mrs Didier, ought to be reading!' I protest, but she is relentless and has confiscated it. 'French literature's all nonsense and immorality anyway. Why don't you try something more edify-ing; some nice English book by Barbara Pym or *Little Women?*'

I laugh out loud.

'But, Sister! That was written for very young girls . . . and has nothing to do with the time we are living in!'

'In that case, Mrs Didier, I'd say it was right up your street,' comes her sarcastic reply.

January

Jean-Paul has brought me some mimosa and some new French books that I suppose I'll have to hide from Sister Ethel. Little 'Get Well Mum' cards from the children, a luxurious nightie and some perfume. Jean-Paul and I are are madly in love – if it weren't for the peep-hole in the door we would *faire l'amour*. He kisses me, caresses me, praises my shapely new self; no question that I have put on weight during my stay in hospital. Funnily enough it doesn't bother me in the least. Anyhow it turns Jean-Paul on, gives him a hard-on; I respond, feeling wet and voluptuous. But the nurses' little peep-hole restrains us. In the heat of our new-found feelings we have to remind ourselves that we are, after all, in a hospital, where it is most improper to *faire l'amour*! In the end we have to stay at arm's length to prevent ourselves from misbe-having . . .

For a long time after he has gone I remain where I am, still aroused, yearning for his body. I am his delectable wife again, who has never done anything to harm either herself or others . . . Though I know this is a lie unleashed by amorous feelings, a part of me wholeheartedly believes it – as long as the mimosa's fra-grance fills the room and the wan January sunlight breaks through the brooding overcast sky. I fool myself into thinking I am well, better than I have been for years! And tomorrow I'm going to ask Dr Vlemingck to let me go home, to Jean-Paul and the children; leave the sick life behind me for good, assure him that I am strong enough to forget all those bleak, dreadful things; bury it under three spoonfuls of earth, cremate it – anyway, what was it that was so painful? I don't remember . . .

January

Dr Vlemingck is sceptical. I implore him to let me out. 'I feel so sorry for the other patients,' I say, 'but I'm not all cooped up in myself any more, my wrists have healed, I have no more anxiety. Please let me! I promise there won't be any relapses.'

For some reason he refuses to believe me.

'The burnt child doesn't always shun the fire,' he replies coldly, not like himself at all. And walks out.

I start to cry. In a rage of disappointment I pull out the mirror from my handbag and fling it down on to the floor. Its cracked face shatters instantly.

Just like me.

February

I long for my children, for Jean-Paul. One by one the days, the endless hospital days, are torn from the calendar, out of my life, which seems freshly washed as if it had been to the laundry. The face that greets me in the mirror is youthful, soft, smiling. Defies all the sadness surrounding me. It is not my sadness, my depression. Just as the spring is breaking through out there in the hospital grounds, my new self, neither anxious nor guilty, is breaking through in this hothouse atmosphere. Each day I go down to therapy. At first I sewed cushions, lustrous as Renoir's women, voluptuous as Rembrandt's. Then made lampshades for our home. Then a whole outfit for Rosalind's doll. But now I am drawing and painting. It is so exciting I forget all about mealtimes, pills and the hospital. All around me there is a kind of brilliant, colourful silence. The old stone house in Lindfield grows gradually out of the paper: the oaks, the diseased elms, Muriel's chapel-like house, our red front door, the ivy and the yellow and pink climbing roses, peering in with curious eyes at Jean-Paul's and my naked bodies, our caresses . . . Then I see another house inside our English one: my pale-yellow childhood home, almost like a Swedish manor house. Mother, dark haired and lovely, is sitting at her desk inside, secretively absorbed in her diary, and Father is in his study, looking for a text for his sermon. Suddenly the bright light of inspiration breaks through his troubled search, gilding his brow like one of Blake's visions and splashing a golden sheen over the bookshelves and even down on our poodle Teddy, asleep on the threadbare carpet.

In its great nursery two little girls, the curly-headed brunette Marie and the flaxen-haired Jenny, are playing with their fragile china dolls that live inside a tall Victorian doll's house. Their play is silent, ceremonious; as important to them as their mother's writings in her diary are to her, or their father's Sunday sermon is to his parishioners. In the boys' room Leonard, eyes closed and his hatchet features framed in bakelite headphones, sits listening to Mozart. The rest of us already regard him as a genius. He is also living in a world of his own, in music. Out in the kitchen Fredrik is sampling Tulla's sauces and stewed fruit. He is the only one that has the key to her fretful, old maid's heart, to her gastronomic secrets. He seeks in her soufflés and cheese pies the love that no one else (except maybe Mother) gives him. He is as afraid of Father as Leo, Jenny and Marie are of being guillotined by his sarcasms, of his bitterness and violent tempers. Around Fredrik I paint a black cloud. Then I leave the past – where our house in Lindfield just now seems to belong – behind me and try to sketch the outlines of a new home for Jean-Paul, the children and me, free from mothers-in-law . . . But here imagination and inspiration fail me. All I can produce is a lot of black dots and dashes, an abstraction, a blob. Can neither draw nor paint, nor even think about our future . . .

A fear, hitherto suppressed by tablets, of coming face to face again with our home, especially with Muriel, flings itself at me with a roar, like a provoked lioness. And I can do no more. The therapist, a young Pre-Raphaelite-like girl with long hair and freckles, asks me how I am feeling, brings me a glass of water.

'You are so *good* at it, Jenny!' she enthuses, overdoing it a little. 'You have real artistic talent! And aren't afraid of expressing yourself! You could become a surrealist or naivist painter, you know, if you stuck at it. Why don't you apply to art school? Most of the others here just paint like kids or else daren't do anything at all. Someone has shattered their self-confidence. They are just hide behind their illnesses, curl up inside their shells like snails. But you've got courage! I believe in you! You will make it!'

In her translucent green eyes I mirror my confidence, and lack of it.

February

Conscious of my own fear. But doing my best to cope with my anxiety-devil. By painting, writing, playing on the untuned piano up there in that room that used to be out of bounds. Jean-Paul has brought me some sheet music from home, but my fingers are all clumsy and out of practice.

They have halved my daily dose of pills. Experimenting with me, I expect, to see how soon I can be discharged.

Throughout the day the scene in Notre Dame has appeared vividly in front of me. That rose window high above us, my mother, dark-featured and southern European-looking, standing by the candles, as deep in her prayers as the Catholic women praying for their loved ones' departed souls, burning in purgatory's fires. I too am seated on a hard chair in front of the Madonna and Jesus, determined to tune into my mother and grasp the essence of her being, which has always seemed so complex until now. Again I hear the organ music – can it have been

Couperin? Mother hands me a candle. 'Light it for me when I'm dead,' she says quietly. I remember how shocked, stunned I felt. My childish protests. My unspoken words before leaving the cathedral: 'Mothers mustn't die before their children.'

But I am a mother myself. For the first time this insight flashes through me: it is as if until now I have only been playing at it, playing at Mummy-Daddy-and-children but have been unaware of my responsibility, of unselfish love, what Jean-Paul calls ' *la tendresse infinie*'.

I have not been allowed to die, to abandon them. And now I want to live for their sakes, undo the damage I have done. How much suffering have I exposed them to, unwittingly, senselessly – my four little ones?

February

'Try not to be afraid of the anxiety,' Dr Vlemingck says gently. 'Turn it into creativity!'

'But it's so strong!' I object. 'It completely paralyses you. And then creativity's out of the question.'

'There are always tablets, you know,' he says cheerfully. 'You must admit they've already done wonders.'

That is as far as he can get. It seems to me as if an apparently insurmountable mountain of pharmaceutical drugs were preventing him and his patients from looking for the path that must surely exist behind it. An overgrown path, almost impenetrable: the path that leads to mental health. Dare I defy Dr Vlemingck's knowledge of psycho-chemistry, his experience, and try to find it? What was it Jean-Paul used to quote from Kierkegaard but which for me held no meaning during an anxiety attack? 'Anxiety is nothing but unrealized freedom.' For me freedom is creativity – but how to attain it when, for me, anxiety and creativity still go hand in hand?

The children have just been here. Or rather, Rosalind and

Vicky, not the others. It feels so empty now they have gone, unnatural, heartbreaking. If I could I would have slipped into my overcoat and slunk off with them, out of this hospital, and never come back; gone home to sanity, to my children and their lives. But they are not letting me leave, not yet . . . I must wait a little longer. Always a little longer.

Their visit has shaken me out of my Sleeping Beauty sleep, my routine here. Half-wrenched me out into reality again, where one walks a tightrope between real sorrows, everyday cares, decision making, responsibilities, demands. It has dismissed the drugs, my cotton-wool existence, my alibis as a sick woman.

My first reaction was fear. I am ashamed. Scared of my own children. When they got here I was sitting over by the window, curled up in the armchair, listening to old Rubenstein play Chopin on the radio, while inside me, somewhere as yet only half-heartedly, yet obstinately, I searched for new poems. Something that hasn't happened for years and years! Only in my newly acquired calm and easily shaken peace of mind do they dare venture out of their impalpable twilight. Even this, though, is enough to light up my whole existence, link up obscure thoughts and feelings and throw out everything irrelevant.

After a few shaky moments, as I fumbled enthusiastically to make contact, the timorous bubble of my inspiration burst and I was again one hundred per cent a mum! Hugs and kisses all round, a lava-hot torrent of feelings at being together again. Tender little words flew to and fro between us, all sorts of questions and answers, clear or unclear.

No longer listening to Chopin's mazurkas and waltzes, now voluptuously dreamy, now passionate, I observed my two girls with new attention and awareness. Vicky has changed. She is no longer a clumsy teenager but a very young woman with a clear complexion, wavy hair and eyes that sparkle with a secretive experience. Something has happened to her while I have been away, I know it without asking. There is a certain female self-assurance, a shy reticence about her, standing there by the window looking out over the dreary hospital grounds. Does she realize she is beginning to be a real beauty? Already in her features, in her whole form, one intuits a certain hereditary refinement. For the briefest moment a primitive pang of female envy went through me. For the first time I felt middle-aged, yes, almost old.

Just as I had observed my mother, she was now observing me, sitting here in the armchair with little Rosalind in my lap. Vicky knows, I thought. At least most of what there is to know. Not much escapes those penetrating gentian-blue eyes! During this terrible time she has drilled down as far as she can into the subsoil of our family's complex existence until she has reached a point where her very youth has put a stop to it and her own stability has forced her to forge a life for herself. Her instinct for self-preservation has pushed me and Jean-Paul aside as the weaker parties, either temporarily or for good. She was in love, and that was making her feel protective but also a trifle superior. Had I lost her or will she come back to me? Did she despise me? Or understand me?

Rosalind, for her part, seemed a bit dejected, perhaps not quite well, and clung to me anxiously. And the thought struck me: will we be allowed to keep this child? Something about her seems only half there, as if she were on a journey that is leading her away from us all. A child on loan. She has always been ethereal, like a butterfly, lacking the other children's' robustness, her roots not so firmly planted in the ground as theirs. The blue veins at her temples shimmered through her transparent skin and under her eyes were dark circles. I hugged her tight, cursing myself for my sick egocentricity, this evil that has cut me off from my own children, particularly from her, my delicate little girl . . .

'Does Daddy know you've come to see me?' I asked. 'All alone in London?'

'We aren't alone,' Vicky answered with a slight swaggering movement of her backside, almost visible beneath her miniskirt. 'Roy has come with us! He is waiting down in the entrance hall. First we are going to the cinema, and then we are going to eat hamburgers and chips.'

'And drink Pepsi-Cola!' Rosalind chirped up.

'Roy! But surely . . . that's the boy from . . .'

'Down at the stables,' Vicky put in calmly. 'He is fabulous, Mum, and *ever* so helpful! We wouldn't have managed without him, all this time. It wasn't easy when Violet had to go. But it's OK now, everything's working smoothly. Roy and I see to everything. He is very practical, fixes all the things Dad doesn't have time to. And cooks fantastic dinners. He is even building Rosie and Jojo a Wendy house!'

'But . . . what about Michael?' I asked, interrupting this torrent of information. 'He has always been so helpful, so good with his hands . . . '

'Oh, him!' Taking a pocket mirror out of her handbag, Vicky started applying lipstick and eyeliner – something she had never done before. 'He is a bit off his rocker since you . . . you got ill and Lady died. Hangs out with a gang of little tough guys who're up to no good. That is, when he isn't playing with Jojo and pretending she's a boy!'

'Is this a castle, Mummy?' A wondering look of disappointment flitted over Rosalind's features as she asked, glancing around my stark and sterile room. 'That's what Vicky said it was, on the train coming up. With princes and princesses. We saw some out there in the corridor. But they weren't pretty at all! And why aren't they wearing crowns?'

Vicky's white lie, I realized, that she must have told in order to spare her imaginative little sister a cruel fact: that her mum is in a so-called madhouse.

'Oh, they've probably put them away in their drawers. But they'll put them on when there is a party – this evening!' Vicky lied glibly.

I felt more and more distressed. In Vicky's voice was something both aggressive and mocking. The poor girl has obviously had enough, she is sick to death of having to look after her little sisters and probably feeling a bit revengeful. Everything at home must be upside down. It has all slipped through my fingers, I have been away so long. And what I was being exposed to, now, was a rude, rather ruthless, but none the less necessary awakening – something I only now can cope with. Taking my courage in both hands, I told my heart to stop thumping, my nerves to stop quivering.

'I'll soon be home, Vicky,' I said as calmly as I could. 'Next week. Maybe even sooner . . . Tell me, how's Daddy?'

Vicky had sat down on the bed's edge, from which she was dangling two legs in fashionable red boots.

'Oh, not too bad. Ever so absent-minded though, forgets everything. Reads and writes half the night. The day before yesterday he had such a terrible attack of migraine I had to call Dr Matthews, who came and gave him an injection. He needs you, Mum. Both physically and mentally . . . Well, you know what I mean! We . . . we all need you!'

This last was a cry for help. A tremor of pain passed through her whole being. And she got up abruptly.

'Well, Mum, must be off. Can't keep Roy waiting any longer. Come on, Rosie! Oh, do let go of Mummy, Rosie. You are not a baby any longer, not like Jojo! Bye, Mum. See you soon.'

They disappeared out into the twilight. Standing by the window I watched them cross the hospital courtyard. A dark, quite handsome boy, with his arm around Vicky, was holding Rosalind's hand.

My children.
Hearts of my heart
blood from my blood
tears from my eyes
waves from love's river
twigs from a tree that is broken
fragile but strong today
will you come into bloom
or break – like me?

February

Only a few days left. Vlemingck has just been here, pronounced
me 'almost' well – albeit with all sorts of reservations (understood:
warnings) and with the mournful scepticism of an antique dealer
who sees one of his treasures sold and entrusted, wrapped up in
layer after layer of tissue paper, to some feckless, unappreciative or
ham-handed client. Labelling it with directives, he uttered in the
firmest tone of voice: 'Never, ever again, stop eating or drinking.
Don't smoke. Avoid alcohol and too much physical or mental
exertion, get lots of fresh air, rest and sleep. And, above all, go on
taking my tablets!' (In short, don't go on living!) Under all of
which I detect an uncertainty, expressed in his hesitant, sidelong
glances; in his slightly over-optimistic yet guarded tone of voice.
And adds: 'But for the time being, Mrs Didier, I must ask you to
come for regular check-ups.'

In his mind's eye I am a hurt bird, already flapping its helpless
wings against his gloomy surgery's grubby windows. (No. I don't
want to come in for any check-ups. I won't ever come back!
Never!) There is something about this kindly physician, his gentle,
fatherly understanding, that can't help trying to exert a magnetic
effect on his patients – and ex-patients, for ever drawing them
back to him.

March

On one of my last nights here I dream a bizarre dream. I am sitting in a primitive café amid tropical palms and prickly pear cacti. Opposite me sits my mother-in-law. Muriel has bobbed hair, is wearing a beige dress from the twenties and is smoking a cigarette in a long ivory cigarette-holder. It seems we are somewhere in Africa. A merciless wind is sweeping in from the flat expanses of desert all about us, depositing its sands in our eyes. An unnaturally small waiter, dressed in a doctor's white coat, flits from table to table. Driven by an intense need to confess all my sins and be forgiven and reconciled, I put out my hands to hers, to touch them, stroke them. But Muriel seems indifferent, almost a little amused. Doesn't say a word. Getting no reaction out of her, I become hysterical. Until in the end I am on my knees, cowering at the feet of this woman I have so hated and feared. Humiliating myself like a dog, I howl: 'Forgive me, forgive me!' But all she replies is: 'Get up, you silly girl! There is nothing to forgive. As you see, I'm still very much alive – living backwards, in fact, because I'm getting younger and younger! Try how you will, you can't kill me! But this lot . . . ' In my dream she points a crimson fingernail to one side and I see Jean-Paul. His hair has turned almost completely white. Pale-faced, he is staring into empty space. At another table are a couple of wilted children and at yet another a thin woman who resembles me and never stops peering into her mirror. Lastly, at a fourth table, another woman, old and round-shouldered, is sitting, scribbling away for dear life, defying the wind that is whirling away her scraps of paper.

'They won't be hard for you to crack,' Muriel goes on in a hard voice. 'You can poison *them* with your little daily doses of hysteria until they pine away and die. But not me! I'm made of catgut. As for you, you are a seductress, a murderess, as I have always known, ever since the day I first set eyes on your family . . .'

Now her tapering fingernail points to my dream-scenario's

backdrop. There, in another café, is Mother, this time with Father and my brothers. All four are sitting stiffly upright, waiting to place their orders. Protect their faces though they may, by holding up their hands against the gusts of desert wind I can see how terrified they are of this sterile, unfamiliar moon landscape.

'You are assassins, the whole bunch of you,' Muriel concludes maliciously. 'And of the worst kind. The kind that never get found out!'

'Oh no, no, Muriel! You are wrong, wrong!' I implore, screaming. But the wind muffles my cry. And I wake up.

A pale-blue daylight is driving away the night and my terror subsides. My hand reaches out instinctively for the emergency button to call the night-nurse and ask her to bring me a sedative. But in that instant I realize that I am supposed to be cured, ready to go home. From now on I am on my own and must cope with nasty dreams, corrosive feelings of guilt; perhaps new anxiety attacks . . .

Later that evening

This place is saturated with pain and a life-weariness ever ready to burst out with terrible force as soon as it isn't sufficiently suppressed with drugs. Moments when cooped-up cries of anguish turn into human howls as the anxiety inside one or another of us struggles out of its padded cell of medications and ruthlessly, shamelessly, shows its face, careless of others' reactions. Attempts to break out from the sleepy numbness – out of the state of apathetic inertia, the unnaturally well-behaved state that these drugs have put us in – almost come as a relief. Such as today, for example, when we were washing up after supper and Susanne, who is usually so compliant, started smothering the wet plates with kisses, sobbing 'My babies, oh, my lovely little babies!', only to fling them no less passionately at the kitchen floor and smash them to pieces.

At such moments I run away. To my room or, as I did this evening, up to the roof terrace. There I could be alone, out of earshot of Susanne's shrieks. Violence scares me. Both other people's and my own, always lurking somewhere deep down inside me, even if just now it is half-asleep. The staff tell me that on one of my first nights here I fought with a male nurse . . . screaming I wanted to go home; even tried to get dressed and pack my bag. Can someone have made it up? I can't remember, anyway. When you are mentally sick and can't defend yourself you get capricious. *They* are always in the right, have the upper hand, and their version of events is always true.

Down below me is London. A huge prehistoric monster, it is dropping off to sleep, crouched under an evening sky streaked with pink and with small clouds scurrying overhead, chasing each other frantically. Just as they did that evening, months ago, when Mother had come to stay with us, and my latent illness, after a long period of relative inactivity, broke out again frenziedly and began chasing me like one of those clouds bleeding to death in the sunset. Was it Mother's visit that triggered it all off, made me suddenly so much worse? A mother-cloud pursuing, harrying a guilt-stricken daughter-cloud? I don't know, don't feel like thinking about Mother. Just now I'm not up to thinking about Mother.

Where is she, anyway? She lived inside me for so long, almost bursting me apart. But now, up on this roof high above London, she is no longer in my heart. She has left it a safe dwelling for Jean-Paul and the children; and – if only for the time being – for all these lonely, strange creatures that everyone has abandoned but I have got to know during these last weeks . . .

Far below, down among the Victorian brick houses and the streets that crawl with traffic, in the grimy Underground stations, under the bridges, in the cold, wet parks where the buds are coming out, they swarm: the abandoned, the sufferers, the eccentrics, the poverty-stricken, the drug addicts – all living in the fangs of this archaic monster that cares nothing that their lives have reached the limit of what can be borne and must ultimately shatter. But what about the others – the happy, healthy, normal, well-off? Well, of course, I realize there are plenty of them, too, but I still can't quite identify with them. Not yet . . .

From where I'm standing I can see the dome of St Paul's, the spire of Southwark cathedral. Oh God, my mother's and father's God, are You to be found inside such buildings, thick and drowsy with the past? Or is it in hovels, beery pubs, filthy backyards that You are hiding? Do You really care about my sisters and brothers in misfortune, our pathetically fated lives, crawling about in this anthill? Do You really see every child that gets run over, every sparrow that falls to the ground?

It's impossible! You have neither the time nor the energy. At the sight of all the man-made evil that has reached its monstrous climax in my lifetime, You, like Susanne down there in the ward, have given a howl of rage and disappointment and cleared out, leaving it to a humanity that You once infused with a few sparks of light and spirit, whom you in your crazy, holy love once kissed – like she, a poor manic-depressive woman, kissed those dishes she had just washed . . .

Well enough to be discharged but still not well, I'll soon be leaving. Though the sick patches inside me are no longer so flaming red, their pallor is insidious. The truth is, I'm scared. So little is needed for them to flare up again, like that idiotic pimple in Paris! Tomorrow, brave but with my heart in my mouth, I'm leaving this grim place. Clearer in the head, perhaps, but for that very reason more frightened than before I became ill.

For a long while Jenny Didier lingers up there on the hospital's roof terrace. Below her the chill late winter air spreads out its blanket, little by little rubbing out the city beneath her in a glassy yellow shimmer like the calix of a daffodil just coming into bloom. Can it be the light that is touching her, she who has been so ill, is the very same as in her childhood's garden?

Jenny loves being high up in solitary places, where she feels as if she were transcending all boundaries. In this she is truly her mother's daughter; we only need to go back and remember how Charlotte, one midnight beside a stormy sea in Brighton, had an intimation of her own immortality. Though weaker than her mother, Jenny is not of the fibre that denies its own mortality. Having recently come as close as anyone can to resigning her life, she is not troubling her head about a hereafter. Tomorrow she will be returning to a life with Jean-Paul and the children; and it is enough. She is not made of the same grandiose, audacious stuff as her problematic mother; nor does she have Leo's desperate courage. At such moments, even so, the boundaries of her more confined existence break; the tormenting sense of her own inadequacy evaporates and her prematurely worn features light up with a kind of joy, a certain feeling of trust, not religious like her mother's, rather of self-confidence. A new life, her own, is breaking through inside her, annihilating the dangerously undeveloped child who, even so, still lurks somewhere deep in the vaults of her unconscious.

Jenny's hospital journal

A last entry in this journal . . .

In the drawer of my bedside table I've found a neatly folded scrap of paper. My first impulse was to throw it away, but on closer inspection I see in my own handwriting, though ill, small and shaky, the words: 'Life is a pure flame and we live by an invisible sun within us.'

I hide this memento in my handbag. Then I go on sitting here in the twilight, repeating the words to myself until I know them by heart.

First thing tomorrow Jean-Paul's coming to fetch me. Side by side we will drive through the gentle English countryside, green with early spring, dotted with crocuses and primroses, half-revealing through its sunshine swelling, green hillsides, even a glimpse, perhaps, of the sea. Together we shall step inside our old stone house. And I'll put my hand in his, so as not to be intimidated by memories, by all I've been through inside its walls. Embrace my children. Hold them in my arms, close, very close, and never leave them, even if one day they must leave me – never again frighten them, hurt them, lay waste their lives . . .

Jean-Paul, my love, help me. Help me . . .